A Big Lump of Coal

"Mattie! Matterhorn! Get over here!"

No reply. I couldn't see anything, but I stumbled through the deep snow, following the sound of barking. I want to be a responsible dog owner, so I always carry a flashlight and a pocketful of plastic bags on our nightly excursions. I pulled the flashlight out of my pocket and switched it on. I played the light over the expanse, seeing nothing but snow. A few more steps and there he was: a swiftly moving brown and white tail and furry butt.

"Mattie," I said, sounding very stern. "Come here, right now!"

He turned his head and looked at me. The light caught his brown eyes. But he didn't come at my command and turned back to whatever had grabbed his attention. It appeared to be a black plastic garbage bag.

My blood boiled. Some irresponsible citizen had chucked their garbage into the park.

The dog stopped barking and settled into a low whine. He stood over the bag, looking back at me. Urging me to come closer.

I shined the flashlight on the bag.

Something reflected back at me.

This was no garbage bag. It was person. A man.

Rest Ye Murdered Gentlemen

Vicki Delany

BERKLEY PRIME CRIME, NEW YORK

An imprint of Penguin Random House LLC
375 Hudson Street, New York, New York 10014

REST YE MURDERED GENTLEMEN

A Berkley Prime Crime Book / published by arrangement with the author

ISBN: 978-0-425-28080-5

PUBLISHING HISTORY
Berkley Prime Crime mass-market edition / November 2015

PRINTED IN THE UNITED STATES OF AMERICA

10 9 8 7 6 5 4 3 2

Cover illustration by Julia Green.
Cover design by Sarah Oberrender.
Interior text design by Tiffany Estreicher.

Penguin
Random
House

To Mom

Chapter 1

The tips of the tall turquoise and green hats bobbed in the lightly falling snow as the elves weaved through crowds of painted dolls, toy soldiers, shepherds with their sheep, reindeer, poultry, clowns, sugarplums, gingerbread people, and candy canes.

"I feel like an idiot," Jackie grumbled. "If Kyle dumps me because he sees me in this ridiculous getup, it'll be on your head, Merry Wilkinson."

I paid her no attention. Jackie always grumbled; it was her natural state. I could only imagine the level of grumbling if she'd been left out of our group. She wore a knee-length tunic of gold, turquoise, and forest green over black leggings. Her hat was a foot-high turquoise triangle with a green pom-pom bouncing on the end. Papier–mâché formed into hornlike appendages and then covered with green felt had been attached to the front of her high-heeled, calf-high boots. Turquoise triangles, outlined in gold glitter, were painted on her cheeks, and her eye shadow was a matching shade of turquoise. I thought the playful makeup brought out my shop assistant's natural beauty much better than the overly applied stuff she normally wore. I kept that opinion to myself.

"Shouldn't you . . . ah . . . be helping?" I nodded to the line disappearing into the crowd. One of the littlest of the elves was in great danger of wandering off, so enchanted was he by everything going on around him.

"If I must." She sighed heavily, but hurried to take the boy's hand and, with a soft word, guide him back into the line.

My mother marched at the front, leading the group toward our float. She was singing scales, and even if the children couldn't see over the crowd they should have been able to follow the sound of her voice. My mother had been a diva at the Metropolitan Opera. She knew how to make herself heard.

I adjusted my mobcap and retied the strings of my apron.

It was December first and we were assembling for the Santa Claus parade, the biggest event of the year in Rudolph, New York, otherwise known as Christmas Town. If there's one thing we know how to do in Rudolph, it's Christmas.

I checked behind me for stragglers and then hurried to catch up. The children were from my mom's vocal classes. The youngest ones would sit on the decorated flatbed while the teenagers marched beside, singing carols. They were all dressed in the same colors and style as Jackie, in varying degrees of quality depending on their parents' sewing skills. They were elves, and I was Mrs. Claus.

Jackie had argued for considerably more décolletage in her elf costume and a much shorter tunic. I'd put my foot firmly down on that. Then she stubbornly refused to let her mother make the costume roomy enough to fit over her winter coat. I let her win that one. Jackie could freeze if she wanted to. The children's costumes had been made large enough to fit over winter coats and snowsuits. I wore two wool sweaters under my dress, a pair of thick tights, and heavy socks, all of which added about thirty pounds to my frame. I didn't need thirty pounds, but it was Christmas and if I was going to be Mrs. Claus, I wanted to dress the part.

Up ahead, I saw Mom climb onto the float. Small children scrambled up after her. The teenagers took their positions and immediately pulled out their smartphones while waiting to begin. Parents milled about snapping pictures.

"Ho, ho, ho," Santa Claus boomed, waving greetings left and right as he walked through the crowd, heading for his own float.

The youngest children squealed in delight; the teenagers rolled their eyes and continued texting, while the parents clapped their hands and tried to look thrilled.

It was, of course, not Santa but my dad, the appropriately named Noel. Dad's round stomach was real as was his thick white beard and the shock of white curls only slightly tinged with gray even though he was coming up on sixty. He totally looked the part in the traditional Santa costume of red suit with white fur cuffs, red and white hat, wide black belt, and high black boots.

I was the last one onto my float. I grabbed my long skirts in one hand; Jackie took the other and hauled me up with as much grace as if she were landing a pike through a hole in the ice.

"Everyone ready?" I called. The children cheered. It seemed like we might actually be able to pull this off. This was the first year I owned my own shop in Rudolph, and thus was responsible for my own float, but in the past I'd always tried to get home to help with the parade. Other years, we'd used a handful of the younger kids from Mom's classes to sit on the float, but this year—without consulting me first—she decided to make the parade the focus of their fall program. All told, there were thirty children, aged five to seventeen.

I'd decorated the float so it looked like Santa's workshop. It had bales of hay for the elves to sit on, a couple of battered old wooden tables as workbenches, whatever I could scrounge in the way of hammers for tools, and some broken toys that looked like they were still being assembled. It was, I thought proudly, just great. George Mann, a crusty old farmer who'd been roped into helping by my dad, provided the tractor that would pull the float. I'd tried to get George to dress in costume, but he'd looked me in the eye and said, "No." I doubted George owned anything but muddy boots, brown overalls, and faded flannel shirts anyway. If anyone asked who he was supposed to be, I'd say the farmer in charge of the reindeer.

I had high hopes for my float. My goal was nothing less than the best in parade trophy.

One thing we didn't have to concern ourselves with was creating a north pole-like atmosphere. Here on the southern shores of Lake Ontario we get snow. A lot of snow. It was falling now, big fat fluffy flakes. The temperature hovered just below the freezing point and there was no wind; people would be comfortable standing on the sidewalk or sitting on blankets spread out on the curb while waiting for the parade. All the shops, including mine, Mrs. Claus's Treasures, were closed this morning so everyone could participate in the festivities, but the business development office had set up stands at regular intervals to serve hot drinks and baked goods.

The semiannual Santa Claus parade is the highlight of the tourist year in Rudolph. People come from hundreds of miles away to see it. When I'd walked through town this morning, going to check that the float had survived the night, I'd noticed that all the hotels and B&Bs had "No Vacancy" signs outside. That would make everyone happy. I say semiannual parade, because we have one in July also. What the heck, gotta get those marks, I mean tourists, to town somehow.

The parade assembly area was in the parking lot behind the town's community center. This morning the lot was a churning mass of adults and children in costume, marching bands, flags, floats, some definitely better than others, and tractors to pull them.

"Hey, kids, give us a smile," a voice called out. Russ Durham, editor in chief of the *Rudolph Gazette*, lifted his camera, and the giggling children struck a pose. Jackie, supposedly embarrassed to be seen in her costume, leapt to her feet and cocked a hip as the camera clicked.

At an unseen signal, engines at the front of the line roared to life. Marchers stamped their feet. Trumpeters and French horn players blew into their instruments. Children applauded and the high school cheerleaders did cartwheels.

Nothing, however, seemed to be happening at the front

of my float. I clambered up onto a bale of hay and peered through the plastic-wrap windows. George was in the tractor's seat, where he should be.

"Let's get going," I called.

He shrugged, not bothering to turn around. He might have said something but I couldn't hear over the noise of the parade starting. Then, to my horror, George got out of his seat and jumped to the ground. He opened the flap at the front of the tractor and his head disappeared into its mysterious depths.

My heart dropped into my stomach. I made my way through jabbering kids and climbed off the back of the float.

Russ had gone to see what George was up to. When I reached the engine, the two men were scratching their heads.

"Your kids look great," Russ said to me. His accent was slow and sexy, full of the color and spice of Louisiana.

"They sure do."

"So do you." He gave me a smile full of dancing hazel eyes and straight white teeth.

"I do not. I look like a harassed old lady." I peered at him through my spectacles. The frames contained nothing but plain glass, part of the costume. I'd stuffed my black hair inside the red and white checked mobcap that came complete with attached white curls.

"A beautiful harassed old lady, then," he said. I felt my color rise. Hopefully Russ would think the red cheeks were part of the costume.

But I had more important things to worry about right

then than how I looked. "Please, please don't tell me there's a problem," I begged George.

"Darn thing won't start," the old farmer replied.

"It has to start!"

"What's the holdup there?" someone called.

The floats near the beginning of the parade, where we were, represented a toymaker's front window, a candy store, a turkey farm, a groaning dinner table, and the stable in Bethlehem. The quilters' guild had red and green quilts arranged on their laps, and the high school marching band members were grinches. The book clubbers wore long skirts and bonnets and were led by Ralph Dickerson, wearing a nightgown and cap and carrying a candlestick. The role of Scrooge definitely suited Ralph, the town's budget chief.

It all looked like total chaos, but the town had been doing this for almost twenty years and they had it down pat.

"Why don't you try it again?" Russ helpfully suggested.

"Been tryin'," George replied.

A man vaulted over the bar at the back of the toymaker's float, the one directly in front of mine, and landed lightly on his feet, his movements a considerable contrast to his appearance. He looked to be about ninety years old with his enormous gray mustache and sideburns, nose accented by a lump of putty holding up his glasses, and an outfit of woolen jacket, knee-length breeches, and shoes with buckles, but I knew he was a thirty-year-old by the name of Alan Anderson; occupation, toymaker. Alan was the second-most popular man in Rudolph, after Santa, but only when wearing his toymaker regalia. He was tall and handsome with blond hair that curled around the back of his neck, sparkling blue eyes, and a ready laugh, but he could be quite shy, and he preferred to go incognito, so to speak.

Alan and I had dated for a short while in high school. It didn't last after graduation. He'd been happy to remain in Rudolph, learning woodworking from his father and making beautiful things, slowly and carefully. I had stars in my eyes as I planned a fast-paced life in the hectic, exciting magazine world of Manhattan. We'd each got what we wanted, but one of us—me—had given up the dream and returned to Rudolph.

I'd wondered briefly if the old spark might be rekindled, but December in Christmas Town was not a time to be courting. We were all too darn busy.

Alan gave me a smile before going to join George and Russ. "Need any help here?" He also stared into the depths of the tractor engine, the three men looking as though it would start if only they focused hard enough.

George's tractor might have been at its best during World War II, but that was no reason for it to give up the ghost now. "Can't you do some kind of temporary fix?" I asked.

George didn't dignify that comment with a reply. Russ looked confused—I guessed engines were not his thing, but he didn't like to admit it. Alan patted his pockets as if he might find exactly the right tool.

Jingle Bell Lane, Rudolph's main street, down which the parade would pass, was out of sight of those of us at the back of the community center, but we could hear the excited murmur of expectation.

I groaned. George continued to scratch his chin.

Alan threw me an apologetic look. "I'm sorry, Merry, but I have to get back. We're about to leave."

"Sure," I said, forcing out a smile.

"Are you, uh, going to the post-parade party?" He shuffled his feet in their buckled shoes.

"Wouldn't miss it."

"Perhaps I'll see you there. Good luck with the float."

I might have spent a moment wondering if Alan merely meant he'd be at the party, or if he was trying to say something deeper, but one of the orange vest–wearing marshals arrived at a trot. "What's going on, Merry? You have to get moving."

I waved my arms. "It won't start. We can't push the dratted thing." In the line behind me, drivers began shouting at us to get out of the way. I could see the front of the parade turning into the street. I wanted to cry.

"You'll have to walk," Russ said. "Let's get the kids down."

"But my float! All my work."

"Nothing you can do about that now, Merry."

"What," my mother sang, "is happening down there?"

I glanced frantically around. Some of the kids were only five or six years old. They'd been recruited because they looked so cute in their costumes, not to walk a couple of miles. In any event, many of them wouldn't have adequate boots. A wave of questions washed over me as the proud parents began demanding to know what was going on. The candy store float pulled around mine; the marching band followed.

Jackie yelled at me to hurry up. As if I hadn't noticed that we were being left behind.

"I've an idea," Russ said. "George, where's your truck?"

George jerked his head. "Pine." The small street behind Jingle Bell Lane.

"How long would it take to attach the tractor to the truck?" Russ asked.

"Minute."

"Run and get it. You can pull the dratted tractor."

George's truck was occasionally called upon to retrieve vehicles that foolishly tried to cross the shallow waters of the bay before the ice was thick enough. But I didn't see that it could help us now. I eyed the mess of floats, marchers, bands, clowns, parents waving their children off. "We can't get the truck through. There's no room!"

"Go, George," Russ said. "Fall into line behind the last float, then hitch up Merry, and join the parade. I'll help you."

"Okay." George sauntered off at his usual slow, rolling gait.

"You can bring up the rear, Merry," Russ said. "Wait until everyone's out of the way, and we'll hook up the truck and fall in line."

"But Santa is supposed to be last," I wailed. "Santa is always last."

"Merry, what is the holdup?" My mother appeared. "The children are getting restless. As am I. It is no good for my voice to be out in this cold for overly long, you know." She waved her hands. Her leather gloves were a perfect match to her gown. Mom had flatly refused to be an elf ("hideous little creatures," she'd declared) and instead spent what was probably a mind-boggling amount of money to have a New York seamstress who sewed costumes for Broadway create a gown that wouldn't have been out of place in the ball scene of *Pride and Prejudice*. I'd been furious, thinking she wanted to upstage a bunch of kids. Today, I had to admit (as

I usually did) that she'd been right (as she usually was). Rather than putting herself above the rest of our ensemble, her gown, in reverse colors—forest green with turquoise accents—tied the group together into a very impressive whole.

"You folks need to get that out of the way." Officer Candice Campbell of the Rudolph police—the one person I didn't need right now—arrived on the scene. "It's blocking traffic."

"Gee, I hadn't noticed," I said. "Candy." Her mouth twisted. Candy was what she'd been called in high school. Now that she was an officer of the law, she really hated that name. Which is why I said it. We didn't get on any better as adults than we had in grade nine.

"It's all in hand, Officer," Russ said with a smile.

The hard cop-like demeanor Candy tried so hard to project melted a fraction. Then she remembered who she was. And that I was watching. "I hope so. Otherwise, I'll l have to issue you a ticket, Merry. Blocking traffic. That's for starters."

I ground my teeth.

The quilt guild float passed us. The women wore identical green and red earmuffs and were pretending to sew—despite their heavy mittens—the cloth spread out on their laps. "Problems, Aline?" a woman called, clearly enjoying the spectacle. "Perhaps we'll see you at the finish line." Her fellow quilters laughed.

Mom ignored them. Perhaps only I could tell that inside she was seething. Mother hated to be shown up in anything, whether upstaged at the Met or falling out of order in the Santa Claus parade.

Groups of anxious parents had followed Mom and were milling about. I told them a replacement vehicle was coming and suggested Mom use the opportunity to warm the children's voices—and the children—up.

She went back to the float. Jackie hauled her up. Not quite the sort of arrival on stage Mom was used to, but she didn't miss a beat. "Children, we will begin with 'Jingle Bells.'" She gave the note.

These kids were taking singing lessons, and some of them were showing considerable talent. The perfect notes rose into the cold crisp air to land on gently falling snowflakes.

Listening to them, I almost forgot how upset I was.

Everyone loved being in the parade, but getting ready and assembled in all the chaos was extremely stressful. Children, not to mention their mothers, could be brought to tears, and more than one fistfight usually threatened to break out. Over the years, I'd heard hundreds of people swear never to do it again. A month later they'd be back, signing up for the parade once again.

As the pure young voices rang out, I could see people visibly relaxing. Grins appeared on ruddy faces, and folks gave their neighbors warm smiles and exchanged handshakes.

The Christmas magic was back.

I remembered that I was supposed to be angry when the penultimate float passed us. If I had any competition for best of parade, this was it. Vicky Casey, my closest friend since babyhood, might be the person I loved most on earth after my parents, but when it came to the parade, she was my bitterest enemy. Vicky owned Victoria's Bake Shoppe.

As well as the usual delights to be found in a small-town bakery, Vicky specialized in gingerbread. Gingerbread cakes, gingerbread bread, gingerbread cookies. Even gingerbread hot chocolate mix, and her special ginger tonic that, added to a glass of whiskey, was guaranteed to warm the cockles of your heart on a cold winter's night (whatever cockles might be). Last year she'd won best of parade with the elves' Christmas Day feast. This year her float was done up like an old-fashioned bakery, with cardboard boxes painted and arranged to resemble an open hearth, a wood-fired oven, and a table covered in rolling pins, pie plates, and cookie cutters. Shelves held breads, pies, and cakes so realistic she'd caught one of her nephews trying to steal a fake cookie. The people posing as bakery workers, gathered from the ranks of her vast extended family, were dressed in long skirts and aprons for the girls, and striped gray pants and high white hats for the boys.

Vicky tossed me a worried look as her float passed. "Okay?" she mouthed.

"Engine problems," I mouthed back.

Realizing that neither I nor anyone with me was in life-threatening danger, she pumped her fist in a triumphant gesture and sailed on by. I really hated that smirk. Almost as much as I hated the glare Santa Claus, aka Dad, threw at me as his high golden sleigh, pulled by nine giant stuffed reindeer mounted on a tractor almost as old as George's, passed.

In any other parade Santa might be the star of the show, but in our town that role went to Fergus Cartwright, the mayor. Looking somewhat like a polar bear losing his fur, His Honor was wrapped in a thick white blanket, with a bushy white faux-fur hat plopped on his hairless head and white mittens on his hands. The mayor sat on the golden thronelike chair at the back of the sleigh, waving regally, while Santa stood in front yelling "Ho, ho, ho." Members of the town's fire department, dressed in their firefighting gear and Santa hats, walked on either side of the sleigh, handing candy canes to laughing, clapping children.

At last, George's behemoth of a truck came into sight. Russ ran to meet him, and he and George quickly attached the truck to the front of the tractor. We had no way of moving the tractor aside while the parade was assembling and didn't want to waste precious minutes to do it now.

I ran back to my float.

"You can't start now," Candy said, trotting beside me. "Santa has to be last."

"Is that an official bylaw?"

"If it isn't it should be."

"Arrest me then," I said. I climbed onto my float.

"Can we go now, Merry?" An adorable little girl peeked out from under the brim of her overlarge hat.

"Yes. Let's go!"

George clambered into the cab of his truck, and Russ leapt up after me as, accompanied by the cheers of the singers and their anxious parents, we jerked into motion. Officer Candy looked as though she were mentally searching the legal books, trying to find something—anything—to charge me with.

"Rudolph!" Mother called out. She sounded the note, and the choir began to sing "Rudolph the Red-Nosed Reindeer."

"You can't come with us," I said to Russ. "You're not in costume."

"The way I look at it, Mrs. Claus, you made me miss taking shots of the start of the parade, so you owe me a lift. Just think of me as the official photographer of Santa's workshop." He lifted his camera and snapped a close-up of my scowling face.

Chapter 2

For the crime of falling out of order and thus disrupting the smooth running of the event, my float was disqualified from best in parade.

That the head of the judging committee this year was Vicky's uncle Doug had nothing at all, he assured me, to do with his decision. Then he buried his face in his chest and hurried away.

I didn't even have time to get mad again. I left Mom and the parents to get the kids off the float and calm them down. Russ and his camera had jumped off somewhere along the parade route. George would haul the float to Mom and Dad's place where it would spend the next six months in the carriage house.

Jackie and I had to make our way to Mrs. Claus's Treasures posthaste and get everything ready to open the shop for the crowds of eager shoppers who would, the plan went, soon pour through the doors.

But first I had to run to my own home and let Matterhorn, my dog, out for a stretch. I lifted my long skirts and galloped through town as fast as I dared on the fresh snow. I cut through the park and rounded the bandstand. Not a person was in sight. Everyone was either still at the parade route, sipping hot chocolate and nibbling cookies, or getting their own businesses ready. To my left, the bay off Lake Ontario was a soft blur of white on white. To my right the shops and houses were all beautifully decorated for the season. I had no time to admire my surroundings. I'd been planning to let the dog pee in his crate today, but a horrified Vicky had told me that we were at a very delicate stage of housebreaking, and to do so might set us back months. Why she used the royal "we" when she was neither the one peeing nor the one rushing home to attend to that, I didn't know. I didn't quite know how I'd ended up with a dog, and a Saint Bernard puppy at that.

Matterhorn, or Mattie as I usually called him, knocked me flying as I opened the door to his crate. He then proceeded to stand over me and threaten to lick me to death. I sputtered, wiped a copious amount of drool off my face, and staggered to my feet. My apartment is one half of the second floor of a gorgeous nineteenth-century Victorian, accessible from the narrow servants' staircase that opens onto the backyard. Knowing what was next, Mattie bolted down the stairs and waited for me to catch up. I opened the back door. He still wasn't quite sure about this snow stuff, and stood on the threshold for a moment, sniffing the air. I gave his rear end a slight push with the toe of my boot and out he went.

He did his business, and then, apparently deciding that this snow stuff was okay after all, cavorted about the yard, leaping at flakes, trying to catch them in his mouth. I watched him play, feeling a smile on my face. Next year I might do my float as a Swiss watchmaker's workshop on Christmas Eve. The kids would love Mattie. He could wear a barrel tied under his chin. He threatened to be big enough by then for the kids to sit on.

I snapped myself back to this year. "Come on, boy. Time to come in. Mattie, come here. Mattie!"

He was showing no inclination of giving up his fun to be stuffed back into his crate. Not only had I found myself with a new dog, but over the Christmas season, my busiest time of the year. Cursing my lack of foresight, I stomped into the yard and dragged the resisting thirty-pound, ten-week-old puppy back into the house.

I then ran all the way to the shop. We were ready to open with five minutes to spare.

Jackie refused to wear the elf costume any longer and had changed into the clothes she'd brought to work. I planned to keep playing Mrs. Claus, hoping it would charm the customers. My tights and the bottom foot of my skirt were soaking wet. The snow that had gathered when I chased the dog around the yard was melting in the warmth of the shop.

Ignoring the chill running up my legs, I ran a critical eye over the display areas, pleased with what I saw. As can be assumed by the name of my business, I specialize in Christmas decorations. My stuff tended to be one-of-a-kind items made by local artists or crafters, or occasionally brought in from my sources in New York City. I'd spent five years as a deputy style editor with a well-known lifestyle magazine. Locating items that were unique, beautiful, and yet affordable to the average buyer was what I did best.

I peered through the shop windows. In keeping with the theme of my float, I'd created a display to resemble the elves' jewelry work area. A local jeweler had lent me some of her older or seldom-used tools and I'd scrounged an old-fashioned wooden school desk and a few kerosene lamps for props. Some of the most eye-catching pieces of jewelry were laid out on black velvet cloth next to a cluster of sparking glass Christmas trees, while a brightly painted wooden Santa inspected them through his spectacles. A couple, her wrapped in fur, him in a calf-length black leather coat and gloves, stopped to inspect the display. I saw her pointing at a glittering rhinestone brooch in the shape of a wreath.

I flipped the sign to "Open" and unlocked the door. The couple came into the shop. "Let us know if you need any help," I said.

"Thank you."

"Your first time to Rudolph?"

"Yes, and it won't be our last, will it, honey? That parade this morning has got to be one of the best I've ever seen. Nothing like a good old-fashioned parade to get the holiday spirit flowing."

I grinned at him. A man after my own heart. I left them to browse.

Jackie came out of the back, dressed in black ankle boots, black tights, a short black skirt, and snug blue sweater. I noticed the man give her a quick once-over. I didn't employ Jackie because she attracted male customers, but it was a bonus.

I adjusted my fake spectacles and settled the mobcap and white hair into a better place on my head.

The bell over the door tinkled and customers began to flood in. I assigned Jackie to staff the till, while I wandered the shop floor, answering questions and helping people choose gifts or decorations.

About an hour after opening a man came in. He was alone, but that wasn't unusual. Plenty of women nudged their husbands in the direction of my shop while they went to Diva Accessories next door. He carried a camera and a notebook; that was unusual.

Betty Thatcher, owner of Rudolph's Gift Nook, the shop on the other side of me, burst in, hot on his heels. The Nook sold mass-produced Christmas decorations, most of them made in China. Nothing wrong with that. We shouldn't have been in competition, but as far as Betty was concerned, every hundred dollars spent on an ornament at my shop could have been used to purchase a truckload of discount decorations at hers. Betty hadn't had a float in the parade—she never did—but I'd seen her there, lurking in the crowd and smirking at my misfortune.

"Mr. Pearce!" she cried, "I totally forgot to tell you about my idea for expanding the store."

The newcomer gave her a strained smile. "I have all I want, thank you," he said in a strong English accent. He was probably in his late forties, short and lightly built, with a bad comb-over and a pale complexion that retained the memory of teenage acne. He approached me, while Betty, tiny but formidable, plucked at his sleeve. "Why don't we go for a coffee? Or I suppose you'd prefer tea." She snorted out a laugh. "My treat. You have to see the Cranberry Coffee Bar. It's one of our most popular spots."

"Thank you," he repeated. "I have the coffee shop on my list."

"Can I help you?" I asked.

"No," said Betty. "Maybe after tea. Come along, Mr. Pearce."

"Thank you for your time, Mrs. Thatcher. I have all I need from you."

Even Betty couldn't fail to notice that she'd been dismissed. She threw me a glare that said it was all my fault this Mr. Pearce didn't want to have tea with her.

"I have a few free minutes right now," she said, defiant in the face of defeat. "I expect to be *soooo* busy for the rest of the afternoon. The crowds just never let up at Rudolph's Gift Nook. You are *soooo* lucky, Merry, not to have that problem." Pleased with her parting shot, she left.

I still didn't know who this man was. His coat was wool, his scarf cashmere, his gloves leather, his camera a Nikon. "Nigel Pearce," he said. "I'm with *World Journey* magazine, here to do a feature on your town and its Christmas spirit."

"Welcome," I croaked. "I mean, welcome to Rudolph and to Mrs. Claus's Treasures." *World Journey* was one of the top travel magazines in Europe.

"I saw you at the parade," he said. "Late, were you?"

"Mechanical problems."

"Are you the proprietor?"

"Yes." I held out my hand. "Merry Wilkinson." I spelled

my name, as I always have to, otherwise people think it's Mary.

He touched my fingers with the tips of his leather gloves. He wasn't exactly warm and friendly, but if Nigel Pearce wanted to write about my shop for *World Journey* magazine, he could be as cold as he wanted to be.

"Pretty town. The Christmas stuff is a mite over-the-top for my taste, but they say some people like all this holiday kitsch. We're going to title the article 'America's Christmas Town.'"

"How nice," I said, ignoring the fact that he'd called my beautiful artisanal goods holiday kitsch. I did not leap into the air and high-five Jackie, although I wanted to. My father and the burgomasters and burgomistresses of Rudolph would be beyond delighted. They'd been trying for a long time to have our town known as America's Christmas Town, but we had stiff competition from the likes of Santa Claus, Indiana; Christmas, Florida; North Pole, Alaska; and Snowflake, Arizona. If *World Journey* gave us the label, it would pretty much be official. I could imagine my dad saying, "Take that, Snowflake!"

"Nice shop." Nigel lifted his camera and began taking pictures. He should have asked permission first, but I was hardly going to slap him down for being rude, now was I?

"Nice staff." He focused on Jackie. She tossed her hair, tilted her chin, stuck out her chest, and beamed.

"Why don't you come out from behind the counter and show us some of these pretty things, love?"

Jackie threw me a questioning glance.

"Your boss won't mind," Nigel said. "I'll get some shots of her looking . . . Christmassy."

There wasn't much to do right now anyway. The customers had stopped browsing and were watching Nigel click away. A few stepped politely out of the way; several stepped forward, trying to "inadvertently" get themselves in the frame.

He took pictures of Jackie standing beside the gaily decorated live Douglas fir (replaced every month), Jackie showing a customer a display of quilted place mats, Jackie helping a man choose a gift for his wife, Jackie posing among our collection of three-foot-tall stuffed Santas, Jackie being Jackie, pretty and flirtatious.

He took one picture of me ringing up a sale. He told me not to smile—it made me look too young to be Mrs. Claus.

My mom would kill someone when she heard she'd missed this.

At last Nigel had all the pictures he wanted. I told Jackie to get behind the counter as a line was forming, and I walked with the photographer to the door. I handed him my card. He put it in his pocket without a word.

"Have you heard about the parade reception tonight? Six thirty at the community center. Santa will be there, some local musicians are playing, a children's choir is singing, and there will be plenty of refreshments. Everyone is welcome."

"It's all part of Christmas in America's Christmas Town, right?"

"Right." I smiled, trying to look friendly. He glanced across the room at Jackie. She waved and called out, "Catch you at the party, Nigel!"

He left.

With the speed and agility of a lion catching sight of an

unattended baby zebra, Betty Thatcher leapt out from the door of her shop.

"What an unfortunate thing to happen," Vicky said to me after she'd modestly accepted the first place trophy at the post-parade party. "Tractor breakdown, and you went to so much trouble. Oh, well, better luck next time." The trophy, a hefty two-foot-tall, gold-painted reindeer with a big red glass ball for a nose, was prominently displayed in the center of the room for all to admire. Plaques ran across the base, with the names of the first place winners and their years. Until next December, the trophy would once again sit in the place of pride on the top shelf of Vicky's bakery. A smaller statue, of Rudolph in bathing trunks and sunglasses, was awarded for the summer parade, but it didn't have the prestige of coming first in the main event. It, too, adorned the bakery.

We were gathered in the main hall of the community center for the after-parade festivities. The prizes had been awarded, every group (except mine!) pretty much got something for showing up. Mom's class sang Christmas songs. Their "Silent Night" was so beautiful that a few of the tourists were brought to tears. As was Mom, when she heard there had been a journalist from an internationally famous magazine in the shop that afternoon. She was mollified when Nigel sauntered in, laden with photography equipment, and I introduced them.

Nigel then went on to take more photos of Jackie: in front of the buffet, admiring the trophies, sitting innocently on Santa's knee. Kyle Lambert, Jackie's current boyfriend, glowered all the while.

But even Jackie had to give way to Mom and her school. I had no doubt that if—a big if—we were the cover story of the magazine, as Nigel had hinted, the photo of her, resplendent in her Broadway-worthy gown, surrounded by pink-cheeked, beribboned, turquoise and green elf–costumed kids, would be on it.

The main room of the center was fully decorated for Christmas, with a real tree with all the trimmings, rows of red stockings pinned to one wall, and colorful baubles hanging throughout. Santa held court for the kids in a big, comfortable wingback chair, listening to their wishes and posing for pictures. Alan, dressed in his toymaker getup, was acting as Santa's assistant, taking notes on a lengthy scroll of paper with a pen that had an elaborate feather stuck to one end. His Honor held court, or attempted to, with the adults, accepting praise for how well everything had gone.

Victoria's Bake Shoppe had catered the affair. Hot chocolate, with or without ginger tonic, huge slabs of gingerbread cake, and perfect gingerbread cookies cut in all sorts of interesting shapes. Fortunately, Vicky had forgone the anatomically correct boy and girl cookies that had been served at my last birthday party—to my considerable surprise.

People came from far and wide to Rudolph for parade weekend. I'd talked to people today from California, Quebec, and Wyoming. With the feature in *World Journey*, we might start getting tourists from Europe and Asia. Dollar signs danced in my head.

My skirt and tights had dried over the afternoon, but then I had to make another dash across the park to feed Mattie and let him out before coming to the party, and I was soaked once again. I was beginning to lose contact with my toes.

I was thoroughly beat and wanted nothing more than to go home, put the fire on, pour a glass of wine, grab *Holmes for the Holidays* or *More Holmes for the Holidays,* which I read every year, and go to bed early. But I wouldn't be able to do that until December twenty-sixth. The store was closed, of course, on Christmas Day, but somehow I'd managed to get myself talked into hosting Christmas dinner in my tiny apartment.

I glanced around the crowded room. Russ had given me a wave when I came in, but had spent his time interviewing town dignitaries and taking pictures for the paper. Pretty much everyone who lived in the vicinity of Rudolph, New York, could be counted on to be here: business owners, the farmers and craftspeople who supplied our shops and kitchens, representatives of the service clubs, town employees. About the only people missing would be the restaurant staff. They'd be getting ready to serve dinner.

The politicians had come out in force, including two state representatives. Speaking of which, I spotted Sue-Anne Morrow glad-handing the crowd. (Glad-handing the locals anyway. She ignored the obvious tourists.) Sue-Anne hadn't declared her candidacy yet, but she made no secret of the fact that she would be challenging Fergus Cartwright for the mayoralty in the forthcoming elections. She was going to run on the slogan "Rudolph can do BETTER!" Our town was prospering, but the number of visitors had dropped off from the heights of a few years ago and sales were down. Nothing we could do about the recession that had stung the entire state, but Sue-Anne wanted everyone to know it was all Fergus's fault.

Fergus had been mayor for seven years, and a lot of people—including me—thought he was getting a bit too comfortable with the job. He hadn't had a fresh idea in a long time. In fact, most of his ideas (when he had them) were handed to him by my dad, who'd decided not to run for another term. But I wasn't entirely sure I wanted Sue-Anne as mayor. I suspected she had a nasty streak that she kept well hidden under her sprayed helmet of gray-blond hair and pastel power suits that always matched her shoes. Today she wore a boxy pink suit with three-quarter-length sleeves and a skirt cut sharply at the knee. I doubted that the suit, or the pink and black ankle boots, had been bought at Jayne's Ladies Wear, Rudolph's premier women's fashion store. Sue-Anne's only concession to the season was a tiny brooch representing a decorated Christmas tree pinned on her collar. Maybe that was one of the reasons I didn't trust Sue-Anne. I didn't think she truly *loved* Christmas.

In Rudolph we lived and breathed Christmas all year long. You might think that would make us hard and cynical when the time arrived, but somehow it made me love the real thing all the more. And I knew the majority of my fellow townspeople felt the same.

I glanced around the room. Most of the women, locals as well as tourists, not in some sort of costume had accented their outfits with the worst (meaning the best!) of Christmas jewelry. Gaudy flashing-light necklaces that the Nook sold for two dollars (five bucks for three), earrings of wreaths or trees, giant brooches. More than a few men were in the sort of homemade Christmas sweaters fashion magazines ridiculed. I spotted Betty Thatcher slithering along behind Nigel Pearce, trying to worm her way into every conversation he attempted to have or every picture he tried to take. I watched as Nigel snapped pictures of three attractive teenage singers when it was their turn on stage, and decided that Betty, fifty years old, totally without curves, and dressed in her usual frumpy style, didn't have a chance. I almost felt sorry for her, and then she caught me watching and gave me a look of such disdain, my sympathy dissolved.

"You're a thousand miles away," a voice said at my side; Alan Anderson with two glasses of steaming hot chocolate. He passed me one. A single giant marshmallow, home-made at Candy Cane Sweets, floated on the surface.

"Thanks. I might have been at the North Pole. I was thinking that I love Christmas."

He laughed. It made a strange sound: the notes of a young man, the appearance of one about a hundred years old. No doubt I presented a similar paradox.

All part of that Christmas magic. I grinned at him and took a sip of hot chocolate. Thick and rich. The toymaker gave me a warm smile. The young blue eyes sparked from beneath his spectacles and under bushy gray eyebrows. I took another sip as I wiggled my toes, trying to get some circulation back into them. My sodden skirt weighed about a ton and my lower appendages felt as though ice might be forming on them. The room was freezing, with the door constantly opening, and most people were dressed in heavy winter clothes and parade-suitable costumes.

"Having a break?" I asked.

"Yup. Even Santa has to answer the call of nature."

My dad had returned from the restroom and was in a

little conclave with Nigel Pearce, Russ Durham, Ralph Dickerson, Fergus Cartwright, and my mom. Mom was drinking water, and the men were munching on gingerbread. Sue-Anne Morrow danced at the edges of the group, trying to squeeze herself in while Mom tried to block her. Betty had disappeared.

Alan and I stood in comfortable silence, watching. Alan was a man of few words. His wooden toys—as much art as things for kids to play with—spoke for him.

Soon Dad broke away from the group and went back to his duties. Mom turned to exchange a word with him, and Sue-Anne saw her chance. She darted forward and thrust her hand toward Nigel.

"I'd better get back to it," Alan said. "Do you . . . uh . . . think, Merry, when all this is over that . . ."

"Nice party." The couple who'd been first into my shop today came up to us. Alan nodded to them and slipped away. I gave them a smile, and not only because they'd dropped five hundred bucks on jewelry and Christmas ornaments.

"We've already made a reservation at the inn for next year," the woman said. "We've finally found a way to entertain my parents on their annual visit. They've retired to Hawaii and love it, but Mom still pines for the old-fashioned Christmases of her youth."

"That's the spirit of Rudolph," I said, feeling my smile widening. Old-fashioned Christmases were my bread and butter.

Night had arrived before five o'clock and snow still drifted lazily out of the dark sky. The room was bathed in a soft blue and green light from the tree and decorations. Soon nothing was left of the food but a few armless and headless gingerpeople and a pile of crumbs. And not many of those. We deliberately didn't provide *too* much food; we wanted our visitors to go to one of the town's many restaurants after the party. People chatted and laughed in small groups, still enjoying their hot chocolate and the last of the cookies, reluctant to head out into the night. The youngest children were being folded into their snowsuits to be taken home and put to bed after an exciting day.

Christmas. I might spend the entire month of December in an overworked panic, but I still love it as much as I did when I was a small kid. And in our house, Christmas had been pretty special. After all, my dad was Santa Claus.

The nicest thing about the Christmas spirit, I always thought, was that it was infectious. Everyone was made happy simply by being near it.

Well, almost everyone. Three people standing by the buffet table did not look as though they were about to burst into a spontaneous round of carols. I knew them all. Two were store owners from the next town, Muddle Harbor. The third was the mayor of that unfortunately named town, Randy Baumgartner.

Over the years, as the reputation of Rudolph as *the* place for Christmas activities and shopping grew, the town of Muddle Harbor fell into decline. It wasn't entirely our fault—the town's main industry had closed and the shipyard along with it—but Muddle Harbor folks were convinced that Rudolph was stealing all the visitors that would otherwise be pouring into their town, loaded with cash to spend.

In fact, they did pretty well out of our overflow. When the B&Bs and inns in Rudolph were full, we directed people to Muddle Harbor and that brought customers to their shops and restaurants. Five years ago they'd tried to set themselves up as "Easter Town" with a parade and festival in the spring. That had ended when the former mayor had run through town in an Easter Bunny outfit with a vital part of his costume missing, pursued by the three-hundred-pound trucker-father of the nineteen-year-old Queen of the Easter Parade, titled the "Chocolette." Right now, Randy Baumgartner and his companions were glaring at the group around Nigel Pearce.

George lumbered up to me, a slab of gingerbread clenched in his paw.

"I hope you're able to get the tractor fixed," I said.

"Already done."

"Not too expensive, then?"

"Have to tell you, Merry. It wasn't no mechanical problem."

"What then?" Not that I particularly wanted to hear. I am interested in a lot of things in this world, but the intricacies of a tractor's innards are not among them.

"Spark plug wires switched."

"Oh. How'd you get it into town, then?" I saw Vicky come out of the kitchen with a fresh platter of cookies. I'd been mad at her long enough. Time to go and help. Give her a chance to invite Nigel Pearce to her bakery.

"Merry," George said. The tone of his voice was so serious I turned back to him.

"What?"

"I drove the tractor into town last night, right?"

"Yes."

"Between then and this morning when the parade started,

the wires got switched. The wires start in order. If they ain't in the right order, the engine don't start."

"Why would that happen?"

"It didn't do it by itself, Merry."

"But you fixed it, right?"

"Easy enough once everyone and their dog weren't yellin' at me to start the blasted tractor, and I had a chance to check 'er over."

"George, are you saying . . . ?"

"That the tractor everyone knew would be pullin' your float was sabotaged. Yeah, Merry, I guess that's what I'm sayin'. Hum, I better get another one o' those cookies afore they're all gone." He touched the rim of his ball cap in his polite old-fashioned way and sauntered off.

Chapter 3

Gobsmacked, I stared at George's departing figure. The way George had described it, it certainly sounded as though the inability of his tractor to start this morning hadn't been an accident. The floats and the vehicles to pull them had been assembled yesterday evening and left in the community center parking lot all night. No one in Rudolph had ever even considered we should put a guard on the floats.

Who would do something like that?

And to me!

I watched Vicky exchange a word with one of her helpers. Vicky was the only one who benefited from the disabling of my float.

No, not Vicky.

I hurried across the room to give her a hand. I was beat, but my best friend had also been on her feet all day, and she still had dishes to pack up, the kitchen to clean, and then needed to have the shelves in her bakery fully stocked and ready to open at seven tomorrow morning.

I grabbed an empty tray out of her hands. "You better take a minute and talk to that guy over there. He's a big-time travel reporter."

She pushed the single long lock of purple hair out of her eyes. The rest of her hair was cropped short. "I've been told. He was in the bakery at lunchtime. Had ham and Swiss on a baguette and potato soup. Even took a few pictures before he left. Don't worry, I'm about to wow him with my special cookies."

"That's good, then," I said, meaning the sandwiches as well as the cookies. Vicky's baguettes were exceptional, even better than ones I'd had in Paris: soft on the inside, crusty on the outside, served with thickly spread butter from a local farm. Yummy! More than a few pounds on my hips owed their existence to that bread. I pulled my head back from dreams of warm baking. "Still, you should take a break, freshen up. I can help with the dishes."

We walked together into the large industrial kitchen. Vicky's helpers were washing the serving dishes and tossing unfinished food and crumpled napkins—featuring Santa's sleigh and his nine reindeer crossing a night sky thick with stars—into the trash.

"I'm sorry about what happened to your float, Merry. Really I am. I was sure it was going to win. Although I can't say I'm not entirely surprised that tractor of George's finally went on strike."

I'd decided not to tell anyone about the suspected sabotage. For now anyway. George was mighty handy with an engine, but even he could make a mistake.

I put the trays on the long table in the center of the room. One platter of untouched treats remained. "These look pretty special."

Vicky made plain cookies, just good gingerbread cut into fun shapes. The only decorations were on the reindeer, who were given tiny red candies for noses. She didn't believe in elaborate icing on cookies. Too much work, she said, and it detracted from the pure flavor of the cookie.

But these cookies were works of art. Edible art. The Santa suits had been painted in bright red icing, with a strip of licorice for the belt, chocolate ganache boots, and a white icing beard. The brightly costumed people had pink icing smiles and black licorice-piece eyes, and the sleigh was piled high with candy gifts. The cookies rested on a bed of coconut arranged to look like snow. The biggest and most beautiful cookie was painted with a thick layer of white icing, topped with colored icing to show a bespectacled man wearing a frock coat and a tall hat, carrying a book. I leaned over and peered closely in order to read the delicate writing painted onto the book. *A Christmas Carol.*

"It's Charles Dickens!"

"I decided to do something over the top for our special guest," Vicky said. "I hope he likes it. It was a heck of a lot of work. You're just in time. I'm about to present it. I asked your mom to make sure Mr. Pearce stayed until the end."

She hefted the tray and handed it to me. "You take it."

"I can't! You deserve the credit."

"I'll get the credit, you can be sure of that. But you're dressed for the part, Mrs. Claus. Come on, let's go."

Her helpers stopped working to watch. The door was

held open for me, and I proudly carried the tray of cookies into the room.

"What have we got here?" Dad boomed. "Ho, ho, ho!"

Mom launched into the "champagne" song from *Die Fledermaus*.

"For our distinguished guest," Vicky said as everyone gathered around. Most of the tourists had left after checking their watches and muttering about reservations or getting children to bed. It was now time for the town to congratulate itself on a job well done, to pat itself on the back, and to relax . . . for about five minutes. Then we headed back to work to get ready for another busy day that was Christmas Town in December. The only outsiders remaining were Nigel Pearce and the people from Muddle Harbor. (The Muddites, we called them. They called us those blasted deer people.) Nigel snapped a photo of the gingerbread cookie display. Then he took another shot of a beaming Vicky beside the tray. Vicky indicated that she wanted me in the picture, but Nigel called for Jackie. Giggling and protesting that she had nothing to do with it, all the while shoving people aside, she snatched up a Santa and pretended to take a big bite. Her boyfriend, Kyle, hadn't dropped his scowl all evening. He clearly wasn't about to start now.

Russ, who regularly did triple duty as photographer and the paper's lead reporter as well as editor in chief, snapped a picture of me with an expression on my face that would frighten small children.

"For our English visitor," Vicky said once the cameras had stopped clicking. "I created a cookie in honor of his countryman who popularized many of the Christmas traditions we enjoy today." She smiled at Nigel and made a sweeping gesture toward the treats.

We all applauded and Nigel Pearce, looking quite pleased with himself, stepped forward. He picked up the elaborate Dickens cookie and bit the head off in one big bite. We applauded again.

The mayor cleared his throat prior to making a speech, but he was pushed aside by the rush on the food.

Once the tray had been vacuumed clean, everyone drifted off into the night. Mom declared that she was absolutely *exhausted,* and Dad gave her a fond smile. The Muddites went away mumbling, although I noticed that their mayor managed to snatch a couple of extra cookies and stuff them into his pocket. Nigel Pearce drew Jackie to one side and, peering down the front of her sweater all the while, whispered in her ear. Kyle had gone to get her coat. Russ snapped one last shot of me at the moment I took a bite of the cookie I'd been able to snatch out from under the grasping hands of Sue-Anne. She gave me a look that would curdle Santa's milk before forcing her face into a smile and turning to Russ.

"Why don't you walk me to my car, Russell, sweetie? It's getting so slippery out there, and these boots aren't suitable for ice. I need a man's strong arm."

Vicky wiggled her eyebrows at me, and I stifled a laugh. The sidewalks had been scraped so thoroughly they'd probably lost a quarter inch of pavement, and enough salt and sand had been laid in the parking lot to equip a California beach. The last thing the town of Rudolph wanted was for one of those tourists to slip and break a leg.

But Russ was young and attractive and exceedingly

charming, and Sue-Anne's husband was rarely seen around town. Probably more to the point, however, Russ represented the town's newspaper.

Vicky sent her helpers home, and I gave her a hand with the last of the cleaning.

"The whole day went well," she said, packing dishes into the plastic tubs she used for transporting supplies.

"Other than me being disqualified from the parade, you mean?"

A smile touched the corner of her mouth. "Other than that. Come on, I'll give you a ride home."

We were the last people to leave the community center. Vicky switched off the lights and I made sure the door had locked behind us.

"You're not being fair!"

"Look, Jackie, I . . ."

The voices broke off. Jackie and Kyle were standing against the wall by the back door, in deep shadows where the lights from the parking lot didn't reach. He had his hand on her arm, and his face was set into deep lines beneath narrowed black eyes. Jackie shook him off. "Night, Merry," she called.

Kyle stepped away from her. Embarrassed, he dug grooves in the snow with the toe of his boot.

"Are you okay there?" I asked, cradling one of Vicky's plastic tubs.

"We're fine. Kyle doesn't seem to understand about taking opportunities and making a grab for the brass ring." Jackie walked into the light. Kyle wasn't the brightest star on the Rudolph Christmas tree, but I'd always thought he was a nice guy. Too nice, maybe, for Jackie. Despite her earlier complaint that he'd dump her if he saw her elf getup, we both knew that wouldn't happen. Jackie went through boyfriends at a rate that was beyond my ability to keep track. And when she tired of them, she liked to be the one who did the dumping.

"I understand," he said, "about dirty old men trying to look important."

She laughed. "Isn't he sweet when he's jealous, Merry? Take me home, Kyle. I'm tired." She walked away, head high. Kyle threw me a look and then ran after her.

Vicky and I left them to sort out their problems.

At home, Mattie greeted me with his usual boundless enthusiasm. After I'd wiped away enough drool to fill a horse trough, I told him I'd be back in a minute and ran into my bedroom to change. I needed a bath, a long hot soak with lavender bubbles, to force some life back into my legs and feet, but Mattie needed a walk after spending a boring day alone in his crate. Off came the damp tights and the Mrs. Claus outfit and on went a pair of beloved old jeans and a tattered, but warm, sweater. I ran my hands through my own black curls, happy to have the cap off. Downstairs, Mattie danced around my feet in excitement, but I eventually managed to get the squiggling beast out of the way long enough to pull on my heavy winter boots and down-filled coat, wrap a long scarf around my neck, and pull a highly unattractive but functional hat with earflaps onto my head.

Last of all, I snapped the leash onto Mattie's collar and we set off. I opened the gate, stepped onto the path, and my arm was almost detached from the socket. I might have enjoyed a pleasant stroll but walking Mattie was more of a mad gallop, abruptly interrupted by bone-shaking halts, as the dog found something interesting to sniff at and then charged off in search of the next fascinating object. This was a neighborhood of stately Victorian mansions, built in Rudolph's heyday when it had been one of the most significant ports on the Great Lakes. Some homes were now in a state of gentle decay, many had been broken into apartments, but almost all of the houses were beautifully decorated. Grinches don't live in Rudolph for long. Majestic trees glittered in front windows, lights were draped across porch frames and pillars or wound between tree branches. The bandstand was trimmed in hundreds of tiny white lights, and a white spotlight shone on the town's official Christmas tree. Thick clouds continued to spill snow, and no light came from moon or stars to guide my way. The lake was a solid black void in the distance.

As we reached the park, Mattie veered off to the right, going deeper into the darkness, pulling so sharply on the leash, I staggered. My feet slid out from under me on a patch of hidden ice. My hands flew out as I tried to keep upright, releasing the leash. The dog bounded away. I fell, hard, into the deep, soft snow. For a moment I lay where I'd fallen, facedown, head buzzing. I blinked, shook my head, and struggled to roll over. I did a quick mental check. I wiggled my toes and my fingers. Everything seemed to be in place and working. My right wrist had broken my fall. It hurt like the blazes, but I could still move it, so I didn't think anything was broken.

With a curse and a groan, slipping and sliding on the

hidden ice, I pushed myself to my knees and then staggered to my feet. I blew snow off my face and wiped down my arms. I couldn't see Mattie but I could hear him barking in the dark, toward the rocky shore of the lake.

"Mattie! Matterhorn! Get over here!"

No reply. I couldn't see anything, but I stumbled through the deep snow, following the sound of barking. I want to be a responsible dog owner, so I always carry a flashlight and a pocketful of plastic bags on our nightly excursions. I pulled the flashlight out of my pocket and switched it on. I played the light over the expanse, seeing nothing but snow. A few more steps and there he was: a swiftly moving brown and while tail and furry butt.

"Mattie," I said, sounding very stern. "Come here, right now!"

He turned his head and looked at me. The light caught his brown eyes. But he didn't come at my command and turned back to whatever had grabbed his attention. It appeared to be a black plastic garbage bag.

My blood boiled. Some irresponsible citizen had chucked their garbage into the park.

The dog stopped barking and settled into a low whine. He stood over the bag, looking back at me. Urging me to come closer.

I shined the flashlight on the bag.

Something reflected back at me.

This was no garbage bag. It was person. A man.

I ran forward and dropped to my knees in the snow. Ignoring the pain in my wrist, I reached for the man. I touched his shoulder, intending to give him a good shake.

Perhaps he'd had too much to drink and had foolishly lain down in the snow for a short nap, or had tripped and been knocked unconscious.

He was so very cold. I touched his neck, and nothing moved beneath my shaking fingers.

I realized that I knew him.

Nigel Pearce. The *World Journey* magazine reporter.

Chapter 4

Mattie buried his head into my side with a slow, plaintive whine. I rubbed my hands through his soft fur and closed my eyes, taking deep breaths and sparing a thought for poor Nigel.

My eyes flew open. Nigel was cold, icy cold, but I'd read somewhere that people who appeared to be frozen to death had been brought back to life when warmed up. I struggled to my feet and shrugged off my winter coat. I pushed the emergency call button on my iPhone with one hand while with the other I draped my coat over the man lying at my feet.

"I'm in the Rudolph town park," I said when the efficient voice of the emergency operator answered. "A man . . . I found a man . . . I think he's dead. Almost dead. He's very cold."

"What is your name, please?"

"Merry Wilkinson. He's lying in the snow. Not breathing. Send help."

"Ambulance and police are on their way," she said. "Stay on the line, Merry."

"Okay. Is this Alison?"

"Yeah."

"Hi," I said.

"Are you okay, Merry?"

"I'm okay. It's dark here, but I have my flashlight on so they'll be able to find me."

"Stay there, then. Do you detect any vital signs?"

I swallowed and said, "No."

"How was the parade? I was sorry to miss it, but you know how busy we get parade weekend, so I pulled an extra shift." Alison Grimes was a graduate of my mom's vocal school. I knew she was just making polite conversation to keep me calm until help arrived, and I chatted back, grateful for her relaxed voice and easy manner.

As we talked, Mattie uncoiled himself from me and went to take another look at Nigel. I grabbed his collar and pulled him away. "I'd better secure my dog," I said to Alison. "Hold on."

"I'll wait."

I grabbed Mattie's leash and led him to a tree about twenty feet away to tie him up. I figured that the EMTs and the cops wouldn't want to play with a giant puppy, delighted as he would be at the opportunity to make new friends.

The snow around Nigel had been churned up, first by Mattie's big paws and then by me. The cops probably wouldn't be happy about that but there was nothing I could do about it now. I tried to remember if I'd seen any tracks as I approached, but I couldn't. I had not been looking for clues.

I shined my flashlight across the ground around Nigel. The long lens of his Nikon was partially under his body. I wondered if I should lift it out of the snow. Surely, a valuable piece of equipment like that shouldn't be getting wet. I left it where it lay. Expensive or not, the cops would not be happy if I disturbed the scene any more than I already had.

The light picked up something I hadn't seen before: a circle of melting snow about two feet away from Nigel. A mass of brown lumpy liquid was sinking into the snow, warm enough to melt it. I caught a whiff of the scent, and my stomach lurched. Nigel had been violently ill.

At first, I thought he must have been awfully drunk to throw up like that and then simply lie down in the snow and take a nap. But alcohol hadn't been served at the party, and if Nigel had been dipping into a private stash, he hadn't appeared to be at all inebriated. Had he started to drink when he left the party? I'd last seen him less than an hour ago. Surely no one could get that drunk that fast?

Mattie's sharp ears caught the sound before I did and he began to bark. Sirens, coming toward us, red, blue, and white lights breaking the blackness of the winter night. A voice shouted, and I waved my flashlight in the air, calling, "We're over here!" Mattie strained at the leash, his front paws clawing at nothing but cold air.

I only had a moment to think that perhaps I should have tied him to a bigger tree before a powerful light shone in my face.

"It's you," said the high-pitched voice of Officer Candy Campbell. "I should have known."

"What's that supposed to mean?" I lifted my hand, trying to shield my face. I peeked out from between my fingers. Two paramedics had followed Candy. They crouched on either side of Nigel, blocking my view, and spoke in low, efficient voices as they examined the still figure.

"Don't move him," Candy said. The light shifted and I could see again. The medics were preparing to load Nigel onto a backboard they'd brought with them. No stretcher would be able to get through the deep snow.

"He's gotta get to the hospital, stat," one of the medics said. He shouted a stream of initials and numbers into his radio.

"He's dead. VSA," Candy said. "The detectives will want to examine him in situ." VSA, I knew, meant "vital signs absent."

"They ain't dead until they're warm and dead," the medic replied. "Don't they teach you that in police college?"

"I don't think . . ." Candy began.

"I don't much care what you think." The medic was an older guy, well into his fifties. I suspected he'd seen and done it all. He probably chewed up small-town cops and spat them out before breakfast. "Let's go. If we get him to the hospital fast enough, the docs might be able to bring him back. Hey! You over there." He shouted and waved toward a group of firefighters trudging through the snow to see if they could help. "We need a lift here."

Quickly and efficiently, the two medics rolled Nigel, still draped in my coat, onto the board, and the firefighters lifted it.

While Candy spluttered, Mattie barked, and I watched, they took the reporter from *World Journey* magazine away.

"What do you know about this?" Candy turned to me.

"Me? Absolutely nothing. I was out for a walk with the dog before turning in. We found him." I pointed toward the body-sized indentation in the snow. "There. Like that."

"Why's he wearing your coat, Merry?"

"Because I hoped to warm him up."

She placed her hands on her laden equipment belt and eyed me suspiciously. "You expect me to believe that?"

"Of course I expect you to believe that. Because it's the truth."

She swung her flashlight onto the patch of snow melting in the warmth of poor Nigel Pearce's last meal. "Is that yours?"

"No."

"Are you sure? Did you kill him, Merry, and then, shocked at what you did, were you sick?"

"Hey!" I said.

I might have gone on to say something I would have regretted, but we were interrupted by the arrival of another uniformed officer, followed by a woman casually dressed in jeans and a brown leather jacket.

On the street, a line of official vehicles was forming as colorful lights shone on the snow. Loud voices broke the silence, and more people were trudging across the park toward us.

"Are you the person who phoned this in?" the leather-jacketed woman asked me.

"Yes. I'm Merry Wilkinson."

She was in her forties, attractive with wide green eyes and curly red hair, long legs, and the hint of a trim figure under her winter clothes. "I'm Detective Simmonds. Tell me what happened."

"I suspect . . ." Candy began.

"Thank you, Officer," Simmonds said. "I'll be taking your statement shortly. In the meantime, some crowd control might be in order."

"But I'd rather . . ."

"Such as that gentleman approaching," the detective said.

Russ Durham was picking his way through the snow. He lifted his camera and began snapping. I made a movement to pull my hood over my face and remembered I wasn't wearing a coat. The last thing I needed was my picture in the local paper, as a person of interest in a police investigation. Good thing I wasn't in my Mrs. Claus costume. That would do the reputation of Rudolph no favors.

Candy threw me a poisonous glance, but went to do as she'd been ordered. She turned the full force of her official indignation onto Russ. I figured he could handle it.

"Where's your coat?" the detective asked.

"I put it over . . . over Nigel. It went with him in the ambulance."

"You're freezing." Only when she said the word did I realize that I was. I'd discarded one of my gloves fumbling for my phone. I wrapped my arms around myself to try to control the shivering.

"We'll talk in my car," she said. "I'll turn the heat up."

"I have to bring Mattie."

"Is that your dog?"

"Yes."

"Rather on the . . . uh . . . large size, isn't he?"

We both looked at the Saint Bernard. He was pulling on the leash with enough force that the poor tree was in danger of breaking in half. Drool flew in all directions as he displayed his enormous pink tongue and sharp young teeth to the detective.

"He's just a puppy," I said, "But he's very well behaved." Here I was, lying to the cops already.

"He can come," she said. "But if he makes a mess of my car, you're the one who'll clean it up."

I ran to free Mattie from the tree. His gratitude apparently knew no bounds and he tried to knock me over in a display of affection. "Stay," I said firmly. Then, less firmly, "Heel."

In response he leapt toward Detective Simmonds, pulling the leash out of my half-frozen hand. To my considerable relief, the cop didn't pull out her gun and shoot him. Instead she pointed with one finger and, in a deep, rolling voice, said, "Down, Mattie!"

He dropped to his haunches without a sound.

"Wow!" I said, hurrying over to grab the leash. "How'd you do that?"

"My parents train animals for movies and TV. He looks like a good boy, but with a dog of that size, you're going to have to ensure he gets proper training."

"I know." She was right, and I figured there was no point in making the usual excuses.

"Give me a sec, and I'll be right with you," she said.

As we'd talked, more men and women in uniform and plainclothes had begun to arrive. "This witness has to get warm," Simmonds said. "I'm going to talk to her now. In the meantime, try to keep that area secure, although it looks like a lot of damage has been done already."

"Sorry," I mumbled.

"Couldn't be avoided," she said. "You wanted to help. We could have done without the dog though. Come on."

She led the way to the rows of cars lining the park. We passed Candy ordering Russ to get back to the road. He wasn't arguing with her, just walking so slowly, while his camera clicked all the while, that it might be time for the July parade before he got there.

Simmonds stopped so abruptly that Mattie ran into her. "Are you physically disabled, sir?"

"No," Russ said, snapping a picture of her.

"Good. Because if you aren't behind that tape in ten seconds I'll be taking you in. Got it?"

Clearly he got it, because he sprinted across the snowy field without taking another picture. I wondered if Detective Simmonds's parents trained human actors as well as animals. "Secure the perimeter," Simmonds said to Candy. "And do a better job of it than you did with one reporter."

"Yes, ma'am," Candy said, throwing me a look that said she firmly believed her humiliation was all my fault. I refrained from giving her a smirk. Something about Candy Campbell brought out the seventeen-year-old in me.

Detective Simmonds drove a silver BMW. I wasn't able to admire the car just then because by the time we got to it I was shivering so hard my whole body felt as if it were going to implode under the force. She switched on the engine and cranked the heat up to high. Finally my teeth stopped chattering sufficiently so that I could talk. I told her everything I knew, both about finding poor Nigel in the snow and the times I'd seen him earlier in the day. Her face had remained totally impassive the entire time (except when she was praising a doting Mattie) but when I mentioned that he'd been, as far as I could tell, stone-cold sober an hour before being sick in the park, her right eyebrow twitched.

"You didn't notice any other footprints around him?" She asked me that question more than once.

I always answered the same way. "No. It was dark, and I wasn't paying much attention, but I'm pretty sure there was only the one set. Except for Mattie's and mine." I flexed my wrist. Simmonds saw me wince. "Are you hurt?"

"Nah. I fell hard but nothing's broken. It'll be okay."

"This party you say he was at interests me," she said. "I assume food and drink were served? Tell me about that."

"There weren't a lot of refreshments. It wasn't intended to be a substitute for dinner. Just trays of Christmas cookies, hot chocolate, and jugs of cider. Nonalcoholic. That's all."

"Everyone ate off the same serving dishes?"

"Yes." I thought of the final platter. The specially decorated cookies. One individual cookie prepared for Nigel Pearce. Charles Dickens and *A Christmas Carol*. A cookie decorated by Vicky Casey herself and set aside for a special guest. I swallowed.

"What?" the overly observant cop said.

"Nothing."

She gave me a look, but didn't ask again. Instead she reached for her radio and pushed buttons. "Dispatch, have there been any 911 calls reporting suspected food poisoning tonight?"

"Nope. Except for the call to the park, all's quiet."

"Okay," Simmonds said to me. "I'll take you home now. You need to get yourself into a hot shower."

"I don't suppose I'll get my coat back anytime soon?"

"No."

The streets lining the town park were as busy as if the parade were about to pass by again. Police cars and fire trucks, uniformed officers keeping the curious at bay. Lights were on in many of the nearby houses, and people were gathered on the sidewalk to watch or standing on porches with their coats hastily thrown over pajamas. Simmonds pulled into the road. Many of the onlookers recognized me, and either waved or pointed me out to their neighbor.

Good thing I hadn't been stuffed into the back of the car, but had been allowed to sit in the passenger seat while we talked. Mattie had jumped into the back, and at a single word from Simmonds, hadn't tried to force his whole body between us.

"Christmas seems to be a big deal here," she said as we passed the beautifully lit tree shining on the bandstand.

"America's Christmas Town," I said. "You're not from around here." It was a statement, not a question. I'd never seen her before.

"I'm from Chicago. I moved here a couple of weeks ago. After twenty years as a cop in the Windy City I was looking for some small-town peace and quiet. Guess I didn't find it, eh?"

"We're pretty quiet," I said. "Most of the time."

"'Most of the time' doesn't concern me." Following my directions, she pulled up in front of my house. "I'm sure," she said, "we'll be talking again."

Lights were on in the first floor front room of the house. A shape moved behind the drapes: Mrs. D'Angelo, my landlady and the neighborhood gossip. Not a thing happened on this street without Mrs. D'Angelo knowing about it. And, I feared, nothing happened upstairs, either, that escaped her attention. Not that anything happened in my apartment I didn't want the neighbors knowing about. Not yet, anyway. I shared the second floor with another apartment, which was now wrapped in darkness. That was good. Steve and Wendy had a new baby, and they were having a lot of trouble getting her to sleep at appropriate times.

I clambered out of Simmonds's car and opened the back door for Mattie. He gave his new friend a long look. Simmonds rubbed the top of his head and lavished praise on him because he hadn't ruined the interior of her car. He accepted her scratches and compliments, and when she said, "Go," he leapt out. His big tongue hung out of the side of his mouth, and drool poured all over my pants. The sleeve of Simmonds's leather jacket, I noticed with a considerable degree of envy, was dry and clean. How on earth had she managed that?

The BMW pulled away. Before I could tiptoe around the side of the house, the front door flew open.

"Everything all right out there, Merry?"

"Perfectly fine, Mrs. D'Angelo."

"Are you sure?" She came out onto the porch. She wore a long winter coat over blue satin pajamas. Her bare feet were stuffed into matching high-heeled mules. Her face was thick with face cream, and four huge, round plastic curlers were pinned to the top of her head. "I didn't recognize that car."

"Someone new to town."

"Has there been an accident? Several police vehicles and an ambulance passed by, heading toward the park. They were going very fast."

"An accident. Yes, I think so."

She peered over the porch railing at me. "Why are you not wearing a coat?"

The toasty warmth of Simmonds's car was rapidly depleting as I stood in the snow chatting. "Oh, gosh. Will you look at that? I am getting cold. Better get inside. Good night, Mrs. D'Angelo."

"Good night, dear."

After all the excitement of a walk in the park, coming across wonderful new smells (my stomach rolled over again), making a new friend, and riding in a police car, Mattie was ready to play.

I was not. I'd warmed up enough in Simmonds's car that I was no longer in danger of freezing to death, provided I got inside right away, but I was chilled right down to the bone.

I ran the shower and stood under the steaming spray until the hot water began to turn cold. I thought of Steve and Wendy with a twinge of guilt, and hoped they wouldn't need a sink full of hot water before morning. I wrapped a fluffy sea green towel around my hair and folded myself into a matching bath sheet. While Mattie licked warm water off my legs and I stumbled over him, I went in search of my phone. It was late, but I had a call I knew I had to make.

"If this isn't Ryan Gosling calling for a date, you're a dead man," said a sleepy voice.

"It's not Ryan, but you need to hear this," I said.

"Go ahead," Vicky said with a groan.

"Nigel Pearce, remember him, the English guy from *World Journey*?"

"Of course I remember him. If you're calling to tell me he wants a date you really are a dead woman, Merry."

"I found him in the park earlier, when I was walking Mattie."

"You took the dog for a walk? That's great, Merry. I told you that regular exercise will . . ."

"Listen, this is serious. He's dead. At least he seemed dead."

"Dead? In the park? Why? How?"

"He'd been sick. Really sick."

She was silent for a moment. "He hadn't looked unwell at the party. He seemed to be having a good time."

"I mean sick as in throwing up."

"I hadn't noticed him drinking, had you?"

"No, and I think that's the point, Vicky."

She said a very bad word. Vicky never swore and that she did now showed me that she understood what I was saying. It was entirely possible the *World Journey* magazine reporter had contracted food poisoning at the post-parade reception.

The reception catered by Victoria's Bake Shoppe.

"Are you feeling okay?" Vicky asked me.

"I'm fine. The new detective in town called the dispatcher and asked if anyone else had reported taking sick. And no one had."

"That should be good . . ."

"But it's not. We don't know for sure that Nigel Pierce did get sick from something he ate, but if he did, and no one else did, then he was poisoned. Deliberately."

Chapter 5

f my iPhone had a hook, it would have been ringing off
it. I cracked open one eye and glanced at the bedside
clock. Ten. I'd been so upset, first at finding Nigel, and
then fearing he'd been poisoned by Vicky's Charles Dickens cookie, I'd forgotten to set my alarm.

Mattie had been so tired after his nightly excursion that
he'd slept a dreamless sleep at the bottom of my bed. I
grabbed the phone, and almost dropped it again, as my sore
wrist reminded me of last night's discovery. I passed the
phone to the other hand. "I'm on my way."

"It's not that urgent," said my mother.

"Oh, hi, Mom. I've slept in. Thought you were Jackie."
I threw off the covers. "I can't talk now, I really am late.
Hey, why are you calling this early?" My mom rarely got
out of bed before noon. All those years in the opera world,
she said.

"Your father was roused at some ridiculous hour." On the sleep schedule, as with many other things, my parents were total opposites. Dad was an early-to-bed, early-to-rise sort while Mom still lived a theater routine.

"Roused about what?" I asked. I carried the phone with me as I followed Mattie down the stairs. I let him out, pleased to see a brilliant blue sky and a bright sun throwing diamonds across the fresh snow. Exactly the sort of day to get people into the mood for Christmas shopping. I studied my hand. The wrist looked to be a bit swollen. I swiveled it, and only felt a slight twinge as it loosened up.

"An emergency meeting of the town council," Mom said.

I stopped enjoying the day and Mattie's antics. "What's this about, Mom?" I feared that I already knew.

"It seems as though that English fellow, the one who was taking pictures yesterday, died. In the park. The police suspect he was poisoned. At the post-parade party, of all things."

"Gotta go!" I said.

I dashed upstairs. No time today for the Mrs. Claus getup. I pulled on the first outfit I saw: a plain black knee-length skirt, opaque black tights, and a red sweater. I'd gone to bed with damp hair and it had dried overnight to something resembling Mrs. Claus's mop, but I had no time to wash it. I stuffed the unruly mess into a clip at the back of my head.

Back downstairs, Mattie was waiting to be let in. He might not be well trained, but he knew his schedule. Morning pee was always immediately followed by breakfast.

How on earth, I wondered for about the hundredth time, had I allowed myself to be talked into getting a dog anyway?

I tapped my foot impatiently while he inhaled his food. At least he wasn't a picky eater. Then I dragged him, protesting all the way, into his crate and closed the door. Giant liquid brown eyes gazed through the bars at me. "I'll miss you," they seemed to say.

I tried not to say, "I'll miss you, too."

Last of all, I pulled on my boots and began hunting for my coat.

Oh, right. No coat.

The lightweight tattered old jacket I wore to shovel the path would have to do.

My phone rang as I was heading out the door. This time it was Jackie, wondering why I wasn't at the shop for opening time. "On my way!" I shouted.

I bolted down the street. Conscious of our reputation as a tourist town, most homeowners are pretty good at keeping the patch of sidewalk in front of their homes neatly shoveled and well salted.

My phone again. This time I checked the display before answering. Vicky.

"I'm heading to the shop now," I said.

"The police are here," she said in a very low voice.

I stopped running. "Why?"

"They were waiting when I opened up. Asking all sorts of questions about what I served at last night's party. Who'd done the baking, had I bought any of it, who served. They told me Nigel Pearce was found dead last night like you said. They hadn't been able to revive him at the hospital."

"Yeah, my mom called to tell me he didn't make it. Dad's at an emergency meeting of the town council. Did the police say anything about, well, how he died?"

"They didn't have to. They're in the kitchen now, poking through bags of flour and nosing around inside the refrigerator."

"Your health department inspection's up-to-date, right?"

"Top marks, as always."

"Then you have nothing to worry about," I said. I'd stopped opposite the park. Yellow crime scene tape had been strung between trees, but last night's activity was over. A lone cruiser was parked at the curb with a single cop inside, keeping an eye out and chasing away the mildly curious as well as the outright ghoulish. More citizens than normal for this time of day were walking their dogs, very slowly, down this stretch of the sidewalk.

"I don't share your optimism," Vicky said. "I've been told I can't open the bakery until they're finished, and goodness knows how long that's going to take. Not that I'd want to be open while cops dig through my sugar and sniff my eggs and call out, 'Bring that poison test kit over here, will you, Bob?'"

"Have they said they're looking for poison?"

"No. They haven't said much at all."

"Is the coffee on?"

"Yeah. I figured it would do my standing with the police some good to provide them with coffee and the pastries I'm not going to be able to sell. Funny enough, they don't seem to fear that the cinnamon buns are stuffed full of arsenic. Not if the rate they're going through them is any indication."

"I'll stick my head in the shop door, check to see if Jackie's managing okay, and be right there. A cinnamon bun sounds mighty nice, too."

"Thanks, sweetie."

The death of Nigel Pearce had reached the ears of the locals. The sidewalks were crowded with shop owners exchanging the news in low voices. Business still seemed to be good though. Most visitors wouldn't bother switching on the local radio station when they got up. We could only hope the details wouldn't reach the big city papers.

Habit took over as I reached my shop and, despite my worry, I cast my eyes over the window display. There were a couple of gaps where we'd sold items, but everything looked festive, pretty, and very inviting.

Inside, two women were examining the wooden toys. "A hundred dollars for this train set seems excessive," the older one said to Jackie.

"It's handmade by a local artisan," my assistant said. "Look at the grain and the color of the wood. You'll never get this quality in a big-box store." The trains were beautiful, and crafted with a great deal of care. Each box came with two railway cars, an engine, and a bright red caboose, each piece about three inches long, as well as a stack of wood tracks that locked together to make a circle. Extension sets could be bought with more track and more cars. Alan Anderson made them, and they were hugely popular.

"I don't know . . ."

"Well, I do," her companion said. "Remember that tractor you bought him for Christmas last year?" She turned to Jackie. "Isaac opened the box, slid the tractor across the floor, and one of the wheels fell off. You get what you pay for, Mom, and isn't your only grandson worth it?"

Sold!

Jackie gave me a wink as she carried the train set to the counter. The women continued browsing.

"Sorry I'm late," I whispered to my assistant. "Rough night. I have to go out again. Can you manage for a while?"

"No problem."

"I'll bring you something back from Vicky's." I studied her face. Her eyes were clear and her skin dewy fresh. "Did you happen to catch the news this morning?"

"I never listen to the news. Much too depressing."

"Do you have this ornament in blue?" one of the customers asked, and Jackie called, "I'll have a latte with extra whipped cream," over her shoulder as she went to help.

I never did understand how Jackie could have whipped cream on breakfast coffee, nor how she kept so thin despite consuming several cups of it a day.

The now-familiar silver BMW was parked in front of Victoria's Bake Shoppe, between a cruiser and an unmarked van. I'd seen that van last night, disgorging men and women in white suits carrying evidence boxes. I climbed the steps and hammered on the door. Through the frosted glass I could see people moving about inside.

The door opened a crack. "Closed," said a uniformed officer.

"Vicky!" I called.

My best friend's pretty heart-shaped face topped by a shock of purple hair peeked around the cop's broad back. "This is my friend. Can she come in, please?"

"Let her in," a woman's voice called. The big cop stepped back.

"Good morning, Ms. Wilkinson." Detective Simmonds looked as fresh and bright eyed as Jackie had, but she was wearing the same jacket and jeans as last night. "What brings you here?"

"Vicky's my friend. I popped in to say hi." The bakery was full of its usual smells of warm pastries, bread hot from the oven, sugar, and spices, but this morning a thin layer of something else lay over it all: chemicals, harsh and unwelcome.

I glanced at the top shelf. The light that usually illuminated the golden Rudolph parade trophy was switched off, and the statue itself was wrapped in gloom.

"I heard that Nigel Pearce died," I said.

Simmonds nodded. "Yeah. They couldn't bring him back."

"How . . ." I began.

"Autopsy's this afternoon," Simmonds said. "Until then, we are not going to speculate. And until then, we're finished here. You can have your bakery back, Ms. Casey."

"I can open?"

"For now. Let's go, people."

They began trooping out. Simmonds was last. "Please don't leave town, Ms. Casey. Until I tell you otherwise."

"This is the busiest time of year. I'm hardly going to . . ."

I placed a hand on my friend's arm. "She won't."

"Good," Simmonds said. She gave us both a long, piercing look before following her colleagues.

Vicky dropped into a chair.

"Are you going to open the bakery?" I asked.

Purple hair flew as she shook her head. Her sleeves were rolled up and the matching dragon tattoos on her forearms moved as she rubbed at her face. "No point. The breakfast rush is over, and I can't get ready in time for Sunday brunch. I called the staff and told them not to come in. The cops have eaten most of what I'd already baked, and I haven't started on anything else." Her blue eyes studied me. "Do they think I poisoned Nigel Pearce?"

"I don't know what they're thinking. Simmonds told you that you could open, didn't she? That means they didn't find anything . . . uh . . . incriminating."

We both started at a knock on the door. "Tell them to go away," Vicky said.

Alan Anderson's handsome face was peering through the window. I hurried to the door. "Bakery won't be opening today."

"Just checking if you guys are okay."

"We're okay. Come on in." Despite the seriousness of the situation, I felt myself grinning at him. He grinned back.

"Would you like a cinnamon bun, Alan?" Vicky asked. "I think the cops left one or two."

"Forget the cinnamon buns," I said. "Did you hear?"

"Bun would be nice, thanks. About Pearce? Everyone's talking about it."

"What are they saying?"

"Town council had an emergency meeting this morning. Soon as they broke up, word started going around that Pearce got drunk and went for a walk in the park, where he fell asleep and froze to death."

"Do you believe that?" I asked.

"No. But that story doesn't make anyone in Rudolph look responsible."

"Anyone like me," Vicky said.

"Anyone," Alan said firmly. "The police aren't saying, and until they do there's no point in speculating."

"But people will."

"Speculate? Sure they will. Already are. The mayor and the councilors just gave them a hint of what to speculate about."

"Is anyone wondering why the cops were here?" I asked. "At the bakery, I mean."

"Some are. They went through Pearce's room at the Yuletide Inn and were asking where he'd eaten earlier."

Vicky groaned. "Here. Not only my baking at the party, but he had lunch here."

Alan put a hand on Vicky's shoulder. "Don't worry about things that haven't happened yet. Things that might never happen. The autopsy'll show he had a bad heart or something. I didn't think he looked like a well man. Right, Merry?"

"Right," I said cheerfully. "He was definitely too thin and kinda pasty white."

"Come to think of it," Vicky said, "he only had a couple of sips of soup and never finished his sandwich."

"As we suspected. He was sick already." Alan gave me a smile. I grinned back, pleased at our logic.

Vicky reached up and patted his hand. "Thanks, guys." She pushed herself to her feet. "Now get out of here. You must have work to do. I know I do. This is a chance for me to get ahead of myself and do some prep for tomorrow. It'll be nice to have the kitchen to myself, like when I first started the business. I might even be able to get home early for once and enjoy a glass of wine and a good book. If you're up to it, Merry, pop on over when you close the shop. Good thing today's Sunday. Some of the tourists won't think anything of us not being open."

Alan and I headed for the door. "Hold up!" Vicky called.

She ran to the counter and stuffed blueberry muffins and cinnamon buns into small white paper bags. The bags showed the Victoria's Bake Shoppe logo of two mischievous gingerbread children peeking around a stylized Christmas tree. "These are no good a day old." The smile she gave us was genuine. Vicky never stayed down for long. I gave her a spontaneous hug. We left her whistling to herself and reaching for a long apron.

"Thanks for that," I said to Alan as we stood on the steps, gripping our bags of cinnamon and sugary goodness. "You knew exactly what to say to her."

"I didn't say anything I didn't mean. People die all the time, unfortunately, no need for the town to get into a panic."

I decided not to mention the puddle of vomit next to Nigel. Hopefully the autopsy would reveal that he'd died of natural causes and that would be the end of that.

We began to walk toward Mrs. Claus's Treasures. The street was full of cars and pedestrians. Shoppers browsed the gaily decorated windows and strolled in and out of shops. Most of them came out, I was pleased to see, carrying shopping bags. I saw more than a few with the logo of Mrs. Claus's Treasures. The air was cold but the sun was warm and people had untied scarves, discarded gloves, and thrown open coats.

"Jackie told me where I could find you," Alan said.

Outside The Elves' Lunch Box a waiter was setting up a sandwich board advertising the day's specials. Fish tacos might not be traditional North Pole fare, but they did sound pretty good. "You were at the shop?"

"I dropped off a box of those necklaces you ordered."

As well as toys, Alan crafted bowls, vases, and jewelry out of wood. I particularly loved his necklaces, as did my customers. He strung twelve to twenty-four highly polished wooden disks on a chain, each piece of wood getting progressively larger as the chain descended.

"Great. They've been very popular and we're almost sold out. Is there a problem? You could have left them with Jackie. You know I pay on time."

"I know. I guess . . . well, I . . ."

I yelped as a tiny ball of indignation leapt out of Rudolph's Gift Nook. "Merry Wilkinson, I should have known you'd have something to do with this." Betty Thatcher glared at me.

She then glared at Alan. "Shouldn't you be in your *workshop*, young man? Crafting exclusive *handmade* custom decorations?"

If Betty didn't like me for selling artisan things, she liked Alan even less for making them. He never seemed to mind. "Thanks for reminding me, Mrs. Thatcher, ma'am. Only twenty-three shopping days until Christmas. That's a pretty sweater. It sure captures the mood of the season."

"Why, thank you," she said, softening a fraction. She wore a red fleece sweatshirt (only $29.99!) decorated with a picture of Rudolph (the deer, not the town), his flashing nose powered by a battery concealed on Betty's person.

"Talk to you later, Merry," Alan said. He walked away in his slow, lazy fashion.

He'd been about to say something to me when we'd been so rudely interrupted.

I glared at Betty, and decided to make my escape as well. Unfortunately, I wasn't fast enough. She plucked at my arm. If a pack of well-dressed and obviously highly competitive shoppers hadn't passed us at that very moment, I might have attempted to shake her off. But her grip would have made a professional wrestler proud, and I didn't want to be observed knocking an apparently (appearances can be deceiving) frail woman to the ground.

"What's this I hear about that nice Mr. Pearce being found dead in the park?" Betty demanded.

"So they say."

"They also say you found him. How do you explain that?"

"I don't have to explain that. But I will. I was walking my dog. My dog found him."

Her lip curled up. "That comes as no surprise to me. I've always said they're filthy, disgusting beasts, dogs. Attracted by no end of rubbish."

Whether said rubbish was intended to mean a dead body or me, I didn't know.

"I couldn't help but notice," Betty went on, "that you were spending a lot of time with Mr. Pearce at the reception last night, Merry."

"I . . ."

"Almost smothering him with your demands for attention, it seemed to me. The poor man didn't get much of a chance to talk to anyone else. Not between you and that mother of yours." She gave me a supercilious smirk, waiting for me to respond.

"Have it your way, Betty," I said, walking away.

"I intend to tell the police that, when they come calling," she shouted after me.

Inside Mrs. Claus's Treasures a line was forming at the counter. Jackie rang up sales and handled money in her usual efficient fashion, but it didn't take more than a quick glance for me to know that she'd heard the news. I rushed to discard my outerwear and replace her at the cash register.

"Take a break," I whispered to her.

"Is it true what Mrs. Thatcher's saying?" she whispered back. "About Nigel?"

"I'm afraid so. Although she's adding a healthy dose of malice to a story that's sad enough as it is."

"Excuse me, but do you have any more of those glass vases? I bought one for myself yesterday, but I've decided they'd make lovely gifts."

"We might be all out, but I can check in the back," Jackie said. The door opened and more shoppers streamed in.

"I'll be okay until Crystal gets here," Jackie said to me, referring to my other assistant, scheduled to come in at noon.

We were so busy for the rest of the day that I scarcely had a moment to think about Nigel Pearce. Or to wonder what Alan had been about to say to me when Betty Thatcher had pounced. I overheard a few people talking about Nigel, but they seemed to think he'd either passed out drunk and then froze, or had suffered a heart attack. Crystal arrived, and Jackie went for her lunch break. She came back with red eyes, smeared mascara, and a swollen nose. She hadn't known Nigel well enough to be mourning him, but she was an emotional person. Not to mention that she would have realized that she wouldn't have her picture in *World Journey* magazine after all.

It was a long, hectic, trying, but very profitable day. Jackie, Crystal, and I were constantly on the hop as eager shoppers browsed and bought. Whenever my face began to ache from all the smiling I was doing, I just had to hear the merry sound of the cash register ringing up another sale to feel better. A light snow began to fall around four o'clock as the lights came on, laying a fresh layer of pure Christmas magic over Jingle Bell Lane.

I'd placed Alan's wooden train sets on a prominent table, and they were soon snapped up. When I got enough of a break to check the window, most of the jewelry on display had been sold. "Please tell me you have more merchandise," I said to Crystal. "I never thought it would be so popular."

With a grin, she tucked a strand of silky black hair behind her ear. "I might be able to find some. I'll have Mom bring it over."

"Thanks. You're a gem." I meant that literally. Crystal was an incredibly talented small-metal artist and, although she was a senior in high school, she supplied many of the jewelry pieces I sold at Mrs. Claus's Treasures. She'd been accepted at the prestigious School of Visual Arts in New York for next fall, and I'd miss her terribly. As would my mom. Along with her other talents, Crystal had a beautiful singing voice and was Mom's star pupil. She was busy enough with her music, her classes, and her jewelry workshop, but she worked in Mrs. Claus's Treasures during the busiest times to make money to help with college.

She slipped into the back room to place the call to her mom for more stock, and I went to politely, yet firmly, remove a handblown glass ornament from the clumsy fingers of a five-year-old.

"Do you like the pretty thing, sweetie?" the boy's mother gushed. "It will look wonderful on the children's tree. We'll take the box, miss."

"You spoil that boy," an older man said to her. "In my day we made ornaments out of popcorn, tinsel, and seed packets." I couldn't help but notice that his arms were full of stuffed toys.

"And," the woman said to me, "they walked twenty miles to school. Uphill. Both ways."

As they left the shop, laden with parcels, the boy began demanding, in a piercing voice, ice cream.

Crystal came out of the back room. "Mom'll bring some things around later. She said that newspaper guy from England died last night. That's awful. I was talking to him at the reception. What do you think happened, Merry?"

Before I could answer, Jackie caught wind of our conversation and hurried over. "It's such a shock. He was going to photograph me today. I can't believe it. My big break gone. I mean . . . poor man."

"He didn't look at all healthy," I said, repeating Alan's suggested line. "Thin and pale."

"English people all look like that," said Jackie, who had never been out of New York State.

"Colin Firth doesn't," Crystal pointed out.

"Who?" said Jackie.

"We do have customers," I reminded my staff.

At one minute to six, I was flipping the sign on the door to "Closed" when it almost hit me in the face. Kyle Lambert strode in, head and shoulders flaked with snow. He was a big guy who hadn't quite learned to control his arms and legs. Thinking of the proverbial bull in the china shop, I snatched up two wineglasses painted with delicate lines to represent red and green colored lights and clutched them to my chest.

"Ready, babe?" he said to Jackie.

"I'll be just a minute." A few customers lingered, and Jackie was on the till.

He turned to me with a smile. "Hope your boss lady pays overtime."

I held open the door. "Jackie will be out when she's finished."

"I'll wait," he said.

I wasn't about to make a scene, so I flipped the lock without another word.

Kyle wandered through the shop, looking not at all impressed by my display of merchandise. I let the last of the customers out. Crystal went to get her bag. Kyle spent a lot of time studying the jewelry display. He picked up a pair of earrings, delicate silver filigrees in the shape of snowmen. He held them up. "Do you like these, babe?"

"Sure do," Jackie said. "Aren't they beautiful?"

"I'll take them. You deserve something special."

She preened.

Then he caught sight of the price tag. "Forty bucks!" His face fell.

"They're handmade. Merry will ring them up while I powder my nose." Jackie gave Kyle a hearty kiss on the lips and skipped off to the back.

"You don't have to buy them if they're too much," I said to him.

"I can afford it," he said, almost choking on the words.

"You seem in a cheerful mood today, Kyle."

"Guess I am, at that." He opened his wallet and carefully selected the exact amount. "Too bad about that magazine guy, eh?"

"What about him?"

"I hear he kicked the bucket. How sad." Kyle made a wiping-away-tears gesture. Then he grinned. I knew his family. They were hard-working, well-meaning people, who had four boys and not a lot of money. Certainly nothing extra for luxuries such as dentistry. Kyle worked for a lawn maintenance company over the summer. In the winter he plowed driveways and made extra money helping out at hotels and restaurants over the busy Christmas season.

"What do you know about that?" I asked, handing him the earrings, which I'd wrapped in tissue paper and slipped into a small bag.

"Me? Nothing at all. Except good riddance."

"Ready!" Jackie called. She'd freshened her makeup and combed her hair. "I'm absolutely starving. You have no idea what a slave driver that Merry is. I hope you're taking me someplace nice for dinner, Kyle."

He handed her the shopping bag. "Sure am, babe."

I unlocked the door for them. Jackie threw me a self-satisfied smirk as she left. Sometimes I didn't like her very much. None of my business, though. Kyle was a big boy.

Kyle wasn't exactly mourning Nigel Pearce. I was thinking that the death of the Englishman had turned out rather well for Kyle, when Crystal came out of the back. "I can stay for a while, help you unwrap and arrange the new stuff, if you like."

"I'm sure you have more than enough to do at home. I can manage."

"Are you sure?"

"I'm sure. Good night. Did you remember that we have Midnight Madness Friday and Saturday?"

She rolled her eyes.

"Sorry," I said. "Forgot who I was talking to for a minute there."

"See you Thursday, Merry."

I cleared some space on the main display table—which wasn't difficult as most of the stock there had been sold—and laid out the fresh supply of Crystal's beautiful jewelry. I was ticking off the enclosed packing slip against the items when someone rapped on the door.

I let in my dad. His white hair and beard were full of snow and he stamped more snow off his boots. "It's starting to come down hard out there," he said, giving me a kiss on the cheek. "Need a hand, honeybunch?"

"If you wouldn't mind, there are a couple of boxes in the storeroom that need to be unpacked."

"I hear it was you who found that Pearce guy last night. You okay?"

"I'm fine, Dad. He hadn't been shot or stabbed or anything awful. He was just lying there. Like he'd gone to sleep. It was Mattie who found him, not me. Oh, gosh, Mattie! I forgot all about him. We were so busy this afternoon." An image of Vicky's scolding index finger wagging in my face popped into my head. "I'll have to go home now, and then come back and finish up."

"A few more minutes on his own won't hurt none. I'll

help you with this stuff. You could always ask your mother to walk the dog when you don't have the time."

"Mom? Are you serious? Mom hates dogs."

"She doesn't hate dogs. Sometimes you don't give her enough credit, Merry. She'd be delighted to help. Of course . . ." His voice trailed off. "She might not want to do the picking-up-after stuff." Another image popped into my head, this time of Mom's face when she realized she was expected to clean up after the dog. "She can go around to your place and let him out into the backyard for a break."

"You're sure she wouldn't mind?"

"She'd be happy to do it," Dad said, not sounding entirely sure of his facts.

With Dad's help I was able to get the additional stock unpacked and displayed in record time.

"Was everyone as busy as I was today?" I asked as we worked.

"No complaints. Lots of talk, though, about that Pearce guy and why Vicky was closed all day."

"What sort of talk?"

"Rumor. Speculation. Gossip disguised as interest. 'It is a capital mistake to theorize before you have all the evidence.'" Dad was a Sherlock Holmes fanatic. He could usually be relied upon to come up with an appropriate quote for any occasion.

"What exactly are they saying?"

"One loudmouthed police officer—I won't mention any names, but a female of your acquaintance—who'd been at the scene, let loose with the word 'poisoned.'"

"Oh, dear."

"You can say that again. We've been trying all day to put a lid on that, without appearing to hush it up, which would only stoke further talk. The autopsy was supposed to be done this afternoon." He was arranging boxed sets of tree ornaments on a side table. He shoved the Christmas-themed napkins and place mats I'd placed there earlier to the back.

"The larger things go behind," I said. "Leave the flat napkins in front."

"This works better."

I began to argue, but my phone chirped to tell me I had an incoming text.

Vicky: *Wine and movie? My place.*

Me: *Just finishing up. Then Mattie. One hour?*

Vicky: *Gotcha*

Vicky and I had a fun, relaxing evening. We watched *Jane Eyre*, ate too much microwaved pizza and popcorn, and drank too much white wine. Vicky lives in walking distance of my place, so I didn't have to worry about driving and enjoyed sitting back with my best friend, doing more talking than watching the adventures of poor, plain, unloved Jane and haughty Mr. Rochester. By unspoken agreement, we avoided the topic of Nigel Pearce and *World Journey* magazine. Mattie was always welcome at Vicky's house, and he spent the evening tormenting Vicky's elderly golden lab, Sandbanks, who was not in the mood for playing with an overactive puppy, thank you very much. Mattie dragged me home around midnight and I fell straight into bed, looking forward to sleeping in a bit. Even in December, Mondays were always slow.

I woke around eight, feeling a good deal better than I should have after a night of indulgence. I let Mattie out and popped in the shower. When I walked back into the bedroom, toweling off, I noticed the phone flashing at me. I called up my voice mailbox to hear Vicky's frantic voice.

"You're my one phone call, Merry. I've . . . I've been arrested. Call my dad. Send help."

Chapter 6

I don't know why Vicky hadn't called her dad herself. He was a lawyer, had a small practice in town. Her mother ran a successful catering business, and despite her dad's fondest wish that his daughter follow him into the law, the cooking part of Vicky's genes had won out.

"Casey and Sorenson," said the efficient voice on the other side of the phone in answer to my call.

"Is Mr. Casey there? It's Merry Wilkinson speaking."

"Hi, Merry. John's gone down to the police station."

"Is it about Vicky?"

"I believe so."

"Thanks." Whew! The cavalry had been called. I threw on clothes without checking for color coordination or style. Poor Mattie would have to go without a morning walk, once again. And poor me would once again venture out into the below-freezing temperatures with wet hair and without even a proper coat. The police hadn't returned the coat I'd used to try to warm Nigel. I didn't much care if they gave it back or not. I never wanted to wear it again.

The Rudolph police station is tucked behind the library on Jingle Bell Lane, beside the town council buildings. I could have walked there, but, besides being coatless, I was in too much of a hurry, so I got my ancient, but reliable Honda Civic out of the garage where it spent most of the winter.

I tore into town, parked in the station lot, and bolted up the stairs. I was out of breath when I arrived in the reception area. Unimpressed with my obvious concern, the cop at the desk, who didn't look as though he was old enough to shave yet, wouldn't tell me if Vicky was there, and let me know that I wouldn't be allowed to see her if she was. He also informed me that he wouldn't tell me if Mr. Casey had arrived. I suspected that if he'd had about half an hour less training at police college, he would have stuck out his tongue and said, "I know something you don't know."

I headed back to my car, going out the doors at the highly unfortunate moment Officer Candy Campbell was coming up the steps. "What a surprise to see you here," she said.

"Harrumph," I said, deciding I would not stoop to her level.

"Vicky Casey. Who woulda thought it?"

I stooped low enough to beg for info. "What's happening? Do you know?"

Her eyes flicked to the lobby and then around the parking lot. No one was in earshot. "Pearce was poisoned, all right. In a piece of . . . get this . . . gingerbread."

I didn't have to pretend to look horrified.

Candy chuckled. "Don't worry, Merry. I'm sure Vicky didn't do it on purpose. They'll take that into consideration in determining her sentence." She pushed her way past me.

The old Honda Civic squealed out of the parking lot and headed toward Mrs. Claus's Treasures, which was pretty much across the street. I was so upset, I parked in front of my own shop, taking up a space that could be used by a paying customer.

Jackie was perched on a stool behind the counter, flipping through a magazine. The shop was empty of customers. Business would be slow until Thursday, when the weekend tourists began arriving again.

My assistant took one look at my face and rose half off her stool. "What's the matter?"

"I'll be in my office." I stalked through the shop and slammed the office door behind me.

"Office" is a grand name for what is the storage closet, staff coatroom, overflow stockroom, and the spot where I do the books. I had to weave through piles of boxes to reach my desk. The computer was almost buried under stacks of paper: invoices, accounts receivable, accounts payable, tax forms. All of which would continue to pile up until January, when I would have time to look at everything. I loved owning my own business, but I sure hated all the paperwork that went with it.

I threw the phone book and a couple of catalogues off my chair and dropped down. I put my chin into my hands and stared at the room. The single decoration was a simple poster designed the first year the town of Rudolph, New York, decided to turn its focus to Christmas.

Rudolph had begun life as an important port on the southern shores of Lake Ontario. The town had been incorporated in 1805 and named for one of the original business owners, Reinhart Rudolph, son of proud German immigrants. Reinhart had been a local hero during the War of 1812, when he'd organized a motley collection of farmers and townspeople to rush to the defense of American sailors whose ship had wrecked on the rocky shore during a winter storm, while fleeing a much larger and more heavily armed British ship.

When heavy industry began to die off in this part of the country and the factories and industrial lands were abandoned to fall into disrepair, the town tried to promote itself as a War of 1812 commemorative destination. Funds were raised and an imposing statue erected to celebrate Reinhart Rudolph's patriotism. High school kids were outfitted in period costumes, trained to march in orderly formation carrying muskets, and taught the history of the great man's great deeds with the goal of entertaining and educating the swarms of history buffs soon to arrive. The Rudolph family had owned a Victorian mansion not far from where I currently lived, and in the 1980s, the town had been able to purchase the house for much less than its former value because the place was falling down and the owners were desperate to move to Arizona. Renovations were planned to turn it into a period museum. The more optimistic of the project's boosters began to talk about a rival to Gettysburg.

All of which came to a grinding halt when a postgraduate student from CUNY was doing original research in England, where he came across the previously undiscovered letters of Mrs. Reinhart Rudolph. Mrs. Rudolph boasted to her sister that her husband was, in fact, spying for the British all along, using the convenient widow's walk at the top of their lakeside home to report on the passage of American ships and troops. As for the famous rescue incident? Reinhart happened to know where the Americans would be coming ashore because he and his wife had lit a blaze of lanterns to guide the American ship onto the rocks. No doubt thinking he'd accept the kudos while he could, the wily fellow had then rushed into the streets to rouse the townspeople to see off the British ship, which he knew was bobbing happily in the lake with no intention of landing.

The town might have been able to dismiss Mrs. Rudolph's letters as fiction, but the eager postgraduate student went further and managed to unearth records of payment from a grateful British government to Reinhart.

It had been my dad who'd come up with an alternate plan to save Rudolph. We'd quietly forget all about Reinhart and pretend the town was named after the most famous Rudolph of them all: The Red-Nosed Reindeer.

Thus Rudolph, New York, was reborn as Christmas Town. The statue of Reinhart, nobly holding a lantern aloft to light the sailors' way, was melted down, his former home sold for even less than the town had paid for it, and the high school kids' sailor costumes replaced with red hats and elf-wear.

Every time I thought of that story it brought a smile to my face. But today I remembered Vicky and my smile died.

The morning passed at the speed of the losing entrant in a snail race. I sat at my desk, drumming my fingers on the desktop and pretending to do accounts. I phoned my dad, but he wasn't answering. Mom gave private lessons to adults on Monday mornings so no point in calling her.

The phone at Victoria's Bake Shoppe was picked up by a machine, thanking me for my call and giving the opening hours. That it was now well into opening hours, but no one was there, was not a good sign.

A floorboard creaked and I looked up.

Vicky stood in the doorway. Her short purple hair was standing on end and deep, dark circles were under her eyes. Her thin frame looked lost in a pair of too-large track pants and a faded gray sweatshirt. She wasn't wearing a coat, just a scarf looped twice around her neck and home-knitted red mittens on her hands. I leapt to my feet, sending piles of paper flying in all directions. I kicked boxes aside as I made my way toward her. I wrapped her in my arms and she fell into them.

When we separated, Jackie was watching us, eyes round with curiosity. "Run to Cranberries," I told her. "Two extra-large lattes, full strength."

"Who'll watch the shop?"

"No one. Take the money you need out of the till."

There's only one chair in my office. I pushed Vicky into it. "What's going on? I called your dad, but he'd already left. They wouldn't tell me anything at the police station."

"Sorry about that," she said. "I kinda overreacted. I wasn't actually arrested."

"That's good to hear."

"I was brought in for questioning."

"About?" I asked.

"They got the autopsy results on Nigel Pearce back this

morning. Pearce was poisoned. The poison was in the gingerbread cookies. My gingerbread cookies."

"Rubbish! I had one of those cookies. As I recall, I ate more than one. I didn't get sick. Do they think your eggs had gone bad or something? Maybe Pearce was particularly sensitive?"

"No, Merry. It was GHB."

"What the heck is that?"

"Also called liquid ecstasy. An illegal, but widely available drug, so my dad tells me."

"Keep that to yourselves," my dad said from the hall. "The police are not making that detail public. You shouldn't leave the shop unattended, Merry. Anyone could walk in."

"Let them," I said. "We have more important things to worry about here."

"That's my girl talking," he said.

"I sent Jackie for drinks."

"Nigel Pearce," Dad said, "died of an overdose of GHB, which he contracted through an iced gingerbread cookie consumed within an hour of his death. GHB is not usually fatal in the quantity he consumed, but Pearce was not a healthy man, according to the pathologist. He was taking a prescription drug that reacts very badly with GHB."

"That's a party drug, right?" I said. "Maybe Pearce gave it to himself and misjudged the dose?"

"I'd like to believe that," Dad said, "but it was in the cookie. That no one else who was at the reception at the time in question has reported so much as an upset tummy is leading the police to suspect that one cookie only had been laced with the drug."

"Accidentally?" I added hopefully. "A by-product of cooking, maybe?"

"No," Dad said. "GHB isn't something that's going to be consumed through cream past its sell-by date or uncooked eggs containing salmonella."

Vicky groaned.

"How do you know this, Dad, if it's supposed to be secret?"

"Let's just say the town council has friends who work in the police station and the coroner's office, so we got a heads-up. If this gets out it could kill the Christmas season in Rudolph."

"Never mind the town. My Christmas season is ruined." At last, Vicky began to cry. She favored a lot of makeup, including thickly applied eyeliner and mascara. Black rivers ran down her face. "In the food business, reputation is everything. If word gets around that my baking killed someone, I'll never recover. The police have ordered the bakery closed until further notice."

"Did they say how long you have to be closed?" I bent over her and wrapped my arms around her heaving shoulders. Vicky was a good six inches taller than me. It wasn't often I was able to comfort her.

I felt the force of her head shaking.

We promoted Rudolph as a year-round tourist destination. No matter the time of year, it seemed that folks loved to pretend it was Christmas. Even in the hot, humid days of July and August people came here to see "Santa" enjoying his summer vacation by the lake. Dad had been known to set out a beach umbrella and chair down by the water, dressed in bright red swimming trunks and the traditional red hat topped with a bouncing white pom-pom, while elves with pointed ears and big shoes, wearing bikinis (the girls) and board shorts (the boys) attended to him. We'd even made the *New York Times* travel section with a picture of Dad with kids in bathing suits and sun hats lined up to sit on his knee.

But, no matter how busy we got at other times of the year, December was the lifeblood of all the shops, hotels, and restaurants in Rudolph. Even if no one believed Vicky's food was deadly, if she had to remain closed through the next weekend, it might force her business under.

"As long as it takes, I guess," Dad said in answer to my question. "If they have reason to believe the poison originated in your kitchens, Vicky, they have the right to order you closed."

She pulled free of my embrace. I grabbed a tissue from the box on my desk and handed it to her. She blew her nose and wiped at her face. When she took the tissue away, she'd stopped crying. Her chin was set and her eyes blazed. "We know that didn't happen, so we'll just have to convince Detective Simmonds of that fact." She got to her feet. "That drug was added at the party. Closing my business is intimidation but useless." She headed for the door.

"Not so fast," Dad said. "I've met Diane Simmonds, and she's no fool. It won't help if you're seen publicly arguing with her. Let your father handle it the proper way, Vicky."

"Coffee," chirped Jackie, appearing with two giant takeaway cups. My office was now getting seriously overcrowded, "Hey, Mr. Wilkinson. If I'd known you were here, I'd have brought you one."

"I'm fine, Jackie. Thanks."

"There's a heck of a fuss going on further up the street," she said, passing out the drinks. "A bunch of people are outside the bakery. What's going on?"

Vicky and I looked at each other. My dad plucked the latte out of my hands. "Guess you won't be needing this. I'll help Jackie mind the store until you get back."

Vicky and I ran out onto the street. "What the heck?" Vicky said as Victoria's Bake Shoppe came into sight. A crowd had gathered on the sidewalk, chatting excitedly amongst themselves. As Vicky and I approached, they fell silent and stepped back. Everyone watched as we mounted the steps. Inside, the bakery was dark and quiet. No wonderful smells emanated from its depths. A sign had been stuck to the door.

A yellow county health department notice. "Closed."

Vicky groaned.

I noticed the owner of A Touch of Holly, the town's premier fine dining establishment, edge away from her, as if Vicky were carrying something contagious.

"Move along now, folks. Nothing to see here." Officer Candy Campbell pushed her way through the crowd.

No one moved so much as a muscle. Did they ever, when a cop said, "Nothing to see here"?

"Is there a problem, Ms. Casey?" Candy said.

"No problem," Vicky said.

"Then you can be on your way."

"This is a public sidewalk," I pointed out. "We can stand here if we want. As long as we want."

Candy struggled to bite back a retort. I was perfectly right, and she knew it. She turned to the crowd of onlookers, their numbers growing as news of a potential altercation spread. "You folks are blocking the sidewalk."

"What of it?" a man said.

Russ Durham ran across the street, his ever-present camera at the ready. I cursed under my breath. Just what Vicky needed.

"Problem, Officer?" he asked.

"No," Candy said.

"Glad to hear it," he said. "Andrea, I saw a couple checking out the signboard in front of your place as I passed. You might want to see that they get some service." A plump middle-aged woman, one who clearly enjoyed the fare served at her own restaurant, hurried away. The crowd began to shift.

"Betty Thatcher," Russ said. "I might want a picture of that sweater for our advertising supplement next week. You get extra space with a picture. I'd prefer to shoot it in the Nook rather than out on the street."

"Goodness," Mrs. Thatcher said, patting her hair. "I'd better freshen up." She hurried away. The crowd broke up, and in a matter of minutes only Russ, Candy, Vicky, and I were left. Rather than being grateful to him for diffusing the situation, Candy threw Russ a poisonous glare. I presumed she'd have preferred to drag us all off to jail in handcuffs. "I want no more trouble here," she snapped. She marched away, her head high.

So high, she failed to notice when she'd reached the edge of the sidewalk. She tripped and stumbled into the road with a startled squeak and windmilling arms. Fortunately—for her—no cars were passing at that moment. She recovered her footing with a hop, skip, and a jump, and marched away. The back of her neck was so red it could be used as a traffic stop.

"Don't laugh," Vicky said to me.

"Not a laughing matter. Thanks, Russ. You handled that well. I'm surprised."

He grinned at me. "Surprised I diffused an incident rather than stoked it to make for better pictures and copy for the paper? Believe it or not, Merry, I'm as proud a booster of this town as anyone else. What happens here matters to me." He indicated the sign on Vicky's door. "And that isn't good. Not for you, and definitely not for the town. I assume it has something to do with Nigel Pearce."

"I didn't poison him!" Vicky said.

"I didn't think for a moment that you did. Look, I was coming to find you two anyway. I went by Mrs. Claus's and Noel told me you were here. Something I need to talk to you about." He glanced around, checking for eavesdroppers. The snow had stopped falling, leaving the air icy fresh and the trees lining the sidewalk laden with pure white powder. Cars drove slowly by, and a few pedestrians were window-shopping, but no one was paying any more attention to us. Up and down the street lights glimmered inside shops and businesses, warm and inviting. Victoria's Bake Shoppe, in contrast, stood dark and cold in the center of the block.

"What?" Vicky snapped. "I'm not giving a statement to the papers. Except to say that my bakery is totally safe and we follow the highest standards . . ."

He lifted one hand. "Hold on. I know that. I got a call. An anonymous call, about fifteen minutes ago. I was told that Nigel Pearce had died from eating a cookie laced with GHB, a street drug, served at the post-parade reception Saturday night."

"So," I said. "We know that. That's why the health department has closed the bakery."

"You know because Vicky told you, right?"

"Yes."

"And Vicky knows that because the police told her, right?"

"Yeah," my friend said. "I was taken down to the station earlier and questioned. My dad came with me and they told him what had happened. Why?"

"After I got my anonymous call, I placed a call of my own to Detective Simmonds. She not very helpfully said the investigation was continuing, but she could confirm that at this time they were acting under the suspicion of homicide. She would give me no details of any suspects or of the cause of death."

"So this person who told you . . ." I said.

"Wants to make sure the nasty details end up in the paper."

"This caller," I said. "Was it a man or a woman? Was there anything familiar about their voice?"

Russ shook his head. "It was very muffled, as though they'd placed a piece of cloth or something across the receiver, like you see in old spy movies. Clearly, they didn't want me knowing who it was."

"Why would anyone want it in the paper?" Vicky exclaimed. "Not only will it interfere with the police investigation, but with only three weeks left until Christmas, if news like that gets around, it could ruin Rudolph. No one'll come if they think there's a killer on the loose."

"Not only a killer but one who struck at the town's Christmas party," Russ said. "While Santa bounced their kids on his knee and we passed out free gingerbread and cider."

Vicky and I stared at each other in horror.

Russ's face was grim. "I can only assume the ruin of Christmas in Rudolph is exactly what my mysterious caller wants to see happen."

Chapter 7

Russ had to get back to the paper. He wouldn't report on the anonymous tip, he told us, but he couldn't pretend Nigel Pearce hadn't died in our town. He'd have to write up *something*.

"Try not to worry," he said. "I did some checking into Diane Simmonds's background when she was hired and her record's pretty solid. She was a sergeant in Chicago and a darn good one, if her solve rate is anything to go by."

"Why do you suppose she moved to sleepy old Rudolph?" Vicky asked. Neither Russ nor I bothered to point out that suddenly, rather than being sleepy, it seemed as though Rudolph had become precisely the right place to be for a cop with a good solve rate.

"Something about a bad divorce and a nasty custody battle with a fellow officer," Russ said. "She has the child with her, so I guess the custody case went her way." He gave

Vicki Delany

Vicky a spontaneous hug. "You take care, and try not to worry. I'll let you know what I hear." Then he hugged me. He didn't let go as quickly as he had with Vicky. His arms were warm and strong and for a moment I wanted to melt into them and let him take all my problems away. "You take care too, Merry," he whispered into my hair. "Hard to believe, but there is a killer out there."

He let me go and stepped back. His hazel eyes were dark and serious. "Call me if you need anything." He hefted his camera and dashed across the street.

Vicky turned to me with a grin. "Long hug."

"He's trying to be supportive. That's nice of him."

"Very nice."

"What's that mean?"

"Nothing. I have to get around to my dad's office to go over what we're going to do next. He had to clear his schedule first."

"Do you want me to come?"

"Thanks, sweetie, but no. You have your own business to attend to. Mine"—she cast a rueful look toward the closed, dark bakery—"is not in need of attending."

"Temporarily," I said.

"Temporarily."

We hugged, told each other not to worry, and went our separate ways. I walked back to Mrs. Claus's Treasures deep in thought. Russ might be confident of Detective Simmonds's abilities, but I was not. I thought the police had acted mighty hastily in closing Vicky's bakery. Sure, I could see it if everyone at the party had come down with food poisoning. But one cookie? How anxious was Simmonds to make her mark in her new town anyway? Was she the

96

sort to rush to judgment and then try to find the facts to fit her case?

I wasn't worried that Vicky would be charged with murdering Pearce. She had absolutely no reason to care about him one way or another. But, if she was forced to remain closed through the rest of the season and the reputation of her bakery was destroyed, it would just about kill her.

I was closer to Vicky than to my own sisters. Always had been. She was fun-loving, impetuous, wild at times (that purple hair didn't go over very well at the meetings of the Business Improvement Association, which was part of the reason she wore it like that), but her bakery meant everything to her and she'd worked darn hard to make it a success.

I would do all that I could to make sure Vicky came out of this mess unscathed.

Back at Mrs. Claus's Treasures, Dad was rearranging the window displays. Gone was the assortment of jewelry, and in its place he'd put an arrangement of dinner plates, painted wineglasses, napkins, and tablecloths, all of which had a Christmas theme.

"What do you think you're doing, Dad? I left you here to help Jackie."

Jackie was behind the cash register, flicking through a fashion magazine.

"Jackie doesn't seem to need any help," he replied. "But you do. That window didn't say 'Christmas' well enough."

"Of course it says Christmas! It says nothing but Christmas. It couldn't say Christmas any louder if it went up to the top of the hill and screamed Christmas through a megaphone."

"Christmas is about family. Families getting together

for the holidays, sitting down to dinner at a time of love and peace. Christmas is about food. You might ask Vicky if she has some pies or tarts she isn't going to use to add to the display."

"Christmas is also about presents, Dad. Jewelry makes nice presents. Men like to see jewelry displays. It means they don't have to spend any time thinking about what to buy their wives."

"Christmas presents are for children," said Santa Claus. "Not adults."

In that, Dad practiced what he preached. The moment I turned eighteen, I no longer got gifts from my parents or my siblings, nor was I expected to give any. The bottom of our tree was always piled high with gaily wrapped packages, but those were for the children of my parents' friends (which meant just about everyone in Rudolph) who would drop by for Mom's famous open house Christmas brunch. My parents didn't exchange gifts, either, although Mom and I got gifts from and sent gifts to her family. Dad might not believe in Christmas gifts between adults, but Mom made sure that she got plenty of loot the rest of the year, particularly on her birthday.

Oh, and did I mention that Dad's birthday is December twenty-fifth? Somehow it was okay for us to give him birthday presents. It was always a challenge in Rudolph in December to find wrapping paper that did not have a Christmas motif.

"Not everyone is as hidebound as you, Dad," I said. "If men want to buy their wives gifts I'm not going to tell them not to, now am I?"

"Did I tell you to turn them away? I did not. I merely thought that a nice display in the window would remind people that their holiday table needs updating." His top lip turned down and the sparkle went out of his blue eyes as he peered at me from under his big, bushy white brows.

"Oh, Dad," I said. I threw a glance at Jackie. She was laughing silently.

The bell over the door tinkled and two women came in. "I am so tired of my mother's Spode dishes," one of them said to the other. "Christmas dinner was never anything but an ordeal for my mother, what with *her* mother-in-law, and every time I get out those plates I'm reminded of how much she hated the holidays." She smiled at me. "Those red and gold dishes in the window are simply divine. Do they come in sets? Good, I'll take twelve sets, please. And the gold chargers to go with them. It's time I gave everything that had been my mother's to a good home."

I stared at my father.

"Careful, Merry," he said, "You'll catch flies." I snapped my mouth shut.

I shouldn't have been so surprised: my father was Santa Claus, after all.

Jackie hopped off her stool. "I'll get them."

"Do you know," the woman's friend said, "I've just remembered that at Thanksgiving Tom broke not one but two of the Riedel wineglasses, and then his fool of a brother chipped another. And now I'm expected to put on Christmas dinner as well. I'll take twelve of those glasses in the window, please."

Dad reached under a table and pulled out a box of the glasses. "Anything else, madam?" he said.

"My tree could use an update, too. Do you have any tasteful tree ornaments? Glass balls are always nice."

"Right over here," he said with a flourish, showing her the display he'd set out yesterday.

One of the women went to get their car and she pulled up out front a few minutes later. Dad and Jackie loaded their boxes into the trunk. The car horn tooted as it drove away, while Dad stood in the street waving.

"Isn't that your car parked right in front, Merry?" he said when he came back in. "You're blocking customer parking."

"I'll move it later," I said. "Right now there's a hole in the window display. That's my entire stock of those Christmas dishes gone. What do you suggest I put in the window next?"

"Jewelry might be nice," Dad said. "Men like to give their wives and mothers jewelry for Christmas. Is Vicky okay?"

I brought my head away from thoughts of decorating the shop window and returned to more pressing matters. "Not really," I said. "She didn't say in so many words, but I can't imagine she can keep the business going if its reputation is ruined and she's closed at the busiest time of the year." Jackie hadn't returned to her spot behind the cash register. She was rearranging the rack of cocktail and dinner napkins, her head noticeably tilted in the direction of my dad and me.

"I have to go home and let Mattie out. Come with me, Dad. I have something I need to talk to you about."

Jackie might have muttered, "Aren't you supposed to be working here?" I ignored her.

"Okay," Dad said. "Jackie, lay out some of those brooches, will you? The ones tucked behind the wooden soldiers. No one can see them there."

"Those were a mistake," I said. "They're too old-fashioned to be popular. They're only twenty bucks each, but I'm going to cut the price next week just to get rid of them."

A man came into the shop. He had that deer-in-the-headlights look that many men get when entering a non-hardware store on their annual expedition in search of a present.

"I wonder if you can help me," he said hesitantly. Yup, a once-a-year shopper.

"Happy to," I said.

"I'll wait outside," Dad said.

"Are you looking for a gift?" I asked the new customer.

"Several gifts, in fact. My great-grandmother turned one hundred over the summer and for the first time in her life she can't get out shopping so she asked me to pick some things up for her. She likes to give a little something to the other ladies in her residence. She has ten friends and wants to spend about twenty dollars on each of them."

I left Jackie wrapping ten rhinestone brooches in gift wrap and joined my father on the sidewalk. "Do you want a job?" I asked.

"Nope."

We got into my car, and I pulled into the street. Traffic was building and someone nabbed my spot as soon as I left it.

"What's up?" Dad said.

"Russ Durham knows that Nigel Pearce was killed by GHB. Someone phoned and told him."

"Who?"

"An anonymous call, apparently."

"Why would someone do that?"

"That's the question, isn't it?" I said. "You and I both know that Vicky's bakery is squeaky clean, but that's beside the point. Only one person died that night, even though there must have been more than a hundred people at the reception, every one of them eating and drinking the same food. And that includes children and old folks, the people most likely to contract food poisoning. The cops say the drug was in a gingerbread cookie. I have to accept that because I have no reason not to. I assume they're pretty accurate with that sort of thing these days. But only one cookie was bad."

I pulled into the parking lot behind the library to turn around. And also, incidentally, to see if anything was happening outside the police station. All was quiet.

My dad was a man of few words. "Pearce had a special cookie, as I recall," he said at last.

"Right, Charles Dickens. In honor of our English guest."

"Did Vicky tell people it was for Pearce?"

"I don't know. She probably did, she wouldn't have wanted just anyone helping themselves to it. You're thinking that Pearce was deliberately targeted?"

"That seems likely. Think back to that evening, Merry. I didn't go into the kitchen, but you did. Where were the special cookies?"

"Right out on the counter. With plastic wrap over them and a note that said, 'Do not serve.' Obviously Vicky didn't want her helpers to take that tray out before everything was ready for the presentation."

"So if it was on the counter all evening . . ."

I followed his train of thought. "Anyone could have come into the kitchen, at any time. Not just Vicky and her helpers, but the community center staff."

"People in search of a glass of water. Or pretending to be in search of one."

I envisioned the scene. Countless people came and went throughout the party. The kitchen opened directly into the main room, and a guard hadn't exactly been placed on the door. "What does GHB look like, anyway?" I asked.

Dad pulled out his phone and pressed a few keys. "A fine white powder."

I remembered the Charles Dickens cookie, decorated with a layer of thick white icing. "The poisoner might not have known the cookie was intended specifically for Pearce," I said.

"That seems unlikely. There were what, ten cookies on that tray? The rest of us simply helped ourselves. Unless the killer, and we have to start thinking of him like that, Merry . . ."

"Or her," I said.

"Or her . . . intended this to be some random act aimed at no one in particular, we have to conclude that Pearce was the intended victim."

"It's probably just our rotten luck that he was killed in Rudolph," I said. "No one here had laid eyes on him before Saturday. His enemy must have followed him here. The town was full of tourists, anyone at all could have slipped in, done the deed, and then left town."

"You're assuming no one here knew the man, Merry. 'It is a capital mistake to theorize before one has data.'" With that parting quote from the Great Detective, Dad opened the car door and got out.

We'd reached my house long ago. I'd parked in my assigned half of the double garage and we'd sat in the car for a few minutes. I got out and walked Dad to the sidewalk. Mrs. D'Angelo was on the porch, washing the windows. She had the cleanest front windows in Upstate New York.

"Noel. Merry." She waved her cleaning rag at us. "I heard the news. That nice Englishman murdered. Right here in Rudolph. I shudder to think what this town is coming to. And at Christmastime at that."

"Have the police confirmed it was murder?" Dad asked.

"No, but everyone knows they like to keep things to themselves. That way they can tell who the killer is when he reveals things only the killer would know." Mrs. D'Angelo was a big fan of murder mysteries. "Imagine, a poisoned cookie."

"Who told you that?" Dad said, his voice sharp.

She waved her cloth. "I don't remember. My phone hasn't stopped ringing all morning." She was interrupted by Bing Crosby singing "White Christmas." "There it goes again." She dug the latest model smartphone out of her apron pocket.

"Louise! Have you heard? Yes, it's true. A poisoned cookie. I don't blame dear Vicky Casey at all—clearly the poison was added after the cookies were baked. Hold on, honey, just a minute." She took the phone away from her ear. If children could see the look on Santa Claus's face right now, they'd spend Christmas Eve hiding under their beds rather than trying to catch a peek of him over the banister. "Don't worry, Noel," she said. "Irene Matlow"—one of the town councilors—"called earlier. She said we don't want news of this to get around. I'm only telling people I trust to keep a confidence."

Dad growled. "I'd better go," he said to me. "Clearly the

cat is out of the bag. The news is spreading, and fast." He threw a glare toward Mrs. D'Angelo, who'd leaned up against the snow-covered porch railing all ready to settle into a nice long chat.

I headed around the back to my own apartment, freed Mattie from his crate, and prepared to take him for a short walk. The temperature was dropping and the wind off the lake was picking up. I still didn't have a coat to wear. My jacket would be adequate for keeping the rain off, but little else. But it was the only one I had, and would have to do. I found a big sweater to wear underneath, and at least I still had my heavy scarf and mitts. I got Mattie's leash and we headed out.

At the end of the driveway, I turned right rather than left for our usual route through the park. I didn't feel much like returning to the park today.

Mattie ran on ahead, straining at the leash, sniffing under every bush, barking greetings to everyone we passed. The sun shone through the fresh snow on the tree branches, creating an exquisite winter wonderland. As we walked and I watched the happy dog overflowing with excitement at everything he came across, I felt my spirits rising. All would be okay, I told myself. It was Christmas in Rudolph.

I was so deep in thought that only gradually did I become aware that a car was creeping along behind me, matching my pace. My heart leapt into my mouth. I jerked on the leash, pulling Mattie closer to me. I turned around.

It was a silver BMW. The car pulled up beside me and stopped. The engine was switched off, and Detective Simmonds got out. "I was on my way to your shop," she said.

"How do you know which is my shop?" I demanded.

She lowered her sunglasses. "I am the police, Merry."

"Oh. Right."

"Not that it's any great secret. I only had to ask anyone, officers or civilians, at the station."

"Oh. Why?"

"Why am I looking for you? I have some questions, that's all. It's a nice day and I could use some fresh air. May I walk with you?"

I might not have wanted this woman to spoil my walk, but Mattie turned traitor. He gave a single joyful bark in greeting and rushed toward Simmonds. She crouched down and gave him a hearty scratch behind the ears. His rear end wiggled with pleasure. "May I give him a treat?" she asked me.

"I guess," I mumbled.

"Let's see what we have here," she said, digging in her coat pocket. She found a dog biscuit and held it out. "Sit," she said. Mattie dropped. Simmonds held the biscuit in front of him. He didn't move. "Good dog," she said, and the biscuit disappeared in a flash.

I tried not to look impressed. I'd been attempting to teach him to sit. He would let his butt hover over the floor for a fraction of a second and then lunge for the offered treat and snap it up with enough force to rip off my hand if I wasn't careful.

Simmonds gave him a final pat and pushed herself to her feet.

"You can't park there," I said, pettily. "It's a no-parking zone."

She gave me another one of her looks. "I suspect my car will be all right for a few minutes."

We continued our walk. Mattie trotted respectfully between us.

"Have you thought anything more about Saturday night?" Simmonds asked me.

"I've thought about little else," I said, suppressing a shudder. "But nothing new. Sorry."

"Tell me about the party earlier. You were there."

"The post-parade reception. We do it every year. Ply the tourists with small amounts of Christmas baking and nonalcoholic drinks to get them into the mood to spend money. Let their kids meet Santa. Pretty much everyone comes, townspeople as well as tourists."

"This town has a mercenary attitude toward Christmas."

"We're trying to keep Rudolph afloat. Provide people with a good living. Stop families from moving away in search of jobs or opportunities like they've had to in so many other places. Do you have a problem with that?"

"No."

"Good. Because if you're going to live in Rudolph, you need to realize that Christmas is how people like me, like Vicky Casey, and almost everyone else in town, make their living, in one way or another. But Christmas is above all what we love. Maybe we seem to go overboard at times, but that's like criticizing my mother for going overboard because she sings opera arias rather than advertising jingles. Opera is what she loves."

"I'm not criticizing. Just trying to get a handle on what makes this town and its people tick."

Mattie woofed softly in agreement. I didn't know he could do anything softly.

"Speaking of Vicky," I said. "She needs her bakery open.

Next weekend should be our busiest of the year, probably even busier than last weekend. Most of us rely on December to see us through the rest of the year."

"I'll keep that in mind."

"Besides, it's pretty obvious that the drug in the cookie that killed Pearce didn't originate in the bakery. Not if no one else who ate her baked goods got sick."

"How do you know what killed him?"

"Everyone knows it. They all think they're only telling one or two friends, but then those friends tell one or two friends and in a flash it's common knowledge. Something else you're going to have to understand if you want to live in a small town. Rather than, say, Chicago."

The edges of her mouth turned up. "I get your point. Tell me about this reception, Merry. I've been to the community center, had a look around. Big kitchen, counters open to the main room. A second door off the kitchen leading to the smaller meeting rooms. Door to the outside near the kitchen."

"People came and went all evening. Platters of cookies and gingerbread were laid out on the table for anyone to help themselves. Same with the cider."

"No one did any cooking in the kitchen, did they?"

"Vicky always does the baking at the bakery and drives the food down in her van. She's very conscious of safety requirements and proper hygiene."

"Did you see Nigel Pearce leave?"

"No. I didn't."

"Did you notice him talking to anyone in particular? Arguing with someone, maybe?"

He'd been paying a lot of attention to Jackie. Jackie had

argued with Kyle about that. Kyle had spent the entire party in a sulk. "No," I said.

"This one special cookie was prepared exclusively for him, I've been told."

I nodded. "And the tray was left out on the counter all evening where anyone could get to it. Find a moment when everyone was busy, lift the edge of the plastic wrap, sprinkle a bit of poison, cover it up again, and then sit back and wait for Pearce to bite into it. I hope you're investigating people who might have had cause to wish Pearce dead. No one in Rudolph even knew the guy."

"We're keeping our options open. Thanks for the walk. I enjoyed that." She gave Mattie a scratch.

"One thing you might not know," I said.

"What's that?

"Someone called the *Rudolph Gazette* around eleven this morning. Anonymously. They told Russ Durham, the editor in chief, the results of the autopsy."

One well-sculpted eyebrow lifted in surprise. "That is interesting. I wonder who would do that?"

"That's the question I have. Not someone who has the interests of the town of Rudolph at heart, I can assure you."

Chapter 8

Tuesday morning, Vicky was waiting for me at the door of the shop when I arrived for work. She had two lattes, which I was pleased to see, and a very sour face, which I was not at all pleased to see.

"Any news from the cops?" I asked, unlocking the door.

"No," she said. "And in this case, no news is definitely bad news. My dad's going to talk to Simmonds this morning. He's going to tell her that keeping my business closed is tantamount to an accusation, and the police will either have to charge me or let me open."

I stopped in the act of taking the first welcoming sip. The lattes were in Cranberry Coffee Bar take-out cups, not from Vicky's own bakery. "That doesn't sound good. You don't want him hinting that they should arrest you."

"I trust Dad."

"I haven't heard anyone accusing you," I said. "We all

understand that the police and the health department have a job to do."

"It's not locals I'm worried about. Dorothy gave me these drinks for no charge. She said she knows I wouldn't do anything in the least bit unsanitary, never mind dangerous. It could have happened to her, if Pearce had had his lunch at the coffee bar."

"That's the spirit of Rudolph," I said.

"Yeah, it is. But the good people of Rudolph don't keep my business going at the busiest time of the year. I'm worried about the upcoming weekend. Midnight Madness. I have plans to be open all evening and to put a stand out on the street selling cookies and squares. Even if I'm open, will the visitors come, knowing my baking might have killed a man?"

"You're worrying about nothing," I said, worrying for her. "Tourists don't read the local paper. Everything will be back to normal by Friday. You'll see." I smiled.

"Thanks, sweetie," she said, prying the lid off her cup.

The shop door flew open and Betty Thatcher fell in. Her face was very pale, making the overly applied blush on her cheeks look like the dots of paint on one of Alan's wooden soldiers. She held a copy of today's *Rudolph Gazette* in her shaking hand. "Have you seen the paper?"

"What's happened?" Vicky and I spoke in unison. "Have they caught the person who killed Nigel Pearce?"

Betty thrust the paper toward us. Vicky grabbed it. I read over her shoulder. The paper was folded open to an inside page, and the main item of news was about an upcoming vote to expand the town dump. I hadn't known the handling of garbage was of such concern to Betty. She must have read the confusion in our faces, because she jabbed one long red nail at the bottom of the page. "That!"

It was a half-page advertisement for the Muddle Harbor Café. "Nestled on the peaceful shores of Lake Ontario" was their slogan. Today something extra had been added to the usual advertising copy. Giant black lettering proclaimed, "We serve SAFE baking in an environment SAFE for your family."

Vicky let out a very bad word.

"You can say that again," Betty said. So Vicky did.

"None of our visitors read the *Gazette*," I said, trying to sound optimistic. "They won't see it."

"Perhaps not," Betty said, "but I doubt the Muddites will limit their advertising to this one ad."

"Probably not."

"Why are you upset about it, anyway?" Vicky said. "It's my bakery they're attacking."

Vicky had a point. Betty was one of the few business owners in Rudolph not known for her community spirit. If it didn't affect the Nook, she didn't care.

"This is bound to be the opening salvo in a full-on attack. If people start going to Muddle Harbor for lunch, why, they might never get back here to shop at my store!"

"I'm going to wring Russ Durham's neck," Vicky said.

"You'll have to get in line." The man in question stood in the doorway. "I hear a lynching party is forming even as we speak. In my own defense, I have to say that I'm not in the business of censorship. The Muddle Harbor Café is a regular client of the paper. If they want to change their ad and take out a bigger one, I can't tell them no."

"Yes, you can!" Vicky stamped her foot.

"Russ is right," I said. "If their ad had mentioned your bakery by name as unsafe, then he would have been within his rights to refuse to accept it. But, on the surface, it's just an ad."

"On the surface," Vicky muttered.

"You're nothing but trouble, Vicky Casey," Betty said.

"Hey!" I said. "That's unfair."

Betty snorted. "This was a respectable town, once." With that parting shot, she stalked out.

Russ, Vicky, and I burst out laughing the moment the door was shut.

"What's Christmas," Vicky said, "without a grinch or two?"

"I wonder if she was born miserable," Russ said.

"Her heart is certainly two sizes too small," Vicky said.

My laughter didn't last long. Betty didn't like many people, but she particularly didn't like Vicky or me. Betty had a son named Clark. The word "layabout" had been invented to describe Clark Thatcher. As he was past thirty, it wasn't likely he was going to change his ways, either. Clark had worked for Vicky last summer. That hadn't lasted long. He showed up at work drunk one morning and, especially since he was supposed to be driving the delivery van, she fired him on the spot. Betty had not been happy about that. Betty knew how to hold a grudge.

Russ must have read my face. "Forget Betty. She'd love to destroy every other business in town, but even she's smart enough to know that she needs a prosperous town for her own business to succeed."

I wasn't so sure.

"I gotta run," Vicky said. "I'm off to my dad's office to

hear what Simmonds had to say." The good mood of only a few moments ago had died. "Don't you dare report that, Russell Durham!"

"Headline news. *Well-known Rudolph baker visits loving father.*"

Vicky harrumphed.

The morning was quiet. I left Jackie to handle what few customers we had and made my preparations for Midnight Madness weekend. I'd gotten in plenty of stock, but as always I worried that I'd bought the wrong stuff. Should I have passed on the felt Santas and gotten more of the glassware? I studied the box of Santas. Rows of identical embroidered faces smiled up at me. Somehow they'd looked more appealing in the advertising brochure. En masse they put me in mind of a horror movie.

"Merry!" my dad's voice boomed from the front of the store.

I picked up one of the dolls and carried it out. "I'm glad you're here, Dad. I'm not sure about these things. What do you think? Oh, hi, Mom. You're up early. Is something wrong?"

Dad didn't look much like Santa today. The sparkle was gone from his eyes and his mouth was set into a tight line. My mom had, shockingly, come out without makeup. She probably hadn't done her hair, either, as she had a wool hat pulled down over her head. My heart almost stopped for a moment. I thought of my three siblings. "What's happened?"

"Have you heard from Eve today?" Mom asked. Eve was my youngest sister. She was in LA these days, trying to break through as an actress. She was not, we all knew although never said, having much luck.

"No. Not for ages. Why?"

"Look at this." Dad thrust his phone toward me. It was open to the messages screen.

I read: *Dad, Eve here. In ambulance heading for Good Samaritan. Car accident. Two broken legs. Please come.*

"That's terrible," I said, giving the phone back to him. "When do you leave?"

"I booked the flight immediately," Mom said. "Out of Syracuse at three o'clock."

"Give her my love," I said.

My parents exchanged glances.

"What?" I said.

"We texted that number with the flight information," Dad said. "It was delivered, but unread, which isn't strange. She might be in the ER or even in the operating room with the phone switched off."

"I called Good Samaritan Hospital," Mom said, "to make inquiries. They have no patient by that name."

"Could the ambulance have taken her to another hospital?" I asked.

"But which one?" Mom asked. "We called the apartment and left a message."

"And . . ."

"Lynette called us back a few minutes ago," Dad said. "She knew nothing about any accident." Lynette was Eve's roommate, another struggling actress.

"Maybe Eve was only able to make one call."

"Maybe," Dad said, "but Lynette said Eve has gone hiking and camping in the mountains with friends. They left two days ago and aren't due back until the day after tomorrow."

"Eve went hiking?" I said, shocked. My sister, for whom spas and luxury hotels had been invented, was hiking? Exercise, to Eve, was what you did in a gym to stay thin, not something for fun.

"A new boyfriend," Mom said. "The rugged outdoors type, apparently."

"That's a relationship doomed," I said. "I'll keep trying to get her while you're in the air."

"We've decided that I should go alone," Dad said while a grim-faced Mom nodded. "At least until I can figure out what's going on. This is all very strange. She's not in the hospital that was in the message. The number the text came from isn't Eve's phone. I tried calling it and reached a generic voice mailbox. I left a message, but have received no reply as of yet. Her own phone isn't answering. And her best friend and roommate knows nothing about this accident and says Eve is out of town."

"Weird," Jackie said.

"You think someone's playing a practical joke on you?" I asked.

"If so," Mom said, "we are not laughing. I'm worried sick."

"I'm leaving for the airport now," Dad said. "Call me immediately if you hear anything."

"Of course," I said.

Dad gave Mom a hug. They clung together for a long time, and when they separated, Mom's eyes were wet.

"I'm sure it will all be okay, Mr. Wilkinson," Jackie said.

"Thanks," Dad said. "Merry, why don't you walk your mother home?"

"Sure," I said.

"I'm fine," Mom said. "You have work to do." She dug in her coat pocket and found a tissue. She blew her nose.

"Store's not busy," I said. "As you can see. Jackie doesn't need me."

"I never do," Jackie said.

Dad laughed. He gave my mom another hug and then he left.

"I'll get my coat," I said. "Not that I have one. Speaking of coats, want to do some shopping, Mom?"

"What?"

"I need a new coat. You can help me shop."

"What happened to yours? You bought it at the beginning of the season."

I wasn't about to tell her why I didn't have one, as that would bring us back to Nigel Pearce. I shrugged. "I decided I don't like it."

My phone rang. I pulled it out of my pocket and glanced at the display.

Eve.

"Eve!" I shouted. "Are you okay? Where are you?"

"Hi to you, too, Merry," my sister's bright and perky voice said. "I'm fine. Although that is an experience I will not be repeating anytime soon. Do you know he actually expected me to sleep in a tent? On the ground? When I said . . ."

"Where are you?"

"Heading back to LA. Soon as I got in cell range, and let me tell you I'll never leave it again, my phone lit up like some sort of Rudolph Christmas display. I got a whole string of messages. I couldn't listen to them all, so I called

Lynette first. She said Dad's been trying to get me. I figured I'd check with you. Are Mom and Dad okay?"

My mom was practically jumping up and down. I gave her a thumbs-up. "They're fine. We're all fine. Have you been in an accident?"

"No. Why do you think that? Although I might have been in more than an accident if I'd stayed on that stupid trip. We had to hang our food from a tree to keep it away from bears. I told Craig he was to take me back to the city, or we were finished. Can you believe it, he said he'd take me as far as the bus station. A bus! I am, even as we speak, standing in line to get on a bus!"

I handed the phone to my mom, who promptly burst into tears; perhaps as much in sympathy with Eve having to ride on a bus as with relief that her youngest daughter was uninjured.

"Can I use your phone?" I said to Jackie.

She handed it over without a word, and I called Dad to tell him he could come home.

Chapter 9

Vicky Casey drove a sexy red convertible Mazda Miata. One of her cousins was a car mechanic who specialized in foreign and antique automobiles. He'd gotten it for her cheap, because it didn't run, and fixed it up so it was almost as good as new. She absolutely loved it. She'd put the top down and break land speed records on country roads as the wind ruffled her hair and men whistled as she flew past. Sometimes they were whistling at her, but more often at the car. She loved that, too.

That, however, was in the summer.

In the winter, the Miata, too delicate for snow and ice and whatever the county dumped by the truckload on the roads to keep them clear, was stored in the garage at her cousin's place, covered by a tarp. In the winter, Vicky walked most places, and if she had to drive, she took the white panel van with the big "Victoria's Bake Shoppe" logo painted on the sides.

Today, she didn't even have that.

I eyed the Mercury Grand Marquis, the sort of transportation Vicky called a Medicare Sled.

I got into the passenger seat and fastened my belt. "Where on earth did you get this?"

"It's my great-aunt Matilda's. She uses it to get to church on Sundays and to bingo the other six days of the week. I borrowed it."

"Which forces me to ask, why?"

"We're travelling incognito."

"So I see," I said. Vicky wore a blue and yellow knitted hat with a pom-pom on the top, pulled down to her eyebrows and over her ears so not a strand of purple was on display. The Vicky I knew wouldn't be caught dead in that hat. "Mind if I ask why, again? Your phone call, which woke me up, I might add, was highly cryptic."

More than cryptic. She hadn't said anything except, "be ready to rock and roll in half an hour," and hung up.

We were now rocking and rolling, as the boatlike car jerked into the street.

It was a few minutes after seven, and the residential area of Rudolph was slowly coming to life. Lights shone from most houses, including mine. The lace curtains in the front window twitched as Mrs. D'Angelo clocked my departure. A couple of inches of snow had fallen in the night, and the snowplows were out, scooping it up and stuffing it by the side of the street. People were shoveling or snowblowing their driveways before heading out to work, while others were walking dogs.

"If we're just going for a drive," I said, "I should have brought Mattie. He needs to get used to being in a car."

"Next time," Vicky said.

In a matter of minutes we were leaving the lights of Rudolph behind and hitting the dark county road running along the shores of Lake Ontario. The beginnings of a soft red glow colored the sky to the east.

"Better take warning," Vicky said.

"Huh?"

"Red sky in morning. Sailors take warning, right?"

"So they say."

We'd barely gone a mile before we found ourselves stuck behind a big yellow school bus on its way to pick up country kids. The road was well plowed, but with all the twists and turns and ups and downs, the line in the center of the road was solid yellow. "We could walk faster," Vicky mumbled. The big car lurched and shuddered. Vicky hunched over the steering wheel. "I don't know how anyone in their right mind can drive a car like this."

"Like what?"

"An automatic. When I drive, I like to be the one in control."

I refrained from saying, "In driving, as in life."

About a mile before the next intersection, the school bus put on its turn indicators and began to slow. Vicky cursed as she was forced to tap her own brakes. Then she shot ahead, barely clipping the back bumper of the bus as it made its turn. The Mercury's engine roared. I wondered if it was enjoying the feeling of power for once, or screaming in terror at the unexpected speed.

We passed a sign. "Muddle Harbor, 10 miles."

"Okay," I said. "Unless you're kidnapping me to hold for ransom, in which case you're going to be sadly disappointed, you have to tell me what's up. The only place this road leads to is Muddle Harbor."

"Got it in one," she said.

"Vicky, you can't be thinking of going to Muddle Harbor to argue with them about that ad in the *Gazette* yesterday." I hadn't seen the local paper yet this morning. I feared to ask if the café had placed another ad hinting that Victoria's Bake Shoppe wasn't safe.

"Me? Argue? Perish the thought. I want to check out the competition, that's all."

"This isn't a good idea."

"Look, Merry. That blasted Muddite slandered my business, in writing. I intend to tell them they can't get away with it."

"They didn't even mention you, Vicky. That's not slander. They simply stated that their bakery serves safe baked goods. That's true. Well, I assume it's true."

"And that," Vicky said triumphantly, "is why we're going. I want to check this place out, let them know we're watching them."

"Why am I being brought into this?"

"Because," she said, "they might drag me into a dark alley and beat me up if I'm on my own."

I kept my thoughts on the chances of that happening to myself. "What did Simmonds have to say to your dad when he asked her to let you open?"

"That she'd consider it," Vicky huffed. "She'd better consider fast. I've got to let my casual staff know if I'm not going to be able to use them this weekend. They need the holiday money almost as much as I do. It's only fair to give them the chance to find something else."

The glory days of the town of Muddle Harbor were long gone. It boasts a lovely location on the lake, and was close enough to Rochester that people could spend long hot days in lakeside hotels or enjoying their own holiday homes. But in cold New York State, that only means summer business, which isn't enough to keep a town thriving all year.

The town's decay was in evidence as we drove down the main street. More than a few shop windows were covered in brown paper or filled with the sort of sparse display that indicates there is no thriving business inside. The few open stores had tried to add some Christmas cheer, but it seemed to my experienced eye that their hearts weren't truly in it.

A handful of shop owners were scraping snow off the sidewalks in front of their businesses. No one looked up as we drove past.

The Muddle Harbor Café sat in the center of the main block. It, at least, was brightly lit and looked welcoming. We drove slowly past, checking it out, and Vicky pulled into a parking spot on the opposite side of the street, a few doors down. We got out of the car and walked to the café.

The light displays on the shops we passed were unimaginative, many of the bulbs burned out and not replaced. The window presentations were badly lit and covered in a thin layer of dust.

My fingers itched to get in there, scrub the windows until the glass sparkled, add better lighting, and rearrange the displays to their best advantage. A women's clothing shop had a fake tree in the window. Fake! And not just fake, but so cheap it looked fake. That might not be exactly forbidden in Rudolph, but it certainly would be frowned upon. In a nod to modernity we allowed tastefully decorated trees of silver or pink aluminum. Some stores stocked inexpensive fake trees (and don't get me started on the lumps of nuclear-green plastic Betty Thatcher sold as wreaths), but we tried to ensure that everything used for decoration was as authentic as possible.

The Muddle Harbor Café was decorated in '50s-diner style: black-and-white-checkered tiles on the walls, a long counter with red-topped stools, and booth seating. Everything looked well maintained and tidy. But the décor, mostly pictures of old-fashioned soda bottles and advertising for long-since-departed companies, didn't just look old. It *was* old. There's retro, and then there's seriously out-of-date.

A few customers were in the café: a group of old men filling a booth (as they probably did once a week all year round), two young women with babies in strollers relaxing over coffee and muffins, and an elderly couple who'd long since run out of anything to say to each other, buried behind their newspapers.

Vicky led the way across the room, and I followed. She plopped herself onto a red vinyl–topped stool and whispered to me, "Don't have anything to eat."

"Mornin' hon," the waitress said. "Coffee?"

"Okay," Vicky said. She did not remove her hat or coat.

"Sure. Thanks." I was wearing my new coat. Crisis averted, Eve safely getting on a bus, and Dad on the way home, Mom and I had gone shopping. The word "restraint" isn't in my mother's vocabulary and without quite knowing what had happened I found myself spending far more than I'd intended on a gorgeous knee-length garment of gray wool with an offset zipper, wide sleeves, and high, face-framing collar. Now I glanced around in search of a hook.

"Just leave it on the stool next to you, hon," the waitress said, pouring the coffees. "Not like we're gonna have a full house."

The coffee smelled rich and delicious. I added a splash of cream and took a sip. Excellent.

I plucked a menu from between the salt and pepper shakers. The breakfast was traditional fare, lots of eggs and hash browns. They also had a selection of muffins, coffee cake, and cinnamon buns that were advertised as "homemade." They might be home baked, I thought, but a peek into the kitchen told me they were likely from a commercial mix. I turned the menu over. Lunch offerings consisted of hamburgers and retro fare like hot turkey sandwiches.

"Ready to order?" the waitress said, her pad and pencil at the ready.

"Just coffee's fine," Vicky said.

"I'll have two poached eggs, soft, with the hash browns and the country sausage and wheat toast." I put the menu back. The waitress gave me a strained smile. Barely eight o'clock and she already looked as though her feet hurt.

"Are you trying to give yourself a heart attack?" Vicky whispered when the waitress had gone to put my order in.

"I haven't had a real old-fashioned American breakfast in years," I said.

"That's because it'll clog your arteries and kill you," Vicky said.

"Come on," I said. "Look at this place. It's no competition to you. And you're no competition to it. Different as chalk and cheese."

"I might not fry eggs in grease, but I do make muffins and pastries," Vicky said. She nodded to the shelf behind the cash register where fresh baking was available for takeout.

A heaping plate was slapped onto the counter in front of me.

"Ugh," Vicky said, barely suppressing a shudder.

I added a hefty couple of squirts of ketchup and dug in. The eggs were perfectly done. Bright yellow yolk leaked into the crispy hash browns. *Deeelicious.*

"Aren't you hot in your coat?" I said once I'd enjoyed my first few mouthfuls. "It's warm in here."

"No. How's the toast?"

"I'll have to give you that. It's factory bread."

She sniffed.

"First time in Muddle Harbor?" the waitress asked. She poured coffee without asking. I like that in a breakfast place.

"Yes," Vicky said with a smile. Probably only I, who'd known her since kindergarten, knew it was her pretend smile. "We're thinking of buying property around here. A summer place. Although," she hastened to add, "we'd want something we can use all year round. Kinda quiet here, though."

"That's because it's early in the week. We get busy on the weekend. Plenty of people come from the cities for winter sports, that sort of thing. All winter long, too, not just at Christmas like other towns get."

"We thought we might check out Rudolph next."

"Oh." The waitress glanced around. The old men and the newspaper-reading couple had left. Only the young mothers remained. "I don't know if you heard about what happened over in Rudolph the other day."

"No. What?" Vicky asked, wide-eyed.

"It's not really for me to say," she said. "Being city girls and all, you might not know the way small towns work. But sometimes, when they get overfull, and have too much going on, they don't quite provide the level of care that they should." She shook her head. "Poor Rudolph. Such a tragedy."

Vicky almost levitated off her stool. I gripped her arm and shoved her back down.

"I'm Janice Benedict." The waitress shoved her hand across the counter. I took it and shook. Vicky glugged back coffee. "I'm the owner of the Muddle Harbor Café. Lived here all my life. You won't find a better town anywhere within a hundred miles of here. And, I have to say, not a safer one."

Janice was good, I had to give her that. She'd pretty much hinted, while pretending to be coy, that the entire part-time population of Rudolph had recently been slaughtered in some unspecified incident caused by an inadequate level of care. She dug into her pocket. "Here, take this." She handed me a business card. John Benedict, real estate agent. A man with sprayed hair and false teeth beamed at me from the square of paper. "My brother's one of the finest, if not the finest, Realtors in Muddle Harbor and vicinity. He knows everything that comes up for sale before the owners even know they're lookin' to sell. Tell him I sent you and he'll be sure to cut you a good deal."

She lowered her voice. "Here in Muddle Harbor, you'll find us very . . . tolerant. I don't like to say, but I've heard some stories about Rudolph folk. Sometimes they're, well, not as accepting as modern folks should be."

"Huh?" Vicky said.

"Huh?" I said. Then the light dawned. She thought Vicky and I were a couple. I smothered a laugh as I wiped up yellow yolk and red ketchup with the last of my toast.

A gust of cold air hit our backs as the door opened. "Great timing!" Janice called. "Here's someone you girls will want to meet. Randy, come on over here and give these ladies a big Muddle Harbor welcome."

Randy Baumgartner hurried across the room, hand outstretched, patented politician's smile firmly in place. He grabbed my hand and pumped it. Then he did the same to Vicky's.

"Randy here's our mayor," Janice said. "Randy, these ladies are looking for good vacation property. No need to look any further, is there? Hey, I've an idea. Why don't I call John right now? Tell him to drop everything and come on over and meet you."

"Will you look at the time." Vicky leapt off her stool. "Gotta run. We'll meet your brother another time. M . . . Martha, get the check, will you."

I didn't know who Martha was or why she would be paying for our breakfast. Then it dawned on me. Vicky didn't want to say my name. I dug into my purse. My plate was nothing but a smear of ketchup, egg yolk, and toasted breadcrumbs. My tummy would protest later, but boy had that been good.

Randy Baumgartner was studying me. "I'm sure we've met before," he said.

"Nope," Vicky said. "She has one of those faces." She rubbed at her head, and her hat slipped. A shock of purple hair escaped.

"Hey," Randy said. "I know you, too. You were at the reception in Rudolph last Saturday."

Janice gasped.

"You're the woman from the bakery!" He turned to Janice. "The one who poisoned that man."

"Gotta run," Vicky said. She grabbed my arm and headed for the door.

"The bakery in Rudolph is perfectly safe," I called over my shoulder. I pulled to a halt beside the table with the two young mothers. "The whole town is perfectly safe. My shop sells handmade wooden toys. Nothing full of artificial chemicals or mass-produced. Friday's Midnight Madness. Come early and bring your kids. Santa will be there."

I ran into the street.

A howling mob intent on stringing Vicky and me up from the nearest lamppost did not pursue us, but we ran as though it did. We leapt into the Mercury; Vicky gunned the engine and we squealed out of town.

"That was fun," Vicky said once we had passed the Muddle Harbor town limits.

"Yeah, real fun. Aside from that, I don't know what we learned. It's no secret the Muddites aren't exactly enthusiastic boosters of Rudolph. Although the dig about not being the sort of place for our type was kinda a low blow."

"They're using what happened to Nigel Pearce against us, Merry. You don't think we're the first people to wander into that 1953 relic of a café—and I still can't believe you ate that entire breakfast—and get a warning about not going to Rudolph. What else might she have said if we hadn't been discovered? Something about satanic rituals, I bet. They're going to play this to the hilt, Merry."

"I have to admit you're right," I said. "Which leads me to another conclusion."

"And what might that be?"

"That maybe some people in Muddle Harbor aren't just taking advantage of our misfortune. Maybe they made it happen."

Vicky turned her head and looked at me. "Are you saying they killed Nigel?"

A truck roared past us, horn blaring. "Oops," Vicky said, pulling the Grand Marquis back into our lane. "Close one."

I pried my fingers off the dashboard. "I'm saying *cui bono*."

"And that means?"

"It's Latin, meaning 'who benefits.' When any crime has been committed, the first thing to ask is who benefits. They always say that in English mystery novels."

"I bow to your superior knowledge. Latin or not, you've got a heck of a good point, Merry. The Muddites do stand to benefit, and big-time. If they destroy the Christmas season in Rudolph, they'll get some of the overflow. Safe baking, my left foot." She ripped off her hat and ran her fingers through her hair.

"That mayor, Randy Baumgartner, was at the reception," I said. "That's why he recognized us today. Him and a couple of their town councilors."

"So they had not only motive, but also the means and the opportunity," Vicky said. "Isn't that also what they say in the mystery novels?"

We drove the rest of the way back to Rudolph in silence.

Chapter 10

'd been gone less than two hours, but Mattie greeted me
with as much enthusiasm as if I were returning from an
expedition to the South Pole. I snapped on his leash and
took him for a quick walk.

"You were off bright and early this morning," Mrs.
D'Angelo called as I rounded the front of the house.

"Went for breakfast with Vicky Casey," I said.

"Such a nice girl, Vicky. Too bad about that hair. Is
Matilda ill?"

"Matilda? Who's Matilda?"

"Matilda Alfenburg. Vicky's mother's aunt. I happened
to be washing the dishes and looking out the kitchen window this morning and couldn't help but notice that Vicky
was driving Matilda's car. Matilda loves that car. She never
lets anyone borrow it."

"Far as I know," I called over my shoulder as Mattie dragged me away, "Great-aunt Matilda is in fighting form."

When I'd first seen Mrs. D'Angleo's house, with an eye to renting one of the upstairs apartments, I'd been swept away by the beauty of the garden. It was a big lot with golf club–quality grass, neat and well-maintained English country garden perennial beds, walkways and porches overflowing with huge terra cotta planters of red and white geraniums and trailing vines. I soon came to realize that all that gardening was for the express purpose of allowing Mrs. D'Angelo to keep her eye on the street and everyone in it. Her activities were severely restricted in the winter, when all she could do was peek out the living room window or wash the windows on the front porch. She loved it when it snowed. Not because she particularly cared for snow, but because it gave her an excuse to be outside. Our front path was the most neatly shoveled on our street. Mrs. D'Angelo tried to get out the morning after a fall to clear off the sidewalk itself, but the town usually beat her to it.

A happy Mattie darted from one patch of yellow snow to another. He needed, Vicky had told me, to start getting used to different people. She thought I should bring him into the shop.

I thought she was nuts. A growing, hyperactive Saint Bernard puppy cavorting among the glass ornaments and festive dishes was a recipe for disaster.

Training, training, Vicky reminded me.

Work, work, I reminded her.

Perhaps when the Christmas rush was over, I'd start introducing him to the shop.

I took my dog home and got ready for work.

* * *

It was after ten when I got to the store, but no line of eager shoppers greeted me. Only Betty Thatcher, who'd probably been lying in wait.

"Nothing today," she said, waving the morning's paper at me.

"That's good," I said. I studied the set to her face as I unlocked the door. "Isn't it?"

"I fear the calm before the storm," she replied.

I wondered what it was like to always be looking on the dark side of life. I went into my shop. Betty followed. I noticed her studying the glass balls that my dad had arranged the other day. She saw me looking, and glanced quickly away.

The door chimes sounded, and Russ Durham came in. "Morning, all."

"No ad in the *Gazette* today?" I asked.

"If you mean from the Muddle Harbor Café, they only place an ad once a week," Russ said. "Hopefully that was it. I was driving by, Merry, when I saw you opening up. Do you have time for a quick coffee?"

Betty harrumphed. "Shop owners don't take time for coffee breaks."

Russ ignored her. I'd been about to turn down Russ's offer, seeing as how I'd been late opening up, but somehow I couldn't make myself appear to be agreeing with Betty. I opened my mouth to accept when coffee itself arrived.

"Good news!" Vicky announced from the open door. She clutched a couple of lattes in her mittened hands. I didn't need to see the hem of her baking apron peeking out from the bottom of her coat to know she was back in business. The broad smile on her face was a sure giveaway.

"You've won the lottery?" I said, accepting the drink. I took off the lid and bent down to breathe in the scent of warm milky steam with a trace of vanilla.

"Even better. Detective Simmonds phoned me when I was returning Aunt Matilda's car, and told me I can open the bakery. I'm back in business." She lifted her arms and twirled in a pirouette, not exactly graceful, as she was wearing snow boots and a heavy winter coat.

"That is good news," Russ said.

"Did they catch the killer, do you think?" I asked.

"Simmonds didn't say. She admitted that evidence indicated the poison wasn't baked into the cookies, but added later. Any one of a number of people could have done it."

"I'll drink to that," I said, lifting my latte. We clinked cups.

"It's past ten o'clock now," Vicky said. "Way too late to make bread, or do much baking at all, but I called my scheduled staff and told them we'll be open for lunch at noon. I've lots of frozen soup and my mom's gone on an emergency grocery run to get salad ingredients for me. I have some things in the freezer I can bake, so we'll be able to offer a limited range of desserts, also. Might as well make bread pudding with all the bread in the back of the shop that's going stale."

"I'll be there precisely at noon for lunch," I said. "Show the flag. I'll call Mom and ask her to join me. Jackie's off today, but I can close the store for half an hour."

Vicky gave me a one-armed hug.

"The best thing you can do right now," I said, "is go to

work. Get that bakery open and the ovens fired up. Start enticing people to come in. Anyone who's ever eaten at the Muddle Harbor Café knows how much better your place is."

"Okay," she said. "Traitor," she muttered to Russ as she passed him. He had the grace to look apologetic.

"I understand why Vicky's mad at you," I said, "even though we know you were only doing your job. But to make it up to us, you have to go to Vicky's for lunch."

"Great. It's a date."

"Not with me! Just go. You, too, Betty."

"Why would I do that?" Betty said. "I always bring my lunch from home."

"To support the town," I said through gritted teeth.

She looked blank.

"To help spread the word that Rudolph is a good place to have lunch before shopping for Christmas trinkets?"

"Oh, right. I suppose I can do that."

Betty left. Russ followed her, but instead of leaving, too, he flipped the sign on the door to "Closed."

"What are you doing?" I said.

He gave me a slow, sexy grin. My stomach dropped to my toes.

"I thought we might enjoy a few private moments in what's probably going to be a very busy day." Russ came close. He lifted his hand and ran the tip of his index finger down my nose. My heart joined my stomach. Green flakes danced in his eyes. His strong jaw moved. "Merry . . ."

I leapt backward. "Busy day, you're right. I'll be on the hop all day. I don't have an assistant today. I don't mean I'm going to be here all alone. Oh no. Customers will be pouring through the doors any minute now. Lots of customers." I glanced toward the door. No one was currently clambering to get in.

Russ's phone rang. He made no move to reach for it.

"You should answer that," I said.

"It can wait."

"It might be important. Like advertisers wanting to complain."

He let out a puff of air. "You're probably right." He pulled out his phone and checked the display. His smile faded into a grimace. "Sue-Anne, good morning. What can I do for you?"

Russ left the shop, and I turned the sign back to "Open."

I then made a phone call of my own. "Rise and shine. I'm taking you to lunch."

"What time is it?" my sleepy mother said.

"Ten past ten."

She groaned.

"If you start getting ready now, you can be here by noon," I said. "Lunch is on me."

"Why?"

"I'll tell you later." I hung up.

One customer came into the shop over the next two hours: a woman in her sixties, dressed in a lumpy winter coat, hand-knitted scarf, and practical boots. She picked up every item, turned it over, examined the price tag, grunted, and put it down again.

Then she left.

Precisely at noon my mom sailed through the door. My mom never walked into a room. She arrived everywhere as though she were stepping onto the stage at the Met on opening night. Today she wore a gorgeous double-breasted pale pink wool coat with huge black buttons, a black hat and scarf, and black leather gloves. Deep gray slacks were worn over high-heeled leather boots. She presented her cheek for a kiss. I obliged and was enveloped in a wave of Chanel No. 5.

"Your father was disturbed, once again, at some ungodly hour," she said to me. "He abandoned his breakfast and ran out the door. I didn't even get my tea!" Every morning, Dad carried a cup of tea, brewing in a pot of pink roses and nicely laid out on a silver tray, into the bedroom to wake Mom up. Mom put on airs and liked to pretend that she was still an adored diva, but she lived here, in Rudolph, New York, rather than in an apartment overlooking Central Park, because she loved my father.

They were a mismatched couple, all right, but they adored each other. I only hoped that I'd find a man to love as much some day. I thought I had once—and wasn't that a mistake. Russ Durham was handsome, charming, and clearly interested in me. But I was not going to allow myself to be rushed into anything. My scars were still too raw.

"Where are we lunching?" Mom asked.

"Vicky's been allowed to reopen. We need to support her and show everyone that we know she didn't serve any poisoned baking."

Mom snorted. "Anyone with any sense knows that."

"How was Dad yesterday?" I asked. "After he got back from heading to the airport."

"Fit to be tied," Mom said.

"You've no idea what happened?"

"A practical joke gone wrong, your father says. If I was still singing professionally and someone had done that to us, I'd think it was an understudy trying to get me out of town for opening night. But here, in Rudolph?"

"It might have been a mistake," I said. "A text sent to a wrong number?"

"Yes. Except the message did say 'Eve here.'"

We'd probably never know. I went into the storage room to get my new coat and pull on my boots. When I came out, Mom was rearranging the window display.

"Mom! Stop that!"

"You need more toys in here," she said. "Christmas is about children." She pushed the jewelry display to the back and placed two of Alan's tall wooden soldiers front and center.

"You and Dad should open a decorating business," I said.

"Why would we want to do that?" She added a third soldier and admired her handiwork. "Better symmetry."

I flipped the sign, locked the shop, and Mom and I walked the short distance to the bakery. We passed one of the town clerks stapling a notice to the round column in front of the library that served as a bulletin board. It advertised Midnight Madness on Friday and Saturday. She gave Mom and me a nod of greeting.

I was pleased to see a steady stream of people going into Victoria's Bake Shoppe. They were almost all locals, here like Mom and I were to support one of our own. And, I might add, to have a delicious lunch.

The usual intoxicating scent of baking bread didn't greet us this afternoon, but glistening sugar-sprinkled pies and tarts and plump gingerbread cookies were cooling on the shelves behind the counter and soup was bubbling in three black cauldrons.

"I'm sorry." Jason, one of Vicky's nephews, was behind the counter, talking to the hungry patrons. "We aren't serving sandwiches today as the bread didn't get baked and Vicky never serves anything other than her own baking. We'll have full service tomorrow. But today we have soup and salads and a wide range of desserts."

"You grab a table, and I'll get our lunch," I said to my mom. "What kind of soup do you want?"

We studied the chalkboard. Butternut squash with apple, split pea and ham, and clear vegetable were on offer.

"Pea," Mom said. She elbowed Rachel McIntosh from Candy Cane Sweets aside to get at a free table.

True to her word, Betty Thatcher had come. She was at the end of the line. I took my place behind her. She must have known I was there, but she stood ramrod straight, facing directly ahead. When it was her turn, she said, "I'll have . . . a cup of tea, please."

"Is that all?" Jason asked.

"With milk." She pulled out her wallet and began counting coins.

Oh, well. At least she was here.

I placed our orders and went to join Mom. I'd barely taken my seat when the door flew open with enough force to have the walls shaking, and Sue-Anne Morrow stormed in. She waved a newspaper in the air. "This is an outrage!"

People turned toward her. "We've all seen the ad, Sue-Anne," Betty said.

"This," she said, "is no ad. It's today's *Muddle Harbor*

Chronicle. I knew they'd be up to no good, so I drove over there this morning to check things out." The Muddites must have thought they were being invaded. "I tried contacting our so-called mayor," Sue-Anne continued, "but was told he wasn't in the office. He's taking a *personal* day. As if a public servant can take a day off willy-nilly."

"Spare us the campaign ad, Sue-Anne," my mother said. "And just tell us what has your knickers in such a knot."

One of the waitresses laughed. Sue-Anne threw her a look that might have turned the ice cream on the apple pie she was carrying sour.

Vicky came out of the back, wiping her hands on the front of her apron. She saw Mom and me and gave us a small wave.

With an eye to the theatrical that would do my mother proud (and had my mother muttering, "Get on with it") Sue-Anne put a pair of reading glasses on her nose. She fluffed the newspaper. "The headline in today's *Muddle Harbor Chronicle* reads, 'Death Stalks Rudolph.'"

"What!" People leapt to their feet. Everyone began speaking at once. Rachel dropped her fork.

"Quiet!" my mother sang. "Please allow Sue-Anne to continue."

"'A brutal death has struck at the heart of the neighboring town of Rudolph, New York,'" Sue-Anne read. "'Visiting tourist Nigel Pearce died following Rudolph's annual gingerbread reception, an event popular with out-of-town Christmas shoppers. The autopsy indicated that illegal drugs had been added to the food he consumed at the party.'"

A groan spread through the room. The waitstaff stood frozen, full plates or dirty dishes clutched in their hands.

"We're finished," Betty Thatcher said.

Sue-Anne continued reading. "'Randy Baumgartner, mayor of Muddle Harbor, said in a statement: Our hearts go out to our friends and neighbors in Rudolph in the face of their tragedy, but let me assure the good people of the great state of New York that Muddle Harbor is open for business. Our restaurants and hotels are clean, and our excellent shops are open for your Christmas shopping needs.'"

This time even Mom couldn't quiet the crowd.

People rushed for the exit. Some didn't even bother to finish their lunch. I might have heard someone murmur something about "stringing that so-and-so Baumgartner up by his own lamppost."

Vicky dropped into a spare chair at our table. "That's bad," she said.

"Yup."

"Thank heavens for small mercies. At least they didn't mention that I'd provided the so-called poisoned cookie."

"Of course they didn't," Mom said. "They want to spread the blame around. Imply that nowhere in Rudolph is safe." She put down her spoon. "As much as I was looking forward to a slice of that pecan pie, I'd better be getting home. I assume this is why your father left in such a rush this morning. I'll have to get his heart medication out of the drawer before he sees that paper."

"Dad's on heart medication? Why didn't I know about this?"

"I am speaking facetiously." She stood up and pulled on her leather gloves.

"If you're talking to Noel," Sue-Anne said, "ask him where the heck our mayor is, and when his office will be issuing a response to this slander. I think threat of a law suit is in order." Sue-Anne gripped her newspaper and left the bakery.

"You don't think people are going to believe that, do you, Merry?" Rachel asked me. "I sell candy, for heaven's sake. If people think our food isn't safe . . ." Her voice trailed off.

"Out-of-towners aren't likely to read the *Muddle Harbor Chronicle*," I said. "Sue-Anne had to drive over there to get a copy."

"Let's hope the bigger news outlets don't pick it up," Vicky said.

Chapter 11

I t must have been a slow news day in the wider world.

The *Muddle Harbor Chronicle*'s report made the *New York Times* web page. CNN and Fox News then picked it up. *World Journey* magazine issued a statement mourning the loss of one of their "most renowned" travel writers and mentioning the location of his demise, Rudolph, New York, several times.

Vicky popped by after the bakery closed at three. She was smiling broadly and carried a bag bulging with leftovers. She dropped the bag on the counter.

"What's this?" I said.

"Your dinner for tonight. Because I was shut down so abruptly, I was stuck with loaves of bread going stale, so I made a ton of bread pudding. I sold almost all of it today, but held some back, knowing how much you like it. There are also a couple of loaves of baguette that will be fine for crostini if you toast it. Some tomatoes if you want to make bruschetta, and a jar of the butternut squash soup."

"That's nice of you, but I don't want to eat into your profits."

"Tomorrow, I'll be back in full business. I'll be making bread and croissants and scones and all sorts of yummy things. That's what brings people into the bakery. It was super nice of so many people to come out for lunch today, and I bet you had something to do with it. So here's my thanks."

"No one has to be encouraged to eat your food, Vicky."

She glanced around my empty shop. "People are not happy, Merry. They're worried that this killing is going to drive tourists away. I'm worried."

"It'll blow over," I said, not convincing even myself.

Even for a Wednesday afternoon, business in my shop was slow. Ominously slow. After Vicky left, I brought my iPad to the counter to read while waiting for people to come in. By the time I (gratefully) closed at six, a Google search of Rudolph, New York, was bringing up hits on major news outlets all over the country, pushing our tourist promotion farther and farther down the page.

My dad came in as I was preparing to lock up. "It's bad, Merry," he said, shaking his head.

"What's happening?"

"I've been getting calls all day. People are cancelling reservations. The Yuletide Inn was fully booked for the weekend and now they're a quarter empty. A Touch of Holly's lost a table of twelve for Friday night, along with some smaller parties."

"Surely this will all blow over," I said. "People have short memories. They'll forget."

"That might be the case by next year, but there's only three weeks left until Christmas this year."

I locked up and we walked out onto the sidewalk together. The town reminded me of one of those postapocalyptic movies. Everyone had disappeared; all that remained was their stuff.

Maybe not everyone: a big old pickup truck, held together more by rust than anything else, drove slowly down the street. George lifted one finger forty-five degrees in salute. Dad touched his hat in reply.

George and his truck.

I had totally forgotten.

"The parade! Do you remember, Dad? George's tractor was supposed to pull my float, but he couldn't get it started."

"Caused a minor hiccup, but no harm done," Dad said. "You managed to catch up to the parade."

"No harm except for being disqualified from the trophy," I said, "but never mind that. I didn't tell you, but when George had time to have a look at the tractor, he found it had been sabotaged."

"Sabotaged? What does that mean?"

"I don't remember exactly what he said. Something about the wires being switched. I didn't give it another thought. I assumed George got things mixed up."

"If George said the wires were switched, then the wires were switched. And you can be sure he didn't do it himself." My dad stroked his beard. "That is interesting."

"Thing is," I said, "I didn't give it much thought because

no one would have a reason to disable my float. I can't say everyone in town likes me." I thought of Betty Thatcher and Candice Campbell. "But no one, I hope, dislikes me enough to go to that much trouble to get back at me. And to do it in such a sneaky way. Making one float look bad did have the potential to throw the whole parade out of whack. Suppose Santa's float hadn't been able to get by." My voice trailed off. "Pretty minor stuff, I know."

"Perhaps not," Dad said. "The person who did it might not have been entirely sure of what they were doing, or they were interrupted and weren't able to finish. Suppose the tractor was supposed to start but then get out of control. A crowded street. Floats, marching bands, sidewalks full of excited children. Even if it was just an attempt to disrupt the parade, it wasn't any practical joke. So I have to wonder: Might whoever was responsible have gone on to do something else? Something more serious?"

I finished his thought. "You mean like poisoning a guest of the town at the town's biggest social event of the season."

"Yes, I do mean that," my father said. "Right now I need to talk to the mayor and he seems to have made himself unavailable. He has to make a strong public statement about this. Usually Fergus can be counted on to do the exact opposite of anything I suggest, but this time, I'm going to make him listen to me. I'm going around to his house. If he's hiding in the basement, I'm going to drag him out. In the meantime, I have a job for you."

"Me?"

"Yes. Go to the *Gazette*. Talk to Russ Durham. He must have contacts in the media in New York. Ask him to work them."

"Why me?"

"Why not you?" Dad said.

"No reason."

We went our separate ways. It was a sign of how concerned Dad was that he hadn't even tried to rearrange so much as a stack of Christmas-themed stationery in my shop.

I decided to go home and get Mattie before barging into the offices of the newspaper. I could phone Russ just as easily, but Mattie needed out, and it was time he started to get accustomed to meeting people and venturing into new places.

Besides, if I was going to have Russ Durham staring into my eyes and looking so deliciously sexy, I needed a thirty-pound puppy to distract me.

My plan came to naught, as the offices of the *Gazette* were closed tight when we arrived. I decided it didn't really matter. What could Russ do anyway? Ask reporters not to report on a scandalous story? To pretend a death—a murder—hadn't happened? But my dad had asked me to speak to him, so I'd give Russ a call when we got home.

Mattie had greatly enjoyed the walk. All the wonderful new smells and sights.

I hadn't.

A cold wind was blowing directly off the lake, coming down from Canada, bringing with it more snow; not the light, fluffy sort that gave me such delight, but hard, icy pellets that stung my cheeks and brought tears to my eyes and pierced every bit of exposed flesh.

It was probably my imagination, but as we trudged back home it seemed to me as though the spark had gone out of Rudolph. The lights in the shop windows seemed to have dimmed, the wreaths hanging from lampposts looked limp, the snow underfoot was dirty and treacherous. People hurried by, huddled in their coats, not making eye contact.

What was Rudolph without the magic of Christmas? Just a small, decaying, postindustrial town long past its glory days.

"Merry!"

I turned at a shout. Alan Anderson was running down the sidewalk. Mattie wagged his tail in greeting.

"You look like you're a thousand miles away," Alan said when he reached us.

"Sorry."

"Is something the matter?"

"Of course something's the matter! Christmas is ruined! You must have heard the news. People are cancelling reservations all over the place. And it's almost Midnight Madness weekend. We're doomed."

Even Mattie caught the pain in my voice. He whined.

"I don't think Christmas is ruined," Alan said in his usual slow, thoughtful manner. "Christmas is about more than selling things, Merry."

I took a deep breath. "You're right. But we do have to keep our businesses going."

"We'll continue to do that. The twenty-four-hour news cycle will move on to another story tomorrow."

Unless, I thought, but didn't say, *something else happens in Rudolph to keep us in the news.*

"What brings you to town?" I asked. I'd been to Alan's house to pick up things for the shop. He lived about ten miles out of town in a charming old farmhouse nested deep in the woods. A separate building on the property served as his workshop.

"Grocery shopping."

Mattie soon got bored of our conversation and began tugging on the leash.

"Have you . . . uh . . . had your dinner yet?" Alan said. We were passing The Elves' Lunch Box. The "Open" sign flickered halfheartedly in the window. The place was empty except for the bored waitress wiping down the counter. Several of the tiny colored lights on the string draped across the restaurant roof had gone out. A gust of icy wind whipped down the street, and the sandwich board advertising the day's specials shuddered and fell to the ground with a crash.

Alan bent over and picked it up. Most of the chalk writing had faded.

"I haven't eaten," I said. "But I have to take Mattie home and feed him. Why don't you come with us? I just happen, for once, to have the makings of a quick but delicious dinner at my place. I might even have a bottle of wine in the fridge."

He gave me a smile. "I'd like that."

I smiled back.

Knowing that dinner would be on offer once we got home, Mattie picked up his pace and dragged me down the street. Alan and I followed in companionable silence. He was a big guy, but he moved as softly as the elf he sometimes pretended to be.

If I'd known I'd be entertaining, I'd have cleaned up the place.

"Sorry about the mess," I said, hastily picking up discarded magazines, a single white sock, and a cup half-full of cold coffee. Mattie grabbed his favorite blue and red ball and dropped it at Alan's feet.

"No ball throwing in the house," I said, trying to sound stern. The living area looked like the inside of a playpen. I'd hung an assortment of rubber balls and chew toys on bungee cords from the ceiling, and more balls, ripped and torn stuffed toys, and shredded blankets covered the floor. Vicky had told me that play was as important to a growing puppy as to a young child.

Alan picked up a much loved (and much chewed) stuffed reindeer I'd brought home from the shop. Mattie lunged for it, and they began a tug-of-war while I went into the kitchen.

"White wine?" I called out.

"That would be great, thanks."

I opened the wine first and then got out Mattie's dinner. He bounded into the kitchen and wolfed his food down, scarcely stopping for breath between bites.

"That's a great dog," Alan said, leaning against the kitchen door. "Good teeth." He held a brown reindeer ear in one hand.

"He sure is. I hope he stops growing soon though," I said, thinking of grocery bills.

Alan tossed the ear into the trash. "Not a chance."

I got down two wineglasses and poured the wine and then handed Alan a knife. He chopped tomatoes for the bruschetta while I heated Vicky's soup and sliced the baguette.

Mattie dozed under the kitchen table while Alan and I drank wine, ate, and talked.

"Sue-Anne was on the warpath earlier," I said, munching on a piece of bruschetta. The tomatoes weren't at their best, this being December in New York, after all, but I'd used good quality olive oil and plenty of fresh basil snipped off the plant growing in the sunny kitchen window, and the toasted bread was dense and full of flavor. "And the object of her wrath was the mayor. My dad said Fergus wasn't answering his phone."

"He's hiding out at home," Alan said. "His car was there when I drove into town."

"Does he live near you?"

"Next property over. We're as close to neighbors as you can get out where I am. It's about a five-minute walk through the woods to the back of Fergus's place."

"Do you think he's a good mayor?"

Alan sipped at his wine. His big hands were rough and scarred. The hands of a man who made his living with wood and tools. "Not a bad one," he said at last. "Although it's no big secret that he sometimes makes the wrong decisions only because he's trying to one-up your father."

My dad had been mayor for a long time. A very popular one. People kept asking him to run again, and he always told them he had no interest in the job anymore. I knew he meant it. "But Sue-Anne's right," Alan continued, "much as I hate to admit it. Fergus should be out there supporting the town. The mayor needs to be the visible face of what a nice, friendly place Rudolph is."

"You don't like Sue-Anne?"

"I don't like her ambition. It sits on her like a parrot on her shoulder. She wants to be mayor awful bad. So bad it's embarrassing sometimes."

"So bad," I said very slowly, "that she might do something to make that happen?"

His blue eyes studied me. "What are you saying, Merry?"

"I don't know. I don't know if I'm saying anything. Do you want more soup?"

"Thanks. Don't get up. I can serve myself."

Someone had tipped the *Gazette* off to the results of the autopsy. Dad had said that the town council had been secretly informed of the cause of Nigel Pearce's death. Sue-Anne Morrow was on the town council. That same someone had quite possibly also placed an anonymous call to the offices of the *Muddle Harbor Chronicle*. Sue-Anne herself admitted that she'd gone to our neighboring town, and chief rival, suspecting they'd be up to something. Did she suspect? Or did she know?

Was it possible Sue-Anne was deliberately spreading the news, deliberately harming Rudolph, to make our well-meaning, but generally hapless, mayor look bad?

Was it possible, I thought with a frisson of shock, that Sue-Anne had done more than just spread the news? Had Sue-Anne decided to *make* the news herself?

Ridiculous. Sue-Anne might be ambitious, but show me a politician who wasn't. Besides, if Dad's and my suspicion that the death of Nigel Pearce was somehow related to the sabotaging of George's tractor, I couldn't imagine Sue-Anne Morrow, in her Chanel suit and Jimmy Choo ankle boots, climbing into the front of an antique tractor armed with a wrench, not to mention having the knowledge of how said tractor worked.

Mattie'd had enough napping. He dropped a drool-soaked toy into Alan's lap with a woof.

"Not now, buddy," Alan said, putting the toy on the table. "Mealtime is not playtime." Mattie bounded off to find something else with which to entertain his guest.

I served huge plates of bread pudding for dessert. Mustn't let it go to waste.

Did I mention that I love bread pudding? Vicky made it with her French bread and plenty of cream and eggs, topped with a sauce of maple syrup and brown sugar for a sinfully rich filling and light, crisp topping.

Alan had two giant helpings.

"Coffee?" I asked, scraping the bottom of my bowl.

"Better not. Time I was on my way." He pushed his chair back and got to his feet. "That was great, Merry. Thanks."

"You can thank Vicky."

Mattie shoved his toy up against Alan's leg. Alan grabbed it and gave him a minute of play, and I walked him downstairs to the door.

He put on his coat and wrapped a long scarf around his neck. He opened the door and then hesitated. I wondered if he were going to give me a *proper* good-night.

Instead he mumbled, "Thanks again," and left. I shut the door behind him and leaned against it.

Chapter 12

"You're looking quite pleased with yourself this morning," Jackie said.

"I am not," I replied. "Don't try to distract me. Haven't I told you not to be using your phone at work?"

"I wasn't."

"Jackie, you were!"

"It's not as if we're busy, Merry."

I sighed. Busy or not wasn't the issue. Like most shopkeepers I knew, I had to continually remind my staff to switch off their phones during working hours. We might not have any customers at the moment, but I didn't want to chance someone coming in needing help and being greeted with the back of my salesclerk as she made arrangements for a hot date tonight with her boyfriend.

"Anyway," she said, pouting, "it's important."

"Is the shop on fire? No? Then any calls you have to make can wait until your break."

"I was phoning England. They might be at tea or something when it's my break. The time's different there, you know."

"I do know that, yes." When I opened the shop and became a boss for the first time, I vowed never to discuss my decisions with my staff. I would make firm pronouncements, and that would be the end of it. That resolution had gone out the window the moment Jackie first plopped her skinny rear end on the stool behind the counter. "You were phoning someone in England? Who do you know in England?"

"No one, *now*!"

"You don't mean Nigel Pearce?"

She sighed. "All right, if you must know. I sent an e-mail to *World Journey* magazine last night. I expressed my condolences on their loss and told them that I'd been talking to him just hours, maybe even minutes, before he died. I didn't get an answer, so I figured I'd better phone. Talk to them in person."

"Jackie, please don't tell me you were planning to ask them if they were still going to run his feature on Rudolph."

She tossed her hair. "So what if I was? He took tons of pictures, here in the shop and later at the party. The magazine might still want to use them. Maybe he sent them part of his article before he died. They wouldn't want that to go to waste, would they?" She slapped her forehead. "His camera! I wonder what happened to his camera. Did you see it when you found him? Do you think the police have it? If they need it for evidence they might keep it for months!"

I shook my head. I should have been used to it by now, but Jackie's self-absorption could still take me aback. "If you must know, he had his camera with him when he died. So the police have it. As for phoning the magazine, I don't think it's a very respectful thing to do, but I can't stop you. Just don't phone them when you're working, okay?"

"Do you think they'll send someone else to finish the story? Maybe like as a tribute to Nigel or something?"

I'd worked in magazines for many years, although not on the editorial side. If Nigel was a freelancer, the story had probably been his idea. He'd almost certainly combined it with another trip to the States. Maybe someone back at *World Journey* would pick up on the idea, but they wouldn't have anyone ready to jump on a plane at a moment's notice. Nigel had not been reporting on something that was exactly high priority. "No," I said in answer to Jackie's question.

"It's just that . . . well, it was my big chance, right? He showed me some of the pictures he took of me. They were great. He said *World Journey* has a huge readership. Who knows who would have seen my picture?" She sounded so sad I almost felt sorry for her.

Almost.

I don't know what she expected, but I did know that talent scouts from major modeling agencies or Hollywood casting companies didn't scour random magazines hunting for a random shot of the next big thing innocently waiting on customers in Rudolph, New York.

"Why'd you leave *Jennifer's Lifestyle*, anyway?" she said. "I love love love that magazine. I'm going to have a home decorated exactly like Jennifer's myself one day. Although I'll have an apartment in the city, not out in the country like her. It must have been your dream job, Merry. You lived in Manhattan. Like on *Sex and the City*. You worked with Jennifer Johnstone! But you came back to Rudolph, the most boring place on planet Earth. I guess I could understand it if your folks were sick and needed care or something. But they're not."

"It seemed like the right thing to do at the time," I said. I wasn't going to talk to Jackie about my life. Not that she really cared anyway.

Why did I leave what truly was my dream job in the city I loved?

Jennifer Johnstone is one of the doyennes of modern American style, with an emphasis on casual outdoor living and the enjoyment of entertaining. Her empire includes magazines, TV cooking shows, and a chain of restaurants, as well as patio and garden furniture and accessories. The magazine she founded is one of the most popular in the country. I'd been working for the magazine for five years when Jennifer turned eighty. At a huge party for her staff, Jennifer announced that she was semi-retiring. She would no longer do public appearances or come into the office, but would direct the company from her hundred-acre oceanfront property on Long Island. Her granddaughter, Erica, would be the new face of the magazine part of the company. No one was pleased with the news. Erica was pampered, spoiled, and massively insecure. Unlike her grandmother, Erica had little confidence in her own taste, therefore had no time for anyone who disagreed with her. The editor in chief quit the next day, and several department heads left with him. Erica brought in some friends from Smith College to take their places.

I thought we had to give her a chance. Jennifer was only as far away as Long Island, and we needed to see how much control she was going to exert on her granddaughter.

My longtime boyfriend and unofficial fiancé, Max Folger, was a copyeditor with the magazine. He saw Jennifer's departure and the subsequent shake-up as his chance to grab the brass ring. Instead of working hard to impress the new boss, he took the easy route and slept with her.

Erica was short and thick-waisted, blessed with small black eyes, a large nose, and thin lips. But she was extremely rich, and money can buy a lot of beauty. She had a reputation of being somewhat of a, shall we say, fun-loving single woman. She regularly made the gossip columns, on the arm of one handsome man or another, getting in and out of limousines in scandalously short skirts, dining in the most fashionable restaurants, or partying all night long in the most trendy nightclubs. Rumor had it that when Jennifer handed the business over, it was on the condition that Erica give up the party life and settle down. Some people whispered that Jennifer had a deadline for the arrival of great-grandchildren as tight as any she'd ever had for her magazine.

And so Erica announced her engagement to the guy who just happened to be her current arm candy. Max Folger.

I couldn't continue working at the magazine. Not if I would see Max every day, now an executive editorial director ensconced in a big corner office with a fabulous view of the East River. Nor did I want to run into Erica as she breezed through the offices air-kissing everyone in sight and calling them sweetie and honey pie before stabbing them in the back.

I didn't even want to stay in New York City. And so I

came home to Rudolph and Mom and Dad, licking my wounds. I planned to hide out for a couple of months and feel sorry for myself.

But that wasn't my parents' way, and before I knew what was happening, Dad had found out that the people who owned the small home design shop next to Rudolph's Gift Nook were planning to retire. The town needed, he said, a store that specialized in non-tacky Christmas decorations. The local craftspeople needed a store that would sell their wares. Wasn't interior decoration what I knew best?

Oh, and look, one of the upstairs apartments in Mrs. D'Angelo's big Victorian has just come available.

I hadn't for a moment regretted my decision to take the apartment, open the shop, and stay in Rudolph.

The few of my friends who were still working at *Jennifer's Lifestyle* told me that circulation was plummeting, but everyone was hoping that Erica's giant wedding, planned for the coming summer, would give it a boost. The wedding would run over several special issues. The food. The gardens. The bride. The couple's new home. The honeymoon.

I finally laughed, realizing that I was well rid of Max Folger as well as *Jennifer's Lifestyle*. I hoped Max wouldn't mind having a team of photographers following him on his honeymoon, telling him where to stand and deciding what he would wear.

"Do you think," Jackie said, returning to her favorite subject, "the cops would let me have a peek at the camera? I could send myself some of the best shots, and they could keep the camera?"

"No," I said. "I'll be in the office if you need me."

"It probably doesn't matter," she muttered to my retreating back. "The really good pictures would have been done on Sunday."

I turned. "What do you mean?"

She fluffed her hair. "Nigel was going to have a *private* photo shoot with me. I was going to go around to his hotel after work with my elf costume. The big fireplace and the tree and all the decorations in the lobby of the Yuletide would make a great background. He's what they call a free-lancer, you know. That means that he doesn't work for any one magazine or paper but takes all kinds of jobs. He even"— she leaned over the counter, eyes sparkling and cheeks flushed—"works for *fashion* magazines sometimes."

She slumped back. The sparkle died. "I mean, he worked for. It's so unfair."

"Unfair for Nigel Pearce."

"Kyle's all happy now. Do you think I should break up with him, Merry? He doesn't want what's best for me. He was so mad when I told him I didn't want to go out after the parade party after all. I had to go home early and get my beauty sleep if I was meeting Nigel the next day for my photo shoot."

"Maybe Kyle didn't want you to make a mistake, Jackie."

"What mistake? Just a couple of pictures."

I had my own questions about what these pictures might have entailed and what sort of promises Nigel would have made in exchange for them . . . I could probably guess. One or two shots would have been taken in the lobby. And then the light would have been wrong and people would have been wandering into the background, and Nigel would suggest they go to his room for the close-ups.

Jackie was a pretty young woman, but she knew nothing

about the larger world. Her good looks, slim but curvy figure, and bouncy personality had made her someone special at Rudolph High School and in the small community in which we lived. But in the magazine and fashion worlds she would have been nothing out of the ordinary.

I thought about Kyle. He'd been angry at Jackie at the reception. No, change that. Not angry at Jackie, but at Nigel. Did Kyle realize, as anyone except a young woman with stars in her eyes would, that Nigel was nothing but a slightly sleazy middle-aged man on the make? Or did he think Nigel really did have something to offer Jackie? Something that would whisk her away from Rudolph, away from him, into a life of money and glamour Kyle could only imagine?

"What did you and Kyle do after the party?" I kept my tone light, as though I didn't much care. Just making polite conversation.

Jackie's eyes narrowed. "Why do you want to know, anyway?"

Okay, so I had to improve my acting skills. "No reason. Call me if you need anything."

But Jackie never could resist the chance to talk about herself. "We went to The Elves' Lunch Box for dinner. We were supposed to go to some big party over at Muddle Harbor, but I changed my mind. Kyle was mad—he gets so jealous, you know. He dropped me at home and said he was going to the party by himself." She fluttered her eyelashes. "He called me the next morning and apologized. He had a terrible time at the party, all by himself. He can be so sweet sometimes."

I went into my office. Kyle and Jackie had gone for something to eat after the party. Kyle had then dropped Jackie at her house.

It didn't matter, I reminded myself, where Kyle was at the time Nigel took sick. The poison had been in the Charles Dickens cookie served at the reception. The killer didn't have to be anywhere near Nigel when he died.

My hand reached for my phone. Should I call the police? Tell Detective Simmonds what I'd learned? She was new to town; she didn't know these people the way I did. Then again, I didn't want to get Kyle or Sue-Anne into trouble just because I thought they'd benefited from the death of Nigel Pearce. Come to think of it, plenty of people benefited from the death of Nigel Pearce. The entire business community of Muddle Harbor, for one.

Cui bono? Who benefits?

I looked up as Jackie called, "She's in the back."

Rachel McIntosh's thatch of red and gray curls popped around the door. "My niece phoned me last night from Tampa Bay. She invited me to come down and spend the holidays with her if I'm afraid for my life here in Rudolph." I almost laughed, but Rachel did not look at all amused.

"The news has been getting around, but only one person has died. I don't think it's a whole lot safer in Florida."

"That's what I told her," Rachel said. "She was only being kind. I heard that a tour group cancelled their reservation at the Carolers Motel for the weekend."

"I'm sure it will all blow over. I checked the online news this morning, and that brazen bank robbery in Albany has pushed everything else off the front pages."

"I suppose that's good," Rachel said. If the cops were

wondering *cui bono* in the robbery they need look no further than the shopkeepers and hoteliers of Rudolph, New York. "I was thinking maybe we could give the police a bit of a nudge. Hurry their investigation along."

"What kind of a nudge?"

She leaned forward. Her coat fell open to display the outfit she and her assistants wore in the store. A long, white apron decorated with a bold pattern of traditional red and white candy canes, over a red T-shirt and black slacks. A necklace of real candy canes, strung together with red string, hung around her neck.

"You were there, Merry, all the time, weren't you? I left the community center when the candy I'd provided ran out. All I can say is I'm glad they didn't find the drugs in my goods. Did you notice anyone in particular hanging around the kitchen? Looking furtive?"

"I'm not quite sure what furtive looks like."

"Oh, you know. Someone like, well, like Maria Lopez. She was angry, I heard, that Pearce didn't take any pictures in her shop." Rachel sniffed. "Not Christmassy enough, I assume."

Now I got it. Rachel's archrival owned the North Pole Ice Cream Parlor. The shop had a nice location overlooking the lake, near the beach, but it didn't exactly do a roaring trade in ice cream in December. I'd heard Maria was considering branching out into candy and hot drinks.

"Can't say I noticed Maria acting particularly furtive. Sorry."

"Not that I'd suspect her of anything like that," Rachel hastened to assure me. "Just a thought. Gotta run."

She dashed off. I eyed my phone. If I told the police my

suspicions of Sue-Anne or Kyle, would I look to them like Rachel looked to me? Trying to cast suspicion on someone just because I didn't like them? Or worse, because I was an interfering busybody.

I went back to my computer. I decided to be optimistic, and sent a quick e-mail to Alan, asking if I could order another box of his toy soldiers. And some of those gorgeous wooden balls that looked so good on a Christmas tree decorated in farmhouse style.

He must have been at his own computer, because the answer came back almost immediately.

> *Balls are ready now. Drop off tomorrow?*
> *Soldiers by the weekend?*

He said nothing about last night's dinner, nor did I. I wanted to. I wanted to ask if we could do it again. And soon.

But I held back. We had been close once, when we were young. We were friends now. Did Alan want to be more than friends?

Did I?

"Hey, Merry!" Jackie shouted from the front of the shop. "You are gonna wanna see this."

I hurried to see what she was fussing about. Jackie was standing at the window, clapping her hands in delight. I could see people coming out of shops, pointing, and calling. Cars were pulling off the road into parking spots, or if they weren't near a spot, in front of fire hydrants or onto the sidewalks. It was snowing again, lovely light fluffy flakes drifting out of a pewter sky.

Jackie and I ran out of the shop, laughing.

George's tractor was coming slowly down the street, pulling a float. And not just any float, but Santa Claus's float. My dad was there, dressed in the full regalia. Fergus Cartwright, the mayor, sported an elf hat pilfered from the pile of children's costumes at Mom's studio.

Dad lifted a bullhorn. "Ho, ho, ho," he shouted.

All along the street, people had stopped whatever they were doing to watch. Everyone clapped, and some cheered. iPhones came out of pockets and people began snapping. On the other side of the street, in front of A Touch of Holly, a woman dressed in a camel coat, red leather boots, and red gloves took pictures with an expensive-looking camera with a long lens.

Fergus took the bullhorn from Dad. "It's Christmas in Christmas Town!"

George blew into a trumpet. More cheers.

"Crafty old guys." Russ Durham had slipped up beside me. He snapped away with his own camera. The tractor shuddered to a halt as if at a signal. Dad and Fergus turned and waved at the camera. Even George waved.

A man ran into the street. He lifted a little boy and passed him to Dad, aka Santa. The child, all red hair and freckles, screamed in delight and Santa stroked his beard and looked serious. Fergus handed the boy a candy cane and patted him on the head. The camel-coated woman took more pictures and then the boy was passed back to his parent. Who happened, I knew, to be the owner of the Carolers Motel. Russ's camera clicked rapidly.

"Where," Fergus shouted to the onlookers, "do you want to be at Christmas?"

"Christmas Town!" people shouted back.

"And where is Christmas Town?"

"Rudolph!"

Then, with a cough and burst of thick black smoke from its rear end, the tractor shuddered into motion and the procession sailed slowly down the street to repeat the whole performance on the next block.

"It's all well and good," I said to Russ, "getting the people here pumped up and having pictures in the *Gazette*. But we need to get the word out to all those tourists who are not here, the ones who are thinking of changing their shopping plans and going to New York or Rochester instead."

"Fabulous show, Russ." The camel-coated woman ran up to us. "Thanks for the tip. I love the spontaneity." She looked right through me. "Nice shop. I'll check it out when I'm done." With that she headed off down the street in pursuit of the impromptu one-float parade.

"Who," I said, "was that?"

"Renee Spencer. She's just started at the *New York Times* as an editor for the style section. Renee and I dated for a while back when I worked in the city. I called her last night, asked for a big favor."

"Oh," I said. "I was supposed to ask you to contact some of your reporter friends. I was going to phone you last night, but I got . . . distracted. I guess I forgot."

"Fergus gave me a call. I suspect your dad was standing over his shoulder ordering him to do something. He said we had to get the good news about Rudolph back in the public eye. And fast. I agreed, and called Renee." He gave me his slow, sexy grin. "Think it worked?"

"If those pictures get into the *Times*, either in print or online, it will. Thanks, Russ."

"You can thank me later. Say, dinner tonight?"

"That'd be great," Jackie said. "Merry would love to, wouldn't you, Merry? Oh, gosh, she said she'd be back to look at the shop. My hair!" Jackie disappeared into Mrs. Claus's Treasures.

"Great, I'll call you later, Merry." Russ set off at a quick clip after the disappearing parade. He turned around and began running backward. "Oh, and check out Twitter."

I pulled out my phone and clicked a button. I typed in Rudolph and the screen began to fill up with tweets such as:

> *#Christmastown! NY shopping and fun*
> *destination. Meet Santa on Main Street.*

A link led to the town's tourist promotion page.

Another click on *#Christmastown* brought up a page of similar stuff, all of it about Rudolph.

Someone had been busy last night.

"It was Fergus's idea," Dad said later when he popped into the shop. "I didn't even know what Twitter was. He called us last night, needing council approval for the cost."

"The cost? It doesn't cost anything to tweet. It's free."

"It may be free, but the people who know how to create the buzz aren't."

"How does Fergus know this? He's about as high-tech as you are."

"His daughter, the one who lives in California, is up on all this social media stuff. She told us that one or two people here in Rudolph tweeting wouldn't be enough to get any momentum going. We hired a company that specializes in that sort of thing."

"Let's hope it's worth it, then."

"It will be, "Jackie said, for once using her phone with my permission. "*#Christmastown* is trending."

"I dare not ask," Dad said, "what 'trending' means. I hope it's something good." He'd come straight from returning the float to the back of the community center, and was still in costume.

"Oh, oh!" Jackie said. "Two can play at this game."

"What?"

"Here's one that just popped up."

> *#Christmastown. Death by gingerbread in Rudolph. Come to Muddle Harbor, NY for #safeXMASbaking*

"The nerve," I said. "They can't say that, can they?"

"Anyone can say anything on social media," Jackie said.

"That doesn't seem fair," Dad said. "Never mind counterproductive. People will stay away from this whole area if that sort of talk gets out." His white beard shook in indignation.

"Tell it to the politicians," I muttered.

Wonder of wonders, a group of customers came in. Four women, all short, all plump, all gray haired. Jackie shut down her phone and hurried to serve them.

"Can we have a picture, Santa?" one of the women giggled.

"Ho, ho, ho," Dad said.

"Let me take it," Jackie said, "so you can all be in the shot."

They scooted over to the corner so the big Douglas fir would be in the background, and Dad put his arms around two of the women's shoulders. They crowded together and beamed identical smiles, identical brown eyes sparkling. Jackie told them to say "cheese" and clicked. Then the women shifted places, additional phones were handed to Jackie, and more pictures taken.

"Imagine," one of them said, "actually meeting Santa himself." They giggled identical giggles.

"What brings you lovely ladies to town?" Santa, I mean Dad, asked.

"These are my sisters," the first one said. "We live so far apart now, and we all have kids and those kids have kids . . ."

". . . and ex-husbands, and second husbands, and in-laws of their own . . ."

". . . that we can't get together anymore for Christmas. So we always have a sisters' day . . ."

". . . in early December. We usually go to the city, but this year we thought we'd do something . . ."

". . . different . . ."

". . . and we're so glad we did. At first we thought the town's awful quiet . . ."

". . . but then the parade started . . ."

". . . and Santa was there. . ."

". . . and it was perfect."

Four identical smiles beamed at me again.

The first one said, "We're quadruplets."

I'd guessed.

As they shopped, the women fussed and exclaimed and continuously called out things like, "June, you have to see this!"

"Friday and Saturday we're open till midnight," I said as I rang up the steady stream of purchases. "As will be the rest of the shops. The butcher'll be grilling hot dogs on the street, Victoria's Bake Shoppe will be selling its gingerbread, and . . ."

"I don't know if I'd like that," one of the women said. "Isn't that the gingerbread that killed that man?"

"No," I said. Technically, I was right. Vicky's cookie hadn't killed Nigel. The drugs someone had added after it was baked had.

"Stuff and nonsense, Rose," one of her sisters said. "It was one of those mob things."

"Mob things?" I asked.

"The English mob followed him here and executed him because he was going to do an exposé on them moving into New York. It could have happened anywhere."

"There's an English mob?" I said.

"Don't you read the newspapers?" she said to me. "It was in the *Empire State Enquirer.*" Not exactly a reputable paper, but if this woman wanted to believe that, I was happy to go along with it.

While the sisters shopped, Dad helped them select gifts and posed for more pictures. He stood at the door waving good-bye as they left, laden with parcels and bags. He went into the back of the shop while Jackie and I rearranged the shelves to fill the holes the women had left.

Dad came out a few minutes later, carrying a large box.

"I found these on the floor. You should put them out." They were glass sculptures: Santa in his sleigh being pulled by his reindeer, led by Rudolph the Electric-Nosed Reindeer. Perfectly tacky, thus absolutely perfect for Christmas.

"Not right now, Dad," I said. "Those women decimated the toy section and the tree ornaments. We need to replace those."

"This should go in pride of place." Dad began arranging space on the main display table in the center of the room.

He had just finished and was stepping back to admire his handiwork when the bell over the door tinkled and Russ came in with the woman from the *Times*. Jackie squealed and hurried over to offer her assistance.

"Renee got some good shots," Russ said.

"Thanks to you, Santa," she said, giving Dad a smile. "This really is Christmas Town. I'm sorry, but I've got to run." She smiled at Russ. He smiled back. "We spent more time," she said, "catching up than I expected, and I have to get going. I'd love to stay and shop, but . . . oh, look at that."

She hurried over to the main table and ran a well-manicured, red-tipped finger across Rudolph's nose. "Russell, this is perfect. My mom will absolutely love it. She collects tacky Christmas things."

"If you want tacky," Jackie mumbled, "there's always the Nook."

Chapter 13

Later that afternoon, Sue-Anne Morrow bustled into the shop. "How marvelous of Fergus to get people talking about Rudolph in a *good* way," she said.

"It was," I agreed.

"And how convenient that Russell happened to have a sympathetic *New York Times* reporter ready to pop down and do a feature."

"We're all supporters of the town," I said.

She peeled off her gloves. "And that's the wonderful thing about Rudolph, isn't it, Marie?"

"Merry."

She tittered in embarrassment. "How silly of me to forget. It was, I'm sure, your father who talked Fergus into getting out the float. And that Twitter campaign. Such a marvelous idea. Fergus would never have come up with something so clever, so modern, on his own."

"It was his daughter's idea, I was told."

She waved her left hand. The giant square-cut diamond caught the lights from the Douglas fir and threw off sparks of green and red. "Noel, being modest again, I suspect. Everyone knows that Fergus couldn't come up with an original idea if his life depended on it."

"Can I help you with anything?" Jackie said.

Sue-Anne glanced around the shop. All my beautiful things, beautifully displayed. I liked to think my shop embodied the spirit of Christmas in one room.

Christmas doesn't mean things—decorations and toys, no matter how lovely they might be—it's about family and community, about hope for the return of the sun and the eventual arrival of spring, and celebration of the arrival of the Christ child. But what's a celebration without showing off a little? Without trying to make your house and home as pretty and welcoming as it can be? At Mrs. Claus's Treasures, we allowed people to do that.

"This is such a lovely store." Sue-Anne ran her fingers lightly over a display of glass balls. "Too bad you don't have any customers."

"We were busy earlier," Jackie said.

"As busy as you'd expect to be, this close to Christmas?" she asked.

Jackie and I exchanged glances. I had to admit, not.

"Fergus's stunt today was too little, too late," Sue-Anne said. "Reservations are down at the hotels and inns. People are cancelling at the restaurants. What do you expect after a guest to our town, a prominent guest, died after eating a piece of gingerbread at a Santa Claus party?"

"Vicky didn't . . ."

"Yes, yes. I am well aware that Victoria didn't deliberately poison that cookie. Or, at least, that's what the police have concluded. But it doesn't matter, Merry, don't you see? Not once the news got spread far and wide. We needed strong leadership the minute the news got out. A powerful response in defense of our town. And what did we get? Fergus Cartwright cowering behind his curtains, waiting for the storm to pass.

"A strong mayor would have made an immediate show of calling the media. He should have done something the very next day. He should have invited reporters from all the local and state papers to Rudolph. A strong mayor would have served them all gingerbread cookies. After taking a big bite for the cameras first." She snorted. "But we all know that Fergus is not, and never has been, a strong mayor."

"He's doing stuff now," Jackie said.

"Like I said, too little, too late. But don't give up hope yet. Your father, Merry, has some more tricks up his sleeve, I've no doubt." She sighed heavily. "I only hope Fergus knows what an invaluable resource he has in Noel. Although I doubt it. Fergus can be too fond of doing things his own way, if you know what I mean, and too quick to disregard advice, no matter how good, if it doesn't align with his thinking. Oh, well, I must be off. I'll come back next week to do some of my own shopping."

"You should get what you like now," Jackie said. "Most of our stock is individual artisan pieces, and when they're gone, they're gone."

What I think of as The Look settled over Sue-Anne's carefully made-up face. The look of someone finding themselves trapped by their own words. In retail we know that *I'll come back later* means *get me the heck out of here*. "I'm sorry," she said, "but I've come out without my pocketbook. Silly of me."

"I'm sure Merry will be happy to extend you credit, Sue-Anne," Jackie said. Her own face was set into serious lines, but nothing could hide the twinkle in her eyes. Jackie was having fun. She was an expert at turning The Look into a sale.

"No. No. I wouldn't think of it. I want no favors." Sue-Anne lowered her voice and leaned forward. Jackie and I bent our heads into the circle. How could we not?

"I have been undecided for a long time," she whispered, "about taking the plunge and declaring my intention to run for the office of mayor. When I realized how badly Fergus has handled this . . . incident . . . my mind was made up for me. My phone's been ringing all week with people begging me to run. I hope you'll remember our chat today at election time, Merry and uh . . ."

"Eleanor," Jackie said.

"And you, too, Eleanor. Merry, your father's support would be invaluable." Sue-Anne pulled her gloves on. "Now, I really must run. I want to check on the other shops, see how everyone's doing. Give them moral support."

She sailed out the door with a wave of her fingers.

"Eleanor?" I said to my shop assistant.

"I was going to say Clementine, but that might be going too far. It doesn't matter, she's forgotten my name already."

"Are you going to vote for her?"

Jackie shrugged. "I don't vote. Waste of time. It's almost six. Are you leaving?"

"In a minute. What do you know about Sue-Anne?"

"Me? Nothing. Almost nothing."

"She's not local," I said. "She moved here when I was in Manhattan. Where does she live?"

"Not far from you. Willow Trail, I think. Somewhere near the lake, anyway. Why do you ask?"

"She's married, right? Any kids?"

"Yeah, she's married. No kids, far as I know. Her husband doesn't get out much. At least he's never seen around. It's rumored he has no political smarts, so she keeps him out of sight. Chained to a wall in the basement, probably."

"Do most people know Sue-Anne's thinking of running for mayor?"

Jackie's eyes glinted. "That's why I never vote. They're all such hypocrites. All that stuff about people begging her to run, and being forced to make a decision. She's been hinting so loudly for months, she might as well hang a flashing sign around her neck: 'Sue-Anne for mayor.' She'll be back, all right, and she'll buy something, too. Probably right in the middle of our biggest crush of the year so we don't notice that, after making sure everyone knows she's here, she buys an ornament for a dollar ninety-nine."

"We don't sell any ornaments for a dollar ninety-nine."

"Whatever. You get the point."

"I do."

I glanced at the clock on the wall. Ten to six. Crystal would be here soon to help Jackie staff the store until closing at nine. I was looking forward to a hot bath, a thick robe, warm slippers, a good book, and an early bedtime. Tomorrow was going to be a heck of a day. I had to open the store at nine, and we would remain open until midnight. Jackie and Crystal would be here in the afternoon and evening to help, but I was facing a solid fifteen hours on my feet.

The mere thought of it made me yawn.

"Early night?" Crystal asked as she came in.

"I must be getting old," I said. "It's six o'clock and all I want out of life is a bath, a book, and bed. The three *b*'s."

"You are old." Crystal unzipped her coat. She was one of *those* people: so talented and intelligent they didn't sometimes realize that not everyone wanted to hear their heartfelt opinions.

"Yeah," Jackie piped up. Now she, on the other hand, always knew exactly what she was saying. "Old and responsible. Ugh."

"I'll be at home if you need me." I headed for the back to get my own coat. "But it had better be an emergency with a capital *E*."

My phone beeped with an incoming text. I pulled it out.

Russ: *Reservation at A Touch of Holly for seven. Meet you there.*

I groaned.

"Something wrong?" Crystal asked.

"An appointment I forgot," I said.

She peeked over my shoulder at the phone in my hands. I jerked it away, but I wasn't fast enough.

"An appointment!" she squealed. "Merry has a dinner date with the hottest guy in Upstate New York and she calls it an appointment."

"You're going out with Alan at last?" Jackie said. "Good."

"Not Alan," Crystal said, "Russ Durham."

"You think Russ is the hottest guy? No way. Alan is.

After my Kyle, that is. But I'm thinking of men more Merry's age."

I left them arguing over the merits of men "Merry's age" versus the younger ones they dated, and went home.

I couldn't believe I forgot all about dinner with Russ. I couldn't believe I wanted to go home and have a bath before crawling into bed rather than eat at the best restaurant in Rudolph with the "hottest guy in Upstate New York." I had less than an hour to get home, walk Mattie, shower, and dress for an evening out. I broke into a run.

I tended to Mattie before leaping into the shower. What to wear, what to wear. When I lived in Manhattan, I'd bought plenty of clothes suitable for dining at good restaurants, but I didn't want to look like I was putting on airs. I also didn't want to look as though I was deliberately dressing down to fit into Rudolph.

I tossed clothes onto the bed.

No one would ever accuse my mom of dressing down. Then again, I am not my mom.

I held up a sleek black linen dress. Nah, I had to wear something that would go with boots. I hate carrying my shoes in a little bag. The dress joined the pile of discarded garments on the bed. Mattie watched the proceedings with a tilt to his head and a question in his eye. He hadn't realized yet that he was being abandoned once again. When he did, the question would turn to a look of pure heartbreak.

I finally decided on black slacks with a blue and green jacket over a black silk shell. I could wear that outfit with my ankle boots. I debated between a chunky green necklace or a green and blue scarf, and decided on the scarf in case the restaurant was chilly. I applied a light coat of pink lipstick and dusted some blush across my cheeks. I studied myself in the mirror, gave my black curls one last fluff, and decided I'd done the best I could with what I'd been given by God and my parents.

By the time I got to the restaurant, Russ was waiting. He spotted me as I came in, and his face lit up. He got to his feet as I crossed the room.

"You look lovely," he said. He moved in close, helped me slip off my coat, and handed it to the hostess.

I mumbled my thanks at the compliment. His physical presence seemed to fill the room. I was aware of the closeness of him, of the scent of aftershave and male hormones. He wore close-fitting tan trousers, a crisp open-necked white shirt with a thin blue stripe, and a black jacket. The jacket stretched over the muscles of his shoulders and upper arms. He fixed his hazel eyes on me and smiled. My heart raced.

"Madam?" the hovering waiter said.

I dropped into the offered chair. Russ rounded the small table and took his own seat. My heart settled back to something resembling its normal rhythm and I found that I could breathe again.

I leaned back to allow the waiter to place the menu in front of me. The place was about half-full. The lights were low, and a single candle in a glass bowl burned on our table. The table was covered in a cloth of starched white linen, the napkins matched, the flatware was silver. Wine and water glasses sparkled in the clear, soft light.

"Shall I order a bottle of wine?" Russ asked. "Neither of us are driving anywhere tonight."

"That would be nice," I said. Then, just in case he had ideas about sleeping over at my house, I asked, "Where do you live, anyway?"

"East Street. Not far from the lake." Walking distance from downtown.

I unfolded my napkin.

We chatted comfortably about life in Rudolph and our past lives in New York City. He'd been with one of the smaller city papers and when the paper was bought by a multinational the usual round of layoffs began. Russ wasn't let go, but he figured the writing was on the wall, and so he started looking around.

"Newspapers are dying everywhere. Those that aren't closing shop are being bought out or implementing efficiencies, whatever that means. I got a tip about the editor in chief job at the *Gazette* coming open. One of my dad's old friends had owned and run the paper established by his father for almost forty years. He had one heart attack and made noises about cutting back on his workload, but the second attack forced him to listen to his doctor. He wanted to keep the paper in the family but hand over the day-to-day running of it. Some of the longtime staff, I knew because my dad had told me, weren't too happy at an outsider coming in, but my dad thought it was a good idea. The newspaper world was changing, and fast, and the *Gazette* needed someone who'd bring new ideas and a fresh way of doing things. Not the sort to say, 'But we've always done it that way.'"

Russ grinned at me over the rim of his wineglass. He'd ordered an excellent pinot noir from Oregon. "Not a lot of newspaper people want to move to a small town or work for a local paper, but it came at the right time for me, and

I don't have a wife or kids to worry about uprooting. My family's from Louisiana . . ."

"I noticed."

He gave me a grin. ". . . and my parents figure New York City, New York State, it's all one and the same. Foreign. Might as well be in France."

I laughed.

"It's been a heck of a learning curve, I can tell you. From New Orleans to New York City to Rudolph, but I'm glad I made the move. There's something about this town . . ."

"I know. I don't think I realized how much I'd missed it until I came back."

The waiter delivered our first course. I'd ordered a salad, and Russ had the potato and leek soup. As this was Rudolph in December the menu featured a roast turkey dinner "with all the trimmings" and prime rib. Desserts included candy cane cheesecake, traditional plum pudding with brandy sauce, and plenty of homemade pies.

"Do you have a sense," I asked, "about the upcoming local election?"

"That question came out of nowhere," he said.

"Something happened today that got me thinking."

"Fergus is planning to run again, but he's facing some stiff competition. Mostly from Sue-Anne Morrow."

"Does she have a chance?"

Russ put down his soup spoon. "Last week I might have said it would be a close race. Fergus is a known quantity. Solid, reliable. Dull as dirt, but people like that in a mayor. If things are going well they don't want someone who will upset the apple cart. That's Fergus. On the other hand, there are people worried that things aren't going to keep going well. That if the tourists are going to continue coming, we have to innovate, make some changes. That's Sue-Anne."

"You said 'last week'?"

"This Nigel Pearce thing has changed the dynamic. Even the slightest hint that tourists will stop coming has people in a panic." Russ waved his hand, indicating our surroundings. "This is probably not a bad turnout for a Thursday night, but they'd rather be full. What's this week been like in your shop?"

"Quiet, I have to admit."

"I made a few phone calls before coming to meet you, and it seems like the Twitter campaign and Renee's pictures on the *Times* web page have done some good. A bus company rebooked at the Yuletide Inn, and the Carolers Motel says they have a couple of new reservations."

"That's great," I said.

"It is. But people, some people, are saying Fergus should have acted sooner, and faster."

"Some people are always complaining. We should give him credit for what he did do."

Russ lifted his wineglass. "I'll drink to that." The candlelight picked out the green specks in his hazel eyes. He hadn't shaved before coming to dinner, and the stubble on his jaw was dark.

I took a quick drink. "So," I said when I had my thoughts back on track, "Sue-Anne Morrow stands to gain from the disruption of the Rudolph Christmas season."

"What are you getting at, Merry?"

"I don't know. She was in my shop earlier. She's going

public with her run for mayor. She's openly saying that Fergus's reaction was, and I quote, 'too little, too late.' That a strong mayor would have handled things differently."

Russ put down his wineglass. "You think Sue-Anne poisoned Nigel Pearce?"

All around us conversation hummed, people laughed, cutlery clinked against china, and glasses and serving dishes rattled.

"Someone did," I reminded him. "You're the reporter. What are the police thinking?"

"One of two things. That someone came to Rudolph with, or in search of, Pearce. They took advantage of the situation at the party, added the drugs to the cookie, and left town."

"And the other theory?"

"The poisoning was random, no victim in particular, just a chance sort of thing."

"That would definitely not be good news for a tourist town."

"Exactly. Far better that Pearce brought his enemy with him. And thus, of course, the enemy is long gone."

"Easy enough to have happened that way," I said. "I was at the party. So were you. The place was full of outsiders. That's the entire point of the post-parade reception. It's not a party for townspeople, it's to get tourists in the Christmas mood. Otherwise known as spending money."

"The police have been through the pictures I took that evening," he said. "Looking for someone"—he made quotation marks in the air—"'acting suspiciously.'"

"I've been thinking about that anonymous phone call," I said. "The one telling you the results of the autopsy."

"What about it?"

"Did you think it odd?"

"Not really. We get plenty of anonymous calls in my business. Sometimes people want to stir things up. Neighbors tattling on neighbors, fathers trying to get their daughter's boyfriends in trouble, women reporting the woman they think their husband's having an affair with. Sometimes the calls are legitimate. People who have something to say but for whatever reason don't want to come forward publicly. That call was definitely the latter. It was a piece of solid info."

"You didn't recognize the voice?"

"No. It was disguised."

"Could it have been a woman?"

"It could have been a talking horse. Why are you asking, Merry?"

"Pasta?"

I jumped at the voice over my shoulder. The waiter had our main courses. He placed a bowl of fragrant pasta, rich with seafood and herbs, in front of me. Russ was having steak and fries.

"Russ," I said when we'd enjoyed our first few bites, "do you remember the parade? Remember my float?"

"I remember that you caused a traffic jam and Candy Campbell was ready to throw the book at you." He grinned.

I opened my mouth to tell him about the tractor. About George discovering that someone had switched the wires.

"Merry, dear. How lovely you look." My mom bent over and brushed my cheek with her lips. "And Russell. How nice." Russ leapt to his feet and took her gloved hand.

"Hi, Mom," I said. "Dad."

My dad gave me a nod. He was not in his Santa Claus attire

tonight, but was instead wearing a hideous and totally tasteless red and green Christmas sweater over jeans. Mom wore a sparkling gold tunic over loose matching trousers, with diamonds in her ears and a thick gold chain around her neck.

"I'd invite you to join us," Russ said, "but . . ." He indicated the table for two.

"We wouldn't dream of interrupting you," Mom said. "Enjoy your dinner."

The hostess was still waiting to seat them. Mom followed her across the room, smiling and waving at people she knew as though she were doing her sixth encore at the Met.

"What brings you guys here tonight?" I asked Dad. My parents rarely went out for dinner together. In this, like so many other things, they were total opposites. Dad liked to eat at home. Mom loved to dine in restaurants, the fancier the better. They compromised, as they usually did, and Mom met up with her friends once or twice a week, leaving Dad to eat his reheated meal on a tray in the company of a good book.

"Aline suggested that we, as prominent citizens of the town, be seen supporting local businesses. She was right, as always, so here I am."

"Good for you, Dad," I said.

"Did you see the pictures on the *Times* web page this afternoon?" Russ asked.

"I did." Dad grinned. "I think we nailed it." He glanced around the restaurant. "Let's hope we can get through the next two weeks without any more tragedies or mishaps." He went to join my mom.

"Your father's a great guy," Russ said. "Is Noel his real name? It's just that he does look like Santa Claus, in or out of costume."

"He was born on Christmas Day, thus the name," I said.

"And your mom. Aline Steiner. Wow."

"You know who my mom is?"

"I'm not a total philistine, Merry." He tried to look offended but the laughter in his eyes gave him away. "My parents are classical music lovers. I even own one of your mom's CDs."

"Ask her to autograph it one day," I said. "She'll be thrilled. She gave up the opera world when she retired from singing, but I suspect she misses it sometimes."

"I'll do that. But right now, I'm going to have a slice of that candy cane cheesecake. Something for you?"

"Just coffee, thanks." We went on to talk about other things, and it was only as I was putting on my coat prior to heading out into the cold, bright night, that I realized I'd intended to tell him about the sabotage to the tractor. But he'd started talking about winter, and how surprised he'd been, as a Louisiana boy, to find he liked it so much.

"You'll fit in perfectly here in Rudolph," I said, taking his arm. "And to make you feel right at home, we do Christmas all over again on July twenty-fifth."

We walked through the dark, quiet streets of Rudolph. Neither of us had said anything, but Russ had simply fallen into step beside me. Perfectly natural for a man to walk his date home, I reminded myself. Overhead the stars were as heavy and brilliant as they can only be in the cold night air. A few people were window-shopping, and as we passed Mrs. Claus's Treasures, I heard a woman say to her companion, "Isn't that the most darling nutcracker soldier."

Russ gave me an exaggerated wink.

I keep the lights outside and in the store window tasteful

and subdued, white mostly with a touch of ice blue for color. Next door, the Nook glowed with enough red and green bulbs to provide energy to a nuclear power plant.

We reached my house. I stopped and gently took my hand out of Russ's grip.

"It's still early," he said. "Are you going to invite me in for a nightcap?"

I took a deep breath. "It's early, yes. But I have a very busy day tomorrow."

"Another time, maybe," he said.

"Another time." I turned and walked up the walkway. The front curtain twitched. Poor Mrs. D'Angelo would be mighty disappointed.

Inside, Mattie began a loud chorus of greeting.

Chapter 14

I stepped back to admire my handiwork. The shop positively gleamed and I was pretty sure the smiles on the faces of the stuffed Santas hadn't been as broad yesterday. The decorations on the Douglas fir in the corner glowed as if lit from inside, the china platters and glass ornaments were brushed clean of the slightest speck of dust. When I'd arrived at the shop, grumbling at the darkness of a December morning, I'd been pleased to see several gaps on the shelves and display cabinets. Crystal and Jackie must have had a busy evening. I happily restocked the shelves while jotting notes on my iPad of what I was running out of and would have to reorder.

I'd stopped at Victoria's Bake Shoppe for a latte and blueberry scone but didn't even have a chance to say hi to Vicky. I could see over the counter and through the glass windows into the bakery, where she and her assistants were nothing but a blur of activity. Tonight was Midnight Madness, the start of what was hopefully the busiest weekend of the year for the shops and restaurants in Rudolph.

Business owners were concerned that numbers were down compared to last year; some reservations that had been cancelled after news of the death of Nigel Pearce got out hadn't been rebooked. But we were an optimistic lot in Rudolph—all that Christmas spirit—and we were determined to pretend that everything was back to normal.

While I worked I put on a CD of my mom singing Christmas songs, and soon found myself singing along. I'd never recovered from the time I overheard her telling a friend that my voice put her in mind of a chorus of frogs in a pond at dusk, calling out in search of mates. I loved to sing, but from that day on I made sure no one was in hearing range. All of my musical talent was inherited from my dad, meaning I had absolutely none.

Fortunately for Mom, who had high hopes of children following in her footsteps, my sister Carole had a marvelous voice as well as the drive to succeed. Carole wouldn't be home for Christmas this year, as she was touring Europe in the chorus of a production of *Carmen*.

At ten to nine I was ready. I was debating whether or not I had time to sprint up the street for another latte, maybe a bagel with cream cheese this time, when a rap sounded on the door. I was about to tap my wrist, to indicate that we weren't open yet, but one look at the face peering in the window put a stop to that.

Detective Simmonds. And she didn't look as though she were a woman on a shopping spree. Officer Candice Campbell accompanied her. Candy's scowl was firmly in place.

I opened the door. "Good morning, Detective. What can I do for you?"

"Do you have a few minutes, Merry?"

I debated saying no, just to see what Simmonds would do. But I didn't have a death wish, so I stepped back. "Come on in. I'm opening in a couple of minutes, but I won't get many customers before eleven."

Simmonds wandered about my shop, checking everything out. Candy stood in the doorway, her legs apart, her hand resting on the butt of her gun. I almost told her to relax, I wasn't going to make a break for it. Then I remembered that death wish thing and kept my mouth shut.

"Beautiful shop," Simmonds said at last. She ran her fingers over the smooth blue stones on a chain of turquoise and silver.

"Thanks. I like it."

"You have some lovely things." She picked up one of Alan Anderson's wooden soldiers.

"Many of our goods are made locally."

"That's good to know."

Candy shifted from one foot to another.

Simmonds put down the soldier. "Tell me about Nigel Pearce."

"I've already told you everything I know. Which isn't much. I never saw him before he came into the shop Saturday afternoon. He introduced himself, took some pictures, left."

"You saw him later, though?"

"I told you that, too. At the reception at the community center. In the presence of a good hundred or more people."

"And that," Simmonds said, "seems to be the problem. A

couple of hundred people saw him there, knew who he was. Many of them spoke to him or had their picture taken by him. I hate to sound melodramatic, but did you notice anyone acting suspiciously?"

I shrugged. "How do you define 'suspiciously'? He was a photographer from a major magazine. People wanted to meet him. They wanted him to photograph them. If I saw anyone deliberately avoiding him, I'd call that suspicious. But I didn't."

"We've been through the pictures on his camera. He took plenty of a woman in a very fancy gown. I've been told that's your mother."

"My mom used to be an opera singer. She was quite the diva in her day." I refrained from saying that she still thinks she is. "She knows how to play for the camera. Besides, she and her students did look mighty good in their costumes. Perfect for photos. Ask Candy, there. I mean, Officer Campbell."

Behind me, Candy's boots shifted once again.

"I did," Simmonds said. "I also interviewed your mother. She claims never to have met Mr. Pearce before that day."

"If that's what she says then that's the truth. My mother is never anything but totally honest." And wasn't that the truth. Whether commenting on my singing voice or what she thought of Max Folger, my almost-fiancé (now ex-almost-fiancé) I could always count on Mom to be brutally honest, and usually right.

"The camera was also full of shots of a woman identified to me as Jackie O'Reilly. I didn't see anything particularly Christmassy about Ms. O'Reilly that Mr. Pearce could use in his story."

"Jackie's pretty," I said. "Men like to take pictures of pretty young women."

Behind me, Candy stifled a snort.

"True," Simmonds said. "Ms. O'Reilly works for you?"

"Yes."

"Does she have a husband? A boyfriend?" Simmonds fixed her cool green eyes on me.

As if she didn't know. I doubted Detective Simmonds ever asked a question she didn't already know the answer to.

"She's not married. She's going out with someone, I think."

"His name?"

"Kyle Lambert."

"Is this Kyle a jealous sort?"

"I have no idea." I don't know why I lied. Maybe because I didn't care for the direction these questions were taking. I didn't want to be getting anyone into trouble. Besides, I had given it some thought. If Kyle had been angry at Nigel for paying attention to Jackie, he wouldn't have poisoned a cookie. He'd have slugged the guy. Then again, was it possible the poison hadn't been what ultimately killed Nigel? Had he thrown most of it up, into the snow in the park, and been followed by Kyle and finished off when he was at his weakest? I knew nothing at all about autopsies, but didn't it take time to get detailed test results back? I'd check with Dad later, see if he'd heard any further results.

"If we're finished here," I said through a strained smile, "it's time for me to open up."

Simmonds walked slowly toward the door. She peered out, looking carefully left and then right. She saw no impatient lines. No one was anxious to begin an orgy of frantic shopping.

"I get your point," I said, "but I have work to do to get ready."

"Tell me about the cookies," Simmonds said.

"I already have," I said.

"Tell me again."

So I repeated everything I knew about the special tray of gingerbread cookies and the Charles Dickens one prepared specifically for Nigel Pearce. "Vicky Casey," I said, "did not kill Nigel Pearce."

"I know that," Simmonds said.

"She wouldn't . . . What?"

"Ms. Casey is an intelligent woman as well as a proud business owner. No one cold-blooded enough to poison a cookie would be dumb enough to do something that would so directly point the finger at herself."

I thought of mystery books I'd read full of double binds and triple-crosses and deliberate misperception. I decided not to point that out.

"Besides," Simmonds said, "I have a passion for croissants and it's been a long time since I've tasted any as good as hers. I wouldn't want to see those pastries being prepared in the kitchen of a women's prison."

"Huh?"

"That was a joke, Ms. Wilkinson."

"A joke. Right." I laughed. Candy laughed, too.

"Thank you for your time. I'll leave you to open. You're going to be part of this Midnight Madness?"

"Yup. I'll be here all night."

"I might stop by later. You do have some lovely things."

Warmed by her praise, I felt bold. "People are saying that someone must have come with Nigel. Either with him, or followed him here. Are you investigating that?"

"Of course we are," Candy snapped. "We're not total fools, you know."

"That's a good question," Simmonds said.

"Humph," Candy said.

"Mr. Pearce arrived in Rudolph, as far as we can tell, alone. He checked into the hotel alone, and the housekeepers say that only one person seems to have used the room. As for whether someone followed him here, it's hard to say. This is a tourist town and there were a lot of visitors on Saturday. He wasn't observed spending any particular amount of time with anyone other than the local people he was supposedly here to write about."

"Was he ever in any trouble, back in England, say? Maybe the person who followed him to Rudolph didn't want to be obvious? Not if he was planning to kill him."

"We have some indication that Mr. Pearce wasn't loved wherever he went," Simmonds said. "He seemed to have used his position as a travel journalist and photographer to, shall we say, get friendly with young women."

"How young?"

"Not so young there was anything illegal going on. That we know of. But his trips didn't always result in him leaving a trail of friends behind."

Jackie. How far would she have gone to get herself featured in *World Journey* magazine, anyway? And, if she did what she thought she had to do, how would she have reacted when not so much as a single photo made it into print?

Her rage would have been something to behold. Fortunately for Jackie, it hadn't come to that. Fortunately for the jealous Kyle as well.

Had some other spurned wannabe model or angry boyfriend followed Pearce to Rudolph? That gave me an idea. "Why would he have been in the park that night? Alone. After dark. That seems strange, doesn't it? You'd think a man like that would go for dinner, have a couple of drinks. Do you think he might have been meeting someone?"

"We've been told that Mr. Pearce was a recovering alcoholic. He'd been sober for many years, but like most alcoholics, he found it hard in strange places. It was apparently his habit to take a long walk before dinner to work off the urge."

"Oh," I said.

"Thanks for your time, Merry," Simmonds said. "Uh . . ."

"Yes?"

"That turquoise necklace. I don't suppose you could put it aside for me?"

"I'd be happy to," I said.

"Thanks. I'll be back later."

The police left. I followed them to the door to flip the sign.

I might have spent longer than necessary looking out onto the quiet street. I couldn't help but notice that Simmonds and Candy's next stop was Rudolph's Gift Nook.

At three o'clock the police closed off Jingle Bell Lane. For the rest of the night Rudolph's main shopping street would be pedestrian only. Carts and tables were set up as shops and eating establishments spilled out onto the sidewalk and into the road. The butcher shop brought out a hot dog stand; Vicky erected a table outside her front door, selling gingerbread and other Christmas cookies; the Cranberry Coffee Bar was serving hot drinks. Crowds began to gather and business was brisk as the day turned to twilight. By five o'clock night had fallen.

My dad wandered the street in full regalia, ho-ho-ho-ing, followed by Alan Anderson in his toymaker costume. Children, wide-eyed and openmouthed, watched them. I always got a particular kick out of the older children, the ones who were starting to question the existence of Santa. My dad and Alan could usually convince them to hold on to their childhood for another year, at least.

My mom also was doing the rounds. She wore a long black cape with an emerald silk lining and matching stitching, and a fake-fur hat. She wouldn't have looked out of place on a Russian troika as it dashed though the snowy woods pulled by three black horses, pursued by a pack of howling, starving wolves. She led four of her adult students, dressed in an assortment of Victorian dresses, capes, and hats. They popped in and out of shops and restaurants, singing carols to the delight of shoppers.

The night was cold and crisp. It didn't snow, but clouds were thick overhead, blocking the moon and stars. The town was illuminated by so many Christmas lights I wondered if it was visible from space.

A small stage had been erected at one end of Jingle Bell Lane, in front of the community center. A children's band played music and clowns walked through the crowd, doing magic tricks or twisting balloons into ornate animal shapes. The object of all this activity was to get people into the stores, and in that, the day didn't disappoint.

At seven Jackie was behind the cash register and Crystal was helping a man select a gift for his wife. Things were slowing down, but that was only temporary. People with little kids would be taking them home for dinner and bed, and adults on their own would be in search of a restaurant. They'd be back, soon enough, for another round of shopping. My mom and her group swept into the shop. She sounded the note, and the singers burst into "God Rest Ye Merry Gentlemen." Everyone in the shop stopped what they were doing to listen to the music, enormous smiles on their faces. I surreptitiously slipped across the room to stand beside the display of Christmas-themed music boxes.

The song came to an end, to enthusiastic applause. The singers bowed and went back out into the night.

"That was perfectly lovely," a woman said to me. "I'm from Toronto and we come to Rudolph every year to do our holiday shopping." She picked up a music box featuring a Santa Claus in his sleigh. She opened the lid and the notes of "Jingle Bells" rang through the shop. "Although I have to confess," she said with a laugh, "I do far more shopping for me than buying gifts. It's really a matter of one for you, and five for me. I love this box. I'll take it."

"I'll put it on the counter for you, shall I?" I said. "So you can continue browsing."

"It's great to see the town so busy, isn't it?" a man whispered into my ear.

I turned to see Fergus Cartwright, our mayor.

"Sure is," I said.

"Looks like that unfortunate incident last week didn't have any long-term effects."

"Right."

"My daughter suggested that Twitter campaign," he said. "Clever girl, my daughter. Invaluable help to me sometimes."

"That's nice." I started to edge away. I had customers to attend to.

"Glad I thought of asking Russell to contact his friend at the *Times*."

"I'm glad you did, too," I said. *Hadn't that been my dad's idea?* No matter.

"I'll let you get back to work," he said.

Fergus was dressed in a severe black suit, white shirt, and black tie. A gold pin was attached to his jacket. *Fergus Cartwright, Mayor of Rudolph*, with the Stars and Stripes on one side, the logo of the town of Rudolph on the other. A bright yellow stain marred the pristine whiteness of his dress shirt. I was about to point it out to him and suggest he could use my back room to try to scrub it off, when none other than Sue-Anne Morrow came into the shop.

The mayor and mayor-wannabe glared at each other. Then they broke into smiles. They met in the center of the shop and shook hands warmly.

"Looks like a successful night, Fergus," Sue-Anne said.

"Yes. Yes." He beamed.

"I heard that some of the guests at the Yuletide Inn were overheard saying they were going to Muddle Harbor for dinner." She lowered her voice. "And we all know that if they eat there, they'll stay to shop."

"Are the stores open late in Muddle Harbor tonight?" I said. "They don't usually do that."

"Apparently," Sue-Anne said, "their mayor suggested they take advantage of all the people coming to the area who might be in search of, and I quote, 'alternate choices.'"

His Honor growled.

"Looks like we need more than a Twitter campaign, Fergus," Sue-Anne said. "I'd be happy to sit down with you and Noel and put our heads together to come up with something . . . original."

"Noel," Fergus snarled. "Noel Wilkinson is no longer the mayor of Rudolph. People keep forgetting that." He stalked out of the store.

"Fergus really is out of his depth, isn't he?" Sue-Anne said to me. "I'd better get back out there. People like to see a calming presence, don't they, Aline?"

"Aline's my mother. I'm Merry."

"Sorry." She waved her fingers at me and left.

I rolled my shoulders and flexed my knees. "I have to take a break," I said to Jackie. "Get something to eat before the rush starts again." I was not in my Mrs. Claus getup tonight, but comfortable slacks, a plain shirt under a good wool jacket, and very sensible shoes.

"We're good here," she said.

I slipped out into the street. The stage had gone quiet as the children's entertainment ended and preparations for the adult stuff began. The town had hired a '50s-era dance band to play. There had only been one objection to the choice: my mom, who wanted nothing to interfere with her group of carolers.

I wouldn't know how this year's sales compared to previous years until I had the chance to ask the other shop owners, but I thought we were doing well. I glanced up and down the street. I'd been in Rudolph last year for Midnight Madness weekend. Was the street quieter? Were people more subdued?

Were the folks of Muddle Harbor gloating over their good fortune?

As if I'd conjured him up, I spotted Randy Baumgartner, mayor of Muddle Harbor, across the street, munching on a hot dog. A group of six came out of A Touch of Holly laughing, buttoning coats, and pulling on gloves. They swallowed Randy up. I glanced around, but he'd disappeared. I wasn't sure if it had even been him.

Candy Campbell strolled by on the other side of the street. The police were out in force tonight, walking the beat and keeping an eye on everything. Detective Simmonds had come into my shop earlier to buy the necklace she had her eye on. She left with two toy soldiers as well, which reminded me that I was supposed to be getting more of those soldiers from Alan.

I took my place in the line at the cart in front of the butcher shop. Sausages and hot dogs sizzled, fragrant smoke and the mouthwatering scent of grilling meat rose into the night air. The line was long, but it moved quickly, and everyone was patient and friendly. When my turn came, I asked for a bratwurst, and stood to one side while the plump sausage was tossed onto the grill to heat.

"You look busy," I said to Dan Evans, owner and chief butcher.

"Been better," he grunted.

"Really? You mean other Midnight Madness nights?"

"Yeah." He kept his voice low. "Other places are saying the same."

"Not good."

"No. White or wheat bun?"

"White." Tonight was not a night for being mindful of proper eating habits.

Dan tossed a bun onto the edge of the grill, toasting it lightly. He thrust my food at me as Kyle Lambert came out of the store, carrying a tray of uncooked hot dogs. Jackie had told me Kyle was working here this weekend.

"Take over, will you?" Dan said. "I need a break."

"Sure." Dan passed Kyle the tongs and the younger man took his place behind the barbeque. "What'll you have, buddy?"

I like my sausage well dressed. I'd slathered on mustard, relish, pickles, sauerkraut, hot peppers, onions, and topped it all with a splash of Dan's so-called special sauce.

The town's toymaker spotted me and came over. "That looks good," Alan said.

I chewed happily. "Tastes good, too. Where's Dad?"

"Huddling with Sue-Anne Morrow," Alan said. "So I came in search of something to eat. Careful, you're about to drop mustard all over yourself." He pulled a tissue out of the pocket of his britches and wiped carefully at my lower lip. His touch was light, and all the while his expressive blue eyes were fixed on mine. My lip quivered. I swallowed. Around us, people chatted and laughed. My mom's group was standing on the snowy lawn outside the library, singing "Silent Night," the pure, clear tones rising into the air. From the other end of the street came the sounds of the dance band warming up. A child asked for a hot dog and his dad said he had to wait for dinner. Alan's finger lingered on my mouth.

The world exploded.

Alan leapt back. I yelped and dropped my sausage. A woman screamed, people shouted. I whirled around. The hot dog barbeque was on fire. Flames shot out from the grill, yellow and red fingers of fire reaching up into the night air.

Kyle Lambert screamed in terror. He fell backward, landing against the side of the building, his white butcher's apron wrapped in flames.

Chapter 15

Alan Anderson was the first to move. His arm shot out and he shoved me aside. I would have fallen had not the crush of people, either frozen to the ground in shock or running away, held me up. I barely had time to register what was happening. I might have screamed for Alan to be careful. Then again, I might have just screamed.

Alan rounded the burning grill and reached Kyle. He grabbed Kyle's arm and threw the shocked man to the ground. Kyle landed hard, face-first. Alan dropped to his knees beside him. "Roll, roll," Alan shouted.

Kyle obeyed, and rocked back and forth on his belly. Dan Evans's wife ran out of the building. She held a cell phone in her hand, and was yelling into it.

"Everyone, get back," Alan shouted. Flames were still leaping from the barbeque. "It might explode."

A stampede began as frightened people hurried to get

away. Some were dragging crying children by the hand. I saw Vicky Casey crossing the street, fighting against the crowd. She carried a fire extinguisher.

"Stand back, stand back." Dan Evans appeared with his own fire extinguisher. He and Vicky trained the red canisters onto the barbeque and simultaneously sprayed foam. Sirens sounded in the distance, getting closer. Candy and another uniformed officer were attempting to get people off the street, trying to clear a path for the emergency vehicles.

I ran to see if I could help Kyle. With Mrs. Evans's help, he'd rolled onto his back. The front of his long apron was scorched and his scraggly goatee was singed, but the skin on his face was clear and what clothes I could see looked to be intact.

"Lie still," Mrs. Evans said. "Help's coming."

Kyle swore. He tried to sit up. "I'm okay. Just shocked."

The fire was out now, no match for the strength of Vicky's and Dan's heavy-duty extinguishers. People began returning, curious as to what was going on. Jackie burst through the crowd, her eyes wide with fright. She screamed at the sight of Kyle and dropped to the sidewalk beside him. She reached for him, but Mrs. Evans thrust out a hand. "Let the medics check him out first."

"I'm okay, babe," Kyle said. He tried to stand. His legs wobbled and he fell back with a moan.

"Out of the way, out of the way." A paramedic pushed her way through the onlookers. Her partner followed, bringing a stretcher.

"I'm okay," Kyle said once again.

"Let us be the judge of that," the paramedic said.

I glanced around for Alan. He was gone. I made my way

to the back of the crowd and spotted him standing with Vicky, who was cradling her now-empty fire extinguisher. Both of them had pale faces and wide eyes. I probably looked the same.

"Get off the road," a cop shouted at us. We ran to do as we were told, and a fire truck edged down the street. Men in bunker gear leapt off the truck and began unfurling hoses.

"Are you okay?" I asked Alan.

He nodded.

"That was . . . brave," I said.

"Didn't even think about it," he said. "If I'd thought for a moment, I would have run in the opposite direction. How's Kyle?"

"Darn lucky, I'd say."

At that moment the stretcher was pushed through the crowd toward the ambulance. Kyle was lying down, but high-fiving everyone who approached him. Jackie walked beside him, holding his free hand and weeping copiously. The paramedics loaded the stretcher into the back and then one of them leapt up. A hand reached out and Jackie was hauled inside. The doors slammed and the vehicle pulled away. Some of the onlookers applauded.

"What do you suppose Kyle did?" I asked.

"What do you mean?" Alan said.

"To make the fire go out of control like that."

Vicky and Alan exchanged glances. "Kyle works for Dan on most special occasions," Alan said. "He knows how to operate a simple gas grill."

"A leak in the hose, maybe," Vicky said. "Some kind of fault in the barbeque?"

Excitement over, the crowd began to break up. Detective

Simmonds was talking to Dan Evans. Both of their faces were grim. Simmonds was gesturing to the now-useless barbeque. Evans shook his head.

The firefighters got into their truck and drove away. Children cheered, thinking it was all part of the fun.

Almost as quickly as the excitement had begun, everything returned to normal. Mom and her choir launched into a rendition of "While Shepherds Watched Their Flocks."

My dad ran up to us. His cap was disheveled and his red nose and cheeks owed as much to the unaccustomed exercise as to the touch of Mom's blush he always added when getting into costume. "What happened? Someone said there was an explosion. I heard sirens."

"An accident," Vicky said. "A fire in the hot dog barbeque. Kyle was singed, but thanks to Alan here, nothing more serious."

I glanced at Alan. His hands were shaking. "Hey, you need to sit down."

"I'm okay," he said.

"Merry's right," Vicky said. "Come inside and I'll get you a cup of coffee and a muffin."

"I'm fine."

"Go with Vicky," Dad said. "Santa's orders."

Alan gave me a glance. Then he nodded and allowed Vicky to lead him away.

"Hero of the hour," Dad said.

"He was that, all right. While the rest of us stood around like fools, only Alan moved."

"Santa, Santa," a cute little girl, all pink snowsuit and cat-faced hat, squealed. Dad put on his serious smile, turning his face into the one I always think of as Father Christmas.

The girl's mother grabbed at her arm, almost jerking the child off her feet. "We're leaving, Amber."

"I wanna speak to Santa."

"I said we're leaving." She pointed a finger, tipped with long red nails, at my dad. "I don't know what kind of a town you think you have here, but it's out-and-out dangerous. Christmas Town indeed. More like Horrorville." She dragged the howling, crying child away.

"Oh, dear," I said.

My dad's face changed, and settled into worried lines. "Accidents happen, but after the death of Pearce, this doesn't look good. I'd better get back out there. Call your mom; tell her we need lively and very loud songs." He walked away, belly rolling in the swaying gait that was part of his act. "Ho, ho, ho . . . Have you been good, kids?"

"Real good, Santa," a teenage boy in baggy clothes smirked. His friends laughed and slapped the joker on the back.

I wanted to follow Alan, make sure he really was okay, and maybe try to recover that moment when he looked deeply into my eyes and his hand caressed my lips. But Vicky would ply him with fresh baking and keep an eye on him for a while. I needed to check on my store, so I headed to Mrs. Claus's Treasures. Russ Durham fell into step beside me, his camera bouncing at his side. I'd seen him earlier, following the ambulance siren and then talking to Detective Simmonds. "Close one," he said.

"Yeah."

"Were you there?"

"Yes."

"Wanna tell me what happened?"

"No."

"I saw some people leaving. I think they're spooked at things that have been happening around here."

"Fair enough," I said. "But that had nothing to do with Nigel Pearce. Just an accident."

"Simmonds isn't so sure."

I stopped walking. "What do you mean?"

"She's ordered the grill to be taken in. She wants it sent to the lab and checked for signs of tampering."

"Tampering?"

"That's what she says. Those gas barbeques are mighty safe these days. Dan and Kyle know how to use it."

"Accidents happen. People get sloppy, make mistakes."

"Simmonds knows that. She just wants to be sure. All I'm saying is, I hope word doesn't leak out of the police station that it might not have been an accident."

I swore. He grinned at me. "I didn't know you knew bad words, Merry."

I swore again. "You should hear my dad when he gets stuck in the chimney."

Russ threw back his head and laughed. "Now that," he said, "is the spirit of Christmas Town."

We reached my shop. I peeked through the windows. A couple of people were browsing. Everyone hadn't fled. Horrorville, indeed.

A cold fist gripped my heart. All we needed would be for that woman to repeat that word. The nickname would spread like wildfire.

Was the explosion an accident? My thoughts tumbled all over themselves. My float, the poisoned gingerbread, and now an exploding barbeque. Even the clumsy attempt to get Dad out of town, if that's what Eve's supposed accident had been.

Randy Baumgartner, mayor of our town's chief rival, had been at the post-parade party and I'd seen him not more than a couple of minutes before the hot dog cart caught fire. Had he been at the parade assembly area, too? *Cui bono?*

Muddle Harbor.

Sue-Anne Morrow also stood to benefit. If business crashed just weeks before Christmas, voters would blame the current mayor. Come election time, they'd remember. Sue-Anne would ensure they remembered.

And then there was Kyle. Kyle, who'd been angry at Nigel Pearce. Kyle, who'd been manning the barbeque when it caught fire. Kyle, who I'd never thought all that bright to begin with. How dumb was Kyle to potentially set himself on fire?

Perhaps not so stupid after all. He wasn't harmed, and now he was basking in the weeping adoration of Jackie. If, and it was a big if, he'd caused the explosion deliberately, it was a risky thing to do. Then again, young men in pursuit of a woman's affections were not always known for their careful assessment of risk.

"What are you thinking?" Russ asked me.

"I'm thinking that I'd better get back to work. And put my happy face on." I gave him a big grin.

He shook his head. "Try a less happy happy face. You look like an escapee from a funny farm."

"We wish you a merry Christmas, we wish you a merry Christmas, and a happy New Year," sang the strolling choir. I hadn't phoned Mom yet. I didn't need to. She knew how important music was in creating mood. People stopped to listen, and I saw a good number of smiles. When the song finished, Mom's voice rising into the night air on the last note like a crystal, the audience applauded enthusiastically.

Mom glanced my way, and I gave her a wink. Russ Durham took a picture of the choir.

"I hope you're going to put that one on the front page," I said. "Not the burned-out hulk of a hot dog cart."

"I am, I will remind you, Merry, also a proud supporter of this town."

I went to work. About an hour later Jackie phoned to tell me that the ER doctor had pronounced Kyle unharmed, although slightly shaken up, and released him. He was, Jackie insisted, in no shape to drive, so she would be taking him home and getting him settled.

What could I say, except that I understood.

Cui bono? Accident or not, Kyle certainly had.

Chapter 16

I staggered home at one A.M. Jackie had not come back to work and Crystal and I had been on the move all night.

And tomorrow (now today!) I had to do it all again.

Remind me why I thought owning my own business would be a good idea?

Although the barbeque fire had been terrifying to those of us in the immediate vicinity, it had gone largely unnoticed by the rest of the town. More than a few people, as well as their overexcited kids, thought the fire truck and ambulance were part of the entertainment. For those who did ask what had happened, my dad and others spread it around that there had been a "flare-up" at a hot dog cart.

I tried to put the incident out of my mind, but throughout the busy night, one thought kept swirling around in my head.

Was someone out to deliberately ruin Christmas in Rudolph?

And if so, what might they have planned for tonight when we had another Midnight Madness?

Not many lights were on in the houses I passed on my way home. I didn't take my usual shortcut through the park, and I felt my feet speeding up as I hurried by. The big tree next to the bandstand was brightly lit, a welcome triangle of color against the dark night. I avoided looking into the corners of the park. To where I'd found Nigel.

Think of something more pleasant, I ordered myself.

Alan. He didn't say much; he didn't have to. Sometimes it seemed as if his expressive eyes did all the talking for him. I lingered over the memory of the touch of his finger on my mouth, the gentle way he'd wiped the dripping mustard off my lips. The way his blue eyes had turned dark and serious as he looked at me.

Had he been about to say something when that hot dog cart exploded?

No. That had been my imagination, working overtime.

I'd had a lovely dinner the night before with Russ Durham.

I didn't know what I thought.

I was glad Mattie was waiting, and I wasn't going home to a cold and lonely house. I'd planned on letting him out after enjoying my hot dog, but with all the excitement, I forgot, and then I couldn't leave Crystal to staff the shop alone.

I'd had to give in, phone Mrs. D'Angelo, and beg her to take care of him.

Not that she needed much begging. Her excitement at the idea of popping into my apartment and having a good snoop around, *with my permission*, came over the phone loud and clear.

I tried to remember if I'd picked my underwear up off the bedroom floor. Probably not.

All the lights were off at the front of my house. Even Mrs. D'Angelo couldn't keep watch the entire time. I heard a rustle in the bushes as I rounded the building, heading for the back and the door to my apartment. A cat, maybe? I glanced up. A faint glow came from a single window in Steve and Wendy's apartment, shining on gently falling snow. A night light in case they had to get up to see to the baby. All was quiet.

I flicked on the flashlight app on my smartphone, and found the lock. As the key turned, Mattie began to bark. I always felt dreadful when he barked in the night, thinking of the sleeping baby next door. But Wendy said he didn't seem to bother Tina in the least. Nevertheless, I hurried in and whispered at the dog to hush.

As usual, my orders had absolutely no effect. I opened the crate and Mattie leapt out. I allowed a minute of kisses before putting him outside. He headed immediately for the back corner and began sniffing around. He must have caught the scent of that prowling cat.

I gave him a few minutes before calling him inside, and together we trudged up the stairs. Or, rather, I trudged. He bounded. I filled his food and water bowls, and while he was inhaling his late dinner, I got myself ready to go to sleep.

That took all of about ten seconds. I collapsed onto the bed, barely able to exert the energy required to pull the duvet up around me.

The bed springs protested as Mattie leapt up.

"Only two more weeks," I told him. "And then we can have a normal life again."

If he answered, I didn't know because I was already fast asleep.

Two more weeks. Two more weeks. I repeated the mantra as my alarm sounded. Mattie's happy, smiling face loomed over me. He woofed in delight as my eyes creaked open. I wiped drool off my cheeks and thought that at least one of us was excited to see the arrival of a new day.

I staggered out of bed and downstairs to let the dog into the backyard. I left the door open and staggered back up. Coffee on and into the shower.

When I came out, feeling at least human if not entirely bright and sparkly, I almost tripped over the dog's bulk, lying in wait, stretched across the threshold of the door.

I bent over and gave him a hearty pat. "I think we both deserve," I said, "a good long walk this morning. And I know just the destination." I pulled out my iPhone and checked Google Maps. Strange things were happening in Rudolph, and the police didn't seem to be getting much done about finding out who was responsible. It wouldn't hurt, I figured, for me to do a bit of poking around on my own. Maybe I could shake something up.

I quickly pulled on warm clothes, poured my coffee into a portable mug, and Mattie and I headed out. It was almost eight, and a gray light was spreading across the sky to the east. The temperature had dropped overnight and it was a nippy five degrees according to the thermometer by the back deck. I snuggled into my lovely new coat and took deep breaths of the cold, clear air. I'd slept well and didn't remember my dreams, but when I woke it was to thoughts of exploding hot dogs, disabled tractors, and dead journalists. Less than an inch of snow had fallen in the night, but some people were out shoveling their driveways and paths.

We turned right at the road, heading away from town.

Jackie had told me that Sue-Anne lived on Willow Trail, and Google Maps had told me that Willow Trail was only a few short blocks from my house. I didn't know what I hoped to find there—unlikely Sue-Anne would even be up and about—but I wanted to check out her house anyway.

We turned onto Willow Trail, a pleasant street of gentrified old homes on large lots. Bingo! I slowed as I spotted a black Suburban with a vanity license plate that said SUEANNE1. A man was dusting snow off the Suburban's windows while a cocker spaniel ran about the yard, following his nose. The dog caught a whiff of Mattie and ran toward us, tongue hanging out and bushy tail wagging.

"Eddie, get back here." The man threw down his long-handled brush and chased after the dog. Mattie's own tail wagged and the two animals greeted each other in acceptable doggy fashion, nose to butt.

"She's okay," the man said to me. "She likes other dogs."

"Mattie's just a puppy," I said. "Not quite sure how to make friends yet."

"They seem to be doing fine," he said, giving me a grin. He was in his fifties, lean and trim, and completely bald. His dark brown eyes wandered down. Too bad for him: I was wearing a heavy winter coat and a pair of old baggy sweatpants covered in pills. His eyes returned to my face. He thrust out his hand. "I'm Jim."

I touched my mittens to his leather gloves. "Merry Wilkinson."

"Noel's girl?"

"Yes."

"How did ugly old Noel produce such a beautiful daughter?"

I felt my smile stiffening. I glanced at the Suburban. "I recognize that car. Sue-Anne Morrow?"

"My wife." He winked. "I hope you won't hold that against me."

Ugh.

"I hear Sue-Anne's going to run for mayor," I said.

He shrugged. "I won't stand in her way."

Hardly a ringing endorsement.

"Do you think she'll do a good job?" I asked.

"I think Sue-Anne can do anything she puts her mind to. She's one determined lady. I mean that in a good way, of course."

"You're not from around here," I said. Mattie's new friend had wandered off in search of fresh scents. I had to hold firmly on to the leash to keep him from following. "Small towns can be wary of outsiders."

He laughed, showing a mouthful of strong white teeth and an attractive dimple. He was a good-looking guy. If you could ignore the creep factor. I suspected some women would. "Yup. You're not really a local unless your great-grandparents are buried in the cemetery."

My great-grandparents on my father's side were.

"Sue-Anne and I don't think that will be a problem. We spent a lot of years in the city, but at heart we're country folk. I was lucky enough to be able to sell my business for a good sum and retire. Not that I'm really retired." He laughed. "I'm not that old. Just wanting to do what I love to do.

"I figure my business smarts will come in handy in a place like this. Sue-Anne couldn't get back upstate fast enough. She's always wanted to get back to her roots. Good thing she didn't make me move to some hardscrabble farm like the one she grew up on."

I let out more length on the leash. Mattie headed off down the sidewalk, sniffing at the ground. He began circling. "Looks like I'm being told to continue with the walk," I said.

"Sure. Nice talking to you. Look, I've an idea. How about you and me meet for a drink one night after work? I'd be glad to brainstorm some ideas for your shop. I made a lot of money in business in the city, you know."

"So you said."

"Nowadays, I charge the big bucks for consulting fees, but I'll do it for you gratis. I'll even throw in dinner." He pulled back the sleeve of his jacket, ensuring I got a good look at the heavy Rolex on his wrist. "Always happy to help out a pretty girl."

Mattie found the perfect spot and settled into a squat.

I pretended not to notice.

"Gotta run," I said. I glanced behind Mr. Morrow, toward the house. Sue-Anne had come out and was standing on the porch, watching us. I gave her a wave. She did not smile in return.

Chapter 17

Horrorville.

Our worst nightmare came to pass and that word began to spread. I first heard about it when I came out of Victoria's Bake Shoppe, carrying a latte and croissant prior to opening the store. I almost bumped into my dad. No one would mistake him for Santa Claus today, not by the look of pure rage on his face.

Russ Durham was with him. He didn't look a whole lot happier.

"What's happened?" I said.

"Someone, probably that woman who wouldn't let her daughter talk to me last night, checked out of the Carolers Motel. Said she wasn't spending another night in Horrorville. Not with a child to worry about. Unfortunately, a family of four was checking in, and they asked her what was going on. She told them a bomb had gone off on the main street. They promptly turned tail and left."

I groaned.

"Forfeiting, I might add," Dad said, "what they'd paid for a night in the hotel. And, to add insult to injury, right there in the lobby the father searched for nearby hotels on his phone, and called the Muddle Harbor Inn."

"Which just happened to have a free room," I said.

"When the advertising desk clerk checked the voice mailbox this morning, it was full," Russ said.

I groaned again.

"You guessed it. The Muddle Harbor Inn, the café, some of the shops, all wanting to place ads in the *Gazette*. Something along the lines of 'a peaceful, family-safe Christmas destination.'"

"Maybe it's a good thing," I said, ever the optimist, "that those people checked out of the hotel and left town rather than spread their fears."

"That's not all," Dad said.

"I got a call," Russ said, "from our anonymous friend. Telling me that the police handed Dan's barbeque to the fire inspector and asked him to give it a quick once-over. It was sabotaged."

"Sabotaged how?"

"The caller didn't say. I called Simmonds. She wouldn't confirm or deny it. She keeps herself pretty much under control, but I could tell she was furious. She said that absolutely no one had been given details of the fire department's investigation of the barbeque."

"So your caller knew it was sabotaged, either because they have an inside track to the police or fire department . . ."

"Or they did it themselves," Dad said.

"Who would do something like that?" I asked.

"Deliberately cause a barbeque to explode in a public place? Or make an anonymous call to the papers?" Russ said.

"It has to be the same person," Dad said. "We might have been able to convince ourselves that the death of Nigel Pearce had nothing to do with Rudolph, but now this?"

"Not so fast," I said. "Dan Evans was cooking and serving the hot dogs. Kyle came out and Dan asked him to take over. The explosion couldn't have been more than a minute or two after that. Maybe someone wanted to get revenge or something on Dan, and mistakenly got Kyle. Maybe they took advantage of the fuss over Nigel Pearce to get back at Dan?"

"That would make sense, Merry," Dad said, "except for the anonymous call to the newspaper. "

"You didn't recognize the voice?" I asked Russ.

He shook his head. "Might have been the same person who called me on Sunday about Pearce, but again the voice was disguised."

"Someone wants to cause trouble in Rudolph," I said.

"And they're not keeping quiet about it," Russ added.

I wondered if that was the point.

Vicky came down the steps. "I could see you guys from inside. What's the huddle about?" She wiped floury hands on her apron. A cable-knit sweater was thrown over her shoulders. Dad filled her in.

"I called Fergus and the rest of the town council to an emergency meeting," Dad said. "We have to consider cancelling tonight's events."

"No!" Vicky and I chorused.

"Can we take the chance on this escalating?" Dad said. "We were lucky no one was injured last night."

Russ's phone beeped. He checked the display. "I have to take this." He stepped away.

"If we cancel Saturday Midnight Madness," Vicky said, "people will panic. And not just visitors. We can't give in to terrorists."

"Don't glorify this by calling it terrorism," Dad said grimly. "This is some small-minded person with a grudge against Rudolph itself."

Russ joined us again, slipping his phone back into his pocket. "That was Renee. She wanted me to know that she got an e-mail telling her what happened last night. And to let me know that Horrorville is now a hashtag on Twitter."

"That woman last night," I said to Dad. "The one who first said . . . that word. Could she have been a plant? Maybe she's the one who sabotaged the barbeque?"

"I can't see it," Dad said. "She looked genuinely frightened."

"All it takes is one catchy word for an idea to spread," Russ said. "Particularly if someone is eager to fan the flames, so to speak."

"And the good folks of Muddle Harbor are very eager indeed," I said. "Randy Baumgartner was in town last night. I saw him. I think it was him. And eating a hot dog, at that."

"What time's this council meeting?" Vicky asked.

"We're on our way now," Dad said. "If we're going to cancel tonight, we have to get it done."

She pulled a face. "I'm just too busy, sorry. Merry, you go. Tell them I want to keep the town open."

"I guess it won't hurt if I'm late opening the store this morning," I said. "I'd like to know what's going on."

Dad and Russ set off, and I followed, gripping my breakfast. The town hall is tucked in behind the library, only a few doors from Victoria's Bake Shoppe. That, plus the fact that the police station is in the same building, went a long way to providing Vicky with customers in off-season months.

Town councilors were arriving in a steady stream. Dad immediately began shaking hands and exchanging greetings. Russ and I climbed the short flight of stairs to the public gallery. Situated at the back of the library, the council chambers overlook the public park and Lake Ontario. It's a wonderful view, winter or summer. In the distance sunlight sparkled on the dark blue waters of the lake, but closer to shore waves had been captured in ice, giving the shoreline the look of a mad sculptor's workshop. A handful of snowmen, constructed with varying degrees of expertise, were scattered about the park.

Inside, a man was hunched over the railing at the front of the public gallery staring at the activity below as the councilors exchanged greetings and took their seats. Russ gave me a nudge and jerked his head toward the man. "*Muddle Harbor Chronicle*," he whispered.

A few people I recognized as local businesspeople took seats near us. Not many had come. Most of them would be getting ready for the day.

The meeting didn't last long. Dad spoke first, emphasizing that the report of the tampering with the barbeque was still nothing but a rumor, and that the murder of Nigel Pearce remained unsolved, so it might well have nothing to do with Rudolph.

Sue-Anne Morrow leapt to her feet the moment Dad drew breath. She talked about our responsibility to ensure the complete safety of residents and visitors to our town. She didn't come down on one side or the other of the issue of cancelling tonight's Midnight Madness. Some of the councilors nodded as she spoke.

I flashed on the image of Sue-Anne as I'd seen her this morning, standing on her porch steps, watching her husband try to charm me. He'd been almost rudely dismissive of her political ambitions. That sort of mild scorn could often inspire the person to try harder, to care more. *I'll show you!* I was about to whisper something to Russ about it, but then he leaned forward as Fergus got slowly to his feet.

He puffed out his chest and, I thought, looked very mayoral in a three-piece suit with wide lapels and wide-legged trousers. Waistcoats hadn't been popular in men's fashion for at least twenty years, and designer suits today were cut tight for a lean silhouette. Just as well Fergus kept his old clothes: tight and lean wouldn't have suited our rotund mayor. He peered over the top of his glasses at Sue-Anne, who looked very up-to-date in a power suit with three-quarter-length sleeves and a straight, knee-length skirt. "That might be," he said, "how things are done in the city, where everyone's afraid of lawsuits and lawyers tell them what to do. But here in Rudolph, we can figure out for ourselves what's best for our town."

"I didn't . . ." Sue-Anne protested, but Fergus hammered on the table with his gavel, cutting her off. I wondered if the suit had been deliberately chosen to look old-fashioned. When it came to political instincts, he was no fool, our mayor.

"Time for a vote," Fergus said. He then launched into a ten-minute speech about love of community, respect for traditions, the importance of small-town America, and above all the spirit of Christmas that was personified by the town of Rudolph. Sue-Anne glowered throughout it all. A couple of times she looked as though she were going to interrupt, but then thought better of it. As Fergus spoke, heads began to nod.

At last he stopped. He nodded to the town clerk.

"All in favor of continuing with tonight's Midnight Madness," she said, "as originally planned, say aye."

It was unanimous. Sue-Anne glanced around the chamber and then put up her hand.

Down below, my dad caught my eye. He gave me a nod. He was not smiling, and his face looked grim. He'd spoken first, arguing that if we cancelled one of the town's major events at the last minute, Rudolph might never recover from the bad publicity.

It was decided, over the objections of Ralph Dickerson, who had to do the budget, that the mayor would speak to the chief of police and ask for additional uniformed officers on the streets. The meeting then broke up.

The *Chronicle* reporter made a dash for the exit. He tripped at the top of the stairs and would have tumbled all the way to the bottom, with no doubt tragic results, had not Betty Thatcher grabbed his arm.

"Watch where you're going, blasted fool," she snarled in her usual friendly fashion. He snarled back and headed downstairs at a more sedate pace.

Russ smothered a laugh. Fortunately today's *Chronicle* was already printed and distributed. News that extra police were needed to protect the town (which would no doubt be written so the reader would assume we were under red alert and the Department of Homeland Security had been called in) would have to wait until Monday.

"Stuff and nonsense," Betty said. "I never had any time for Fergus. He's a dithering fool. But it looks like he's finally found himself a backbone. Some of us can sit around all day, but I have a business to run. I've left Clark minding the shop."

I watched her disappear down the stairs. I stopped so abruptly Russ ran into my back.

Betty had mentioned her son, Clark, and that reminded me that Betty had a grudge against Vicky from the time Vicky'd fired Clark. What better way to get revenge than to make it look as though Vicky sold poisoned goods? Betty had been at the post-parade reception.

Betty also didn't care much for me. I never took it personally; she considered me to be her competition, even though I wasn't.

Betty had been at the parade grounds in the morning. I'd seen her when I arrived to do the last check of my float. I hadn't spared her a thought; lots of people had been there, making sure everything was okay before it was time for the parade to begin. But Betty didn't have a float in the parade. Betty was Rudolph born and raised. At fifty years old, in this area, that meant there was a good chance she'd lived on a farm, which also meant she might know something about tractors.

Okay, so Betty might want to make me look bad, and she might have wanted to get back at Vicky, but she had no reason to blow up the hot dog cart.

Russ and I emerged from the town hall into brilliant sunshine. "So it's full steam ahead," Russ said.

"What?"

"You're a million miles away. Let the shopping begin."

"I'd better get back. Unlike Betty I had no one to mind my shop while I was here."

"I know today's going to be another killer of a day, but tomorrow things will slow down, won't they?"

"Yes, thank heavens. We'll close at six tomorrow."

"Do you have any plans for after that?"

"Sleep. Glorious sleep."

He grinned. "I'd offer to keep you company." Blood rushed into my face. "But you have to eat, too. How about dinner?"

"Thanks, but I'm going to say no. I'll be bushed. Just because the shop's closed doesn't mean work's finished for the day. There's always something else to do to get ready for next week."

"Another time, then?"

"Sure."

He gave me a salute and walked away. My heart settled back into my chest. Business, I told myself. I had to think about nothing but running my business for the next two weeks.

Chapter 18

When I got to the store, the first thing I noticed was that the Douglas fir was looking sad and bare. Other than the strands of lights, everything on the tree was for sale, and yesterday it had been thoroughly picked over. I went into the back and found another box of ornaments made by a local glass artist. I unwrapped the beautiful balls and hung them, one by one, on the tree, keeping my eye on the door for potential shoppers as I worked. No matter how many times I decorated this tree, I always enjoyed it. I turned a ball in my hand, letting beams of green and red light from deep within flash around the shop. Some of the balls were the size of my thumbnail, works of miniature art, and some were bigger than a baseball. All were stunning. As well as the glass, I hung whimsical reindeer made of wooden clothespins and bits of red felt, and strung ropes of cranberry-red wooden beads. I'd put on one of my all-time favorite CDs, Boney M.'s *Christmas Album*, and bobbed to the lively music as I worked.

The bell over the door tinkled and I turned to see my dad come in.

"Someone's in a good mood," he said.

"Christmas always puts me in a good mood," I said.

He kissed me on the top of my head. "That's why we called you Merry."

I laughed and gave him a hug. My mother had wanted to name me Gundula, after Gundula Janowitz, the legendary soprano who was her idol as well as a good friend. Fortunately, Dad had won.

"Are you worried about tonight?" I asked.

"I'll be on high alert, and I'd advise you to do the same. Right now, I'm going home. This old Santa isn't as young as he used to be, and I need a nap."

Dad left, and I went back to arranging the stock. The supply of wooden toys was getting low. I sent a quick text to Alan.

Me: *Need more trains for next week. Got any?*

Alan: *Working on them now. Helping Santa tonight.*

Me: *Can I come around and pick them up?*

Alan: *Paint has to dry. Tomorrow after six. Stay for supper?*

I hesitated. Then my fingers moved without conscious thought.

Me: *If I can bring Mattie.*

Alan: *Sure.*

"Morning, Merry," Jackie called. "Looks like it's getting busy out there already."

"Busy is good," I said. Jackie would be working the day

shift today, ten until seven. At three, Crystal would come in to help me until eleven. I'd staff the store myself for the last hour.

The bell tinkled again, a group of laughing women came in, and I went to work with a smile.

The day passed without incident. To our considerable relief *#horrorville* was picked up by horror fans who thought it was a new book or movie, and they began using it without reference to Rudolph, leaving the town in the clear.

Mom and her group were warming their voices up, my dad and Alan were doing their rounds, the police were closing off Jingle Bell Lane, and the stage was being readied for the early-evening children's performers when I decided I could get away to tend to Mattie and maybe grab something to eat while both Crystal and Jackie were in the store. Business had been satisfyingly steady all day. Crystal sold the last of the wooden train sets and slipped up to me when her happy customers left, laden with parcels.

"Are we getting any more of those trains in?" she asked me. "They're really popular this year."

"Alan's working on them, and I'll have some for next week."

"It's nice of him to give his time to do the toymaker-and-Santa thing," she said.

"It is."

"That's why I love this town so much," she said. "It really is Christmas Town, in more ways than one. I'm sure going to miss it when I'm away at college."

"And we're going to miss you. Not to mention your jewelry. We sold quite a few of your pieces over the last few days."

She smiled modestly. Then she glanced around the shop. No one was in earshot, but Crystal lowered her voice and stepped closer to me. "My mom says someone's deliberately trying to ruin Rudolph."

"Accidents happen," I said. I seemed to have been saying that a lot lately.

"Wasn't an accident what happened to Mr. Pearce, was it?"

"No. But the police suspect he brought his enemy with him."

"That doesn't help us much. You know my mom runs a B and B? She had a cancellation last week and then another yesterday. She can't afford to have empty rooms at the busiest time of the year. She thinks the people from Muddle Harbor are behind all of this."

"I suppose that's possible."

"My mom didn't want me to come into town for work today. Said there's no telling what the Muddites will get up to next. I told her she was being silly."

"She's just being a mom," I said, thinking that the last thing we needed was locals to start panicking and thinking the town wasn't safe. "Moms worry."

"Yeah, I know that. I think she was really saying she doesn't want me to move to the city. She doesn't, but she knows I have to follow my dreams."

"And you do. Sometimes you can follow your dreams and then come back home, where you belong. Your mom knows that."

"I'm glad Kyle's okay."

"So am I." We both looked to the cash counter, where Jackie was ringing up a set of cocktail napkins and matching paper plates. Kyle, she had told us, was fine, although upset at the state of his goatee. He was also disappointed at being out of a job. Still shaken up, Dan had decided not to get another hot dog cart for the time being.

"Back soon," I said to my staff.

I bundled myself up against the cold and went outside. The streets seemed busy. I wasn't as optimistic as I'd tried to sound. By now, I was convinced that someone was deliberately trying to ruin Christmas in Christmas Town. Maybe the Muddites, maybe someone else. I had no idea who, or why, but that didn't matter. I could only hope he or she had had enough "fun."

Across the street, Dad was sitting on the bench in front of the library. A child was on his knee while others in the line shifted with excitement. Alan stood beside him, jotting notes on his long scroll of paper.

"That's the true spirit of Christmas Town," Fergus Cartwright said in a booming voice.

Sue-Anne was with him, as were a couple of other councilors, putting up a united front. Detective Diane Simmonds was also part of the group. The police presence was heavier than it had been last night. But, I hoped, not so obvious to outsiders that they'd be spooked. We were standing in front of Rudolph's Gift Nook, and Betty hurried out. Not quite feeling the community spirit of Christmas Town, she hissed at us to stop blocking her window display.

I remembered what Crystal had said about everyone working together. "It's nice of Alan to give up his time to play the toymaker. I've sold out of his wooden trains, and I hear that the toy shop is getting low also. But he's come into town to help Santa rather than working."

Betty huffed. "I still have plenty of toys left."

"For those who like plastic and chemicals," I said. Looks like I was also losing the Christmas spirit.

"I saw those trains the other day," Simmonds said. "They're marvelous. I want to get some for my brother's kids. Don't tell me they're all gone?"

"The nice thing," I said, addressing no one in particular, "about locally sourcing your stock is that supplies can quickly be refreshed. He's making more trains this weekend. They'll be here on Monday."

"I love Alan's things," Sue-Anne said.

"Plenty of people come to Rudolph every year just for Alan's toys," I said. "They say their kids get a kick out of meeting the toymaker himself."

"I don't think there's anything better for putting one in mind of an old-fashioned childhood Christmas," Simmonds said, "than hand-painted wooden toys."

The small group was quiet for a moment, all of us thinking of Christmases past as we watched Santa Claus and his toymaker greeting happy kids.

Most of us, anyway.

"Will you people get a move on," Betty snapped. "No one can see my window."

Mom and Dad came into the shop around ten, ready to pack it in. Dad was finished anyway, as the children who wanted to see Santa should be long tucked into bed, while dreams of sugarplums danced in their heads. Mom declared that she refused to compete with that "vile cacophony" and had called it a night.

For some reason, the town in its wisdom had hired an AC/DC cover band for the night's street dance. I tended to agree with Mom, but I made a point of never letting her know that I did. I myself enjoy a good AC/DC song, but enough really is enough.

Two women in their late seventies squealed at the sight of Dad. They wanted to sit on his lap. There are no chairs in the sales areas of my shop, so they had to be content with asking him if his beard was real and admiring the cut of his suit. They then admired Mom's cape and were delighted when she sang a few bars of "Jingle Bells" for them. At that moment, I just happened to be arranging a set of bells formed into a wreath designed to hang over the front door. The women spotted it, and before you could say *one horse open sleigh*, they were carrying it home.

"Good night, dear," Mom said to me.

"I'll be with you in a minute, Aline," Dad said.

"No you won't," Mom said, more to me than to her husband. "You'll stop to talk to everyone you pass and won't make it home for hours."

She gave me a kiss, exchanged a few words with Crystal, and left.

"Do you know," Dad said, "what you need over there are some flowers."

"I don't sell flowers. I have plenty of wreaths though." My wreaths are not made of greenery, nothing living that can die, but are arrangements of glass balls or delicately twisted grape vines adorned with bows and ribbons. Some are made of fake (but tasteful!) cedar or fir boughs.

"Nope, flowers," he said.

"Well, I don't have any."

"Those glass vases," Crystal said, "would work with some of the cedar branches in them, and then accented with those small red bows."

"That would look hideous," I said.

My dad began opening a package of the bows and collecting fake greenery. I shrugged and left him to it.

It was a few minutes before midnight and, after stifling a yawn, I was about to announce the immanent closing when the door opened once again. Several people were still in the shop, engaged in that frantic last-minute rush of purchases necessitated by closing time. We'd be open again tomorrow, but perhaps they feared most of the stock would disappear overnight.

Not that I minded frantic last-minute purchases.

Officer Candy Campbell swaggered in, hand on the butt of her gun. She was in uniform, and surveyed my shop as if suspecting I were cooking meth in the back rooms, and she was searching for addicts among my gray-haired, warmly dressed, sensibly shod customers.

"Everything okay here?" she asked.

"Fine, thank you," I replied.

"Is there a problem?" a woman asked.

"No," I said. "Thank you for your concern, Officer." I glared at Candy. She glared back. The police had been told to be unobtrusive. Candy didn't do unobtrusive.

Candy's eyes moved away from me. For a moment I thought I was imagining things, as a look of—could it be?—delight appeared on her face.

"Oh," she said. "That's so lovely." She crossed the room in three quick strides. She stood in front of the glass vase with the, to my eye, hideous display of fake greenery and red ribbons. "This vase would be perfect for my grand-mother! She's living in a retirement home now, and she loves it when the family brings her flowers. At Christmas she can display it just like this! Will you put it away for me, Merry? I'll come in tomorrow before I start work."

"I . . . yeah, I can do that, Can . . . Candice."

She gave me a smile. Will wonders never cease? Candy Campbell knew how to smile. "Thanks. I'm so pleased. Grandma's difficult to buy for, but I know she's going to love it."

She waved her fingers at me and trotted happily out the door.

"What a lovely young lady," one of the customers said to me. "I do love the community spirit in your town. Even the police are cheerful and friendly."

"Yes," I choked.

"Now that I see those vases, I'm going to get one, too. I have a friend it will be perfect for."

Eventually the last purchase was rung up and the last happy customer departed. I locked the door and fell back against it.

I switched out all the lights except for low ones behind the counter and over the display windows, and locked the door behind me. At ten past midnight the streets were still busy. The restaurants were serving the last of their custom-ers, the shopkeepers were locking up and heading home, and people were out for a walk and enjoying the night air. From the end of the street, for about the twentieth time that night, came the sound of "Dirty Deeds Done Dirt Cheap."

It had been a good day. The night had passed without incident. The town had one more special event planned before Christmas, an outdoor children's party next Saturday afternoon. There'd be skating on a cleared patch of the bay, a snowman-making contest, various games, and plenty of food. Dad and his helpers would be busy and Mom's children's classes were scheduled to perform.

I dared to hope that whoever our grinch was, they'd achieved whatever they'd wanted.

When I walked into my apartment, a foul smell greeted me. A few sniffs brought me to the trash can under the kitchen sink and the realization that I hadn't thrown the garbage out since I didn't know when. I'd had fish a few nights ago, and had bought more than I needed. The remains were doing what the remains of fish do. I was exhausted, and debated leaving it until morning, but I feared it would attract bugs. I pulled the bag out of the trash can, knotted the edges together, and carried the stinking mess downstairs, while Mattie danced at my feet hoping to get a chance to dig his nose in. I threw the bag into the outdoor garbage can by the back door, hoping it would be frozen solid by morning.

I was absolutely beat and looking forward to a long, luxurious lie-in tomorrow. The store didn't open until noon on Sunday, and it would close at six.

Heaven.

And then I was invited to dinner at Alan's. By staying for dinner, did Alan mean *stay for dinner as long as you're here anyway, Merry* or did he mean something more like *stay for dinner as I want to be with you, Merry?*

I was still trying to decide when I fell asleep.

I woke to the sound of Mattie barking. My room was

pitch-dark, the way I like it when I sleep. I told Mattie to hush, and rolled over.

He didn't hush. His barking got louder, more frantic.

"Mattie! Be quiet. You're going to wake the baby. Come here." I patted the covers. My eyes slowly became accustomed to the ambient light. The bedroom door was closed and Mattie was scratching at it, trying to get out.

I groaned. I could ignore him and have a mess to clean up in the morning, or get up, let him out, and go back to sleep. I climbed out of bed. His potty training was coming along pretty well, considering how little time I had to devote to him. I ought to be pleased that he knew to ask to go out.

I'd be pleased in the morning.

I opened the bedroom door and he charged down the stairs, still barking. I followed, alternately stumbling and grumbling.

I froze, my foot on the bottom step. Mattie wasn't barking now, but whining. His head was down and he was sniffing at the bottom of the door. I smelled smoke. Something crackled. The light coming through the small window in the door was a shifting red and orange.

Fire!

I screamed. And then I, very foolishly, threw open the door. Mattie yelped, turned tail, and headed back upstairs.

Flames were shooting out of the garbage can. The lid was lying about two feet away. I was absolutely certain I'd fastened the lid properly after I put the trash bag into it. I live in a neighborhood of big old trees, meaning lots of squirrels and the occasional raccoon: little creatures with dexterous paws, clever brains, and love of human garbage.

I headed for the lid, intending to snap it down onto the can, hoping that would put the fire out, but before I could reach it my neighbor Steve arrived with a small kitchen fire extinguisher. "Merry, get out of the way," he yelled. I leapt back and he sprayed the garbage.

It went out almost instantly. The fire had been much smaller than it had looked to my frightened eyes, silhouetted against the dark yard and the black sky. Steve and I hesitantly ventured close and peered into the can. The plastic bag on top was smoldering. I held my breath against the acrid scent of burning plastic.

We could hear sirens approaching.

"Wendy called 911," Steve explained.

"You were quick," I said.

"We have a baby. That makes you quick. I figured something was wrong by the way Mattie was barking. Not his usual bark. I looked out the window and could see the fire. What the heck happened?"

"I have absolutely no idea."

"Where is Mattie, anyway?" Steve asked.

"Hiding." At that moment the dog came out of the house, twitching nose first, checking to see if it was safe.

Sirens screamed to a halt in front of our house. "I'll stay here," Steve said, "in case it starts up again. You meet them and bring them around back."

An upstairs window flew open. "What's happening, honey?" Wendy called.

"Fire's out," Steve answered. "You can go back to bed."

Mattie followed me as I ran around the house. Lights

began coming on inside our house, as well as in other homes up and down the street.

"Over here," I called. "At the back."

Firefighters ran past me. "It's out now," I added.

I joined the group standing around my smoldering garbage can.

"Better finish it off," one of the firefighters said. He aimed his hose at the can and flooded the thing.

"What on earth is going on here?" Mrs. D'Angelo demanded. She'd thrown on a coat over her nightgown, but hadn't done it up. I had the presence of mind to be surprised that tonight she was sleeping in a sexy sleek peach nightgown, elaborately adorned with lace and ribbons. Neighbors, in various assortments of hastily grabbed outerwear and pajamas, followed her.

"Whose garbage is this?" the firefighter asked.

"Mine."

He glared at me. "You'd better be more careful about what you're throwing out. Did you forget to extinguish a cigarette or something?"

"I don't smoke."

Mrs. D'Angelo squealed, "You could have burned down my house!"

"I didn't . . ."

"You folks are lucky there's no wind tonight," the firefighter said. "That garbage can's mighty close to the house. A couple of sparks, a finger of flame, and up it all goes."

"Poof," one of the neighbors helpfully added.

"I don't smoke," I repeated. But no one was paying any attention to me. Mrs. D'Angelo was telling Mrs. Patterson from next door that she'd had "the fright of my life," and the firefighter was praising Steve for having a working fire extinguisher and knowing how to use it. Mattie sniffed pajama bottoms and boots.

"One more incident from you," Mrs. D'Angelo said to me, "and I'll be reviewing the terms of your lease. Why, I might have lost my home. Just wait until I tell your father about this."

"I don't smoke," I repeated.

"I'm feeling quite faint," she said to the firefighter, who just happened to be young and very handsome. "Perhaps you could help me inside."

"I've got you, Mable," Mrs. Patterson said, grabbing Mrs. D'Angelo's arm. "Let me make you a nice cup of tea to settle your nerves."

Eventually they all left, the neighbors exclaiming over what a close call they'd had, and the firefighters warning me to more careful disposing of my cigarette ends.

"I don't smoke," I said to Steve when only he and I were left standing beside the remains of my garbage can.

"I know you don't. What do you suppose happened, Merry?"

We studied the soggy ruin. "I've been at the store all day. I came home twice to feed the dog and let him out. I didn't use the stove or light any candles or anything like that. I threw week-old fish out before going to bed. Can rotten fish self-combust?"

"No."

"I didn't think so." I glanced around the yard. Every inch of snow was churned by Mattie's paws, and then overlaid by the footprints of the firefighters and neighbors. Before everyone arrived, I hadn't thought to check for marks in the snow. Probably wouldn't have mattered anyway. The yard was fenced, but the sidewalk had been shoveled after the last snowfall.

"Strange things have been happening around here, Merry," Steve said.

"Don't I know it."

"Wendy says everyone at town hall is on edge. They're all waiting for something else to happen. And I think it just did. Do you want me to call the firefighters back? Someone should check the garbage."

"For what?"

"An accelerant, maybe. You say nothing in that garbage was likely to cause a fire, and I believe you."

"Leave it," I said. "I want to go back to bed. I just want all this to be over."

"You take care, Merry."

"I will. And you, too."

"Count on it," he said, and he went back to his little family and his bed.

I called Mattie and we also went back to bed. But I didn't get another minute of sleep.

Chapter 19

In the weak gray light of an early winter's morning, the garbage can looked like something out of a postapocalyptic movie. I stood on the step in my pajamas, clutching a mug of coffee and studying the remains. Mattie had given the sodden black ruin a good long sniff and then run about the yard checking up on all the wonderful scents that had been deposited last night.

The fire had been terrifying, but overnight I'd realized that we hadn't been in any real danger. If an accelerant had been added, whoever'd done it hadn't used much. Only the top of the garbage was burned. Even if the whole can had caught fire, it wouldn't have been likely to spread. The yard was covered in snow, and the house was a solid brick Victorian. Nothing was lying around that could catch fire, the trees were draped in snow, and the wooden fence was far away, protected by deep drifts.

It was entirely possible this had been nothing but a prank by a bunch of stupid, bored kids.

Except for all the other incidents.

Although I couldn't see how setting my garbage on fire would ruin Christmas in Rudolph, if that was the arsonist's aim. Maybe all they wanted to do was to scare people?

It had worked. I'd been scared. Now I was getting angry. Fire wasn't something to play with, and a baby had been sleeping overhead.

So much for sleeping in. I went inside and made a quick phone call. Then I poured my coffee down the sink and pulled on jeans and a sweater and headed into town.

Detective Simmonds was sitting at a table in Victoria's Bake Shoppe when I got there. It was eight o'clock on the Sunday morning after Midnight Madness and she was the only customer. The whole town would be sleeping in this morning.

I wondered if Simmonds ever slept. She was perfectly put together in a red leather jacket, black slacks, and oxblood ankle boots. Her unpainted nails were neatly trimmed, her hair was curled at the ends and tucked behind her ears, and a touch of blush and pale pink lipstick gave her face some color.

I, on the other hand, had a tumbled mess of curls, black circles under my eyes, chewed fingernails, and I hadn't noticed a grease stain on the front of my shirt until now.

Without asking what I wanted, Vicky brought me a mug of coffee and a blueberry scone. Simmonds was having coffee, black.

"You should have called me last night," she said after I'd related my story.

"I was tired and wanted to forget about it. No harm done. Except that I now have to buy a new garbage can. And my landlady is looking for ways to get rid of me."

"Don't make jokes, Merry," Vicky said. "It could have been serious."

"That's the point," I said. "It couldn't have gotten out of control. Whoever did it must have known that." I threw up my hands. "Who knows, maybe I did light a candle last night or something."

"I'm sending someone around to pick up that garbage can," Simmonds said. "I want to have it looked at. Are you in the habit of lighting candles late at night when you get home from work and then throwing them in the garbage?"

"No."

"Then it's unlikely you did so last night."

"This is all getting seriously weird," Vicky said.

"I agree," Simmonds said. "What I find interesting is how minor these events seem to be. Minor, except that we have to remember that a man died."

"Yeah, after eating one of my cookies," Vicky said. "Would you like something to eat, Detective?"

Simmonds grinned. "To show my support, I'll have one of those scones. They do look great."

Vicky snapped her fingers and pointed to the last bit of scone disappearing into my mouth. I've always wanted to be able to snap my fingers and have food appear. In this case, Vicky's assistant brought over the pastry on a plate. In New York if you snapped your fingers at a waiter, they'd throw you into the street so fast you wouldn't know what was happening. But everyone who worked at the bakery was some relative or other of Vicky's and they knew that was just her way and not to take offense. Besides, the employee Vicky was hardest on was herself.

"Anything new happening with the murder investigation?" I dared to ask, hoping the delicious baking would mellow Simmonds.

She obliged. "Very little. Unlike what you see on TV it can be surprisingly difficult to find a killer if there are no friends or relatives in the picture and the killer hasn't bragged about what he's done or left a trail behind him. We've been in touch with the police in England, where Pearce lives, and they're running some checks, but so far, nothing. We may never know. I'm pretty sure someone followed Pearce here and then slipped out of town without being noticed."

"I'd buy that, if it wasn't for all the other strange things. Starting with my float."

She raised an eyebrow. "What about your float?"

"The tractor pulling my float in the Santa Claus parade was deliberately incapacitated. I put it down to someone playing a practical joke." I avoided looking at Vicky. "But these jokes are no longer funny."

"No," Simmonds said. She finished her scone and got to her feet. She pulled her wallet out of her pocket.

"It's on me," Vicky said.

"No it isn't. I can't be accused of taking bribes." She put a couple of bills on the table. She then took out a square of white card and a pen. She turned the card over and scribbled on the back and handed it to me. "Keep this. I've put my personal cell number on the back. Call me anytime, day or night, if you have reason to be concerned. I'll let you know what we find in the garbage can. Take care."

A lot of people seemed to be saying that to me lately. "I will."

I shoved the card into my coat pocket as we watched the detective leave. She held the door open for George, who greeted her with a nod of the head. He gave the same greeting to us and ambled up to the counter to order a loaf of white bread and six dinner rolls. He was dressed in his usual attire of farm overalls and heavy work boots.

George looked like what he was. A farmer.

A twinge niggled at the back of my head. Someone else had grown up on a farm. I'd been told that recently. I couldn't remember who.

"Are you going to tell your dad what happened?" Vicky asked.

"I don't want to worry him."

"No matter how old we get, it's always our parents' job to worry about us."

"True. But not this time."

"I'm thinking another trip to Muddle Harbor might be in order this afternoon," Vicky said.

"Why?"

"They have got to be behind this. If they kill tourism in Rudolph, visitors'll go there."

"If they kill tourism in Rudolph," I said, "visitors will stay home or go to the city. They come here because it's Christmas Town. Muddle Harbor has nothing to offer."

"You're assuming the Muddites are sensible people," Vicky said. "That's an incorrect assumption. It's time for a show of force. Let them know we know what they're up to. I'll pick you up at closing. I'll bring some of my nephews, too."

"Can't," I said. "I have to head out of town and get some stock for the shop."

"Leave it."

"Don't wanna."

She sighed. "I guess you're right. I don't think I could face another meal in that so-called café, anyway."

I was grateful she didn't pursue the topic of where I was going for the stock. Back in high school, Vicky had maintained that Alan and I were "soul mates" and "meant for each other." She'd been more upset than I when he and I went our separate ways after graduation. When I'd come back to Rudolph I could count on long, meaningful looks from her whenever his name was mentioned. Today, I did not need long, meaningful looks, nor did I need to find my own thoughts heading in that direction.

"What do you mean 'another meal'?" I said. "You didn't have anything."

"Simply being around all that grease was enough."

"Vicky!" We looked up at a shout from the counter. "Phone call."

She stood up. "Want another coffee?"

"Yes, please. And I'll have another scone, too. Make it one of those white-chocolate pecan ones this time." What the heck, after the night I'd had I needed a two-scone day.

Vicky took the phone, and her assistant put a mug of hot coffee and my treat in front of me. The coffee smelled wonderful and the plump scone was thick with nuts and glistening with white chocolate.

I picked up the cup and cradled it in my hands, enjoying the warmth.

Think, Merry, think.

So far everything that had happened—my float, the poisoned cookie, the hot dog cart explosion—seemed designed to interrupt the Christmas celebrations. But the attack on my garbage can (and I felt foolish simply thinking that) was personal. The only person it scared was me. All the neighbors thought I was a careless smoker.

So, the question I had to ask was:

Why me?

Assuming the fire was not a teenage prank, why was I being targeted? What was special about me?

Nothing at all.

That I'd left Rudolph and gone to the city for a number of years and then come back? That was common enough around here as to be normal. That I owned a shop on Jingle Bell Lane? Again, why me? There were lots of shops on Jingle Bell Lane.

I did own the shop next to Betty Thatcher's Gift Nook. Betty didn't like me or the goods I sold. But if Mrs. Claus's Treasures were forced to close and I headed out of town with my tail between my legs, even she would know there's nothing worse for business than boarded-up shops on Main Street.

Did she want to get rid of me so much that she'd risk her own business in the process?

I tried to imagine Betty creeping around my backyard with a bottle of accelerant and a match. It wasn't a hard image to conjure up. I'd keep my eye on Betty.

Meanwhile, I could think of nothing special or unusual about me here in Rudolph. I was such an established part of Christmas Town; my dad was Santa Claus.

A fist closed over my heart. My dad was Santa Claus.

Who represented Christmas more than Santa Claus? What better way to ruin Christmas in Rudolph than by getting to my dad? Had I been the target from the very beginning, with the disabling of my float, or was it something new with the fire last night? I'd told Vicky I wasn't going to say anything to Mom or Dad about the fire. I didn't want to worry them.

Should I?

Should I warn Dad that he might be next?

I'd scarcely given another thought to that text message supposedly from Eve out in Los Angeles. I was thinking about it now. The message had not been from Eve. Eve was supposed to be out of cell phone range for a few days. Did whoever had been responsible know that, or was it just a lucky (for them) coincidence? The message had to have been intended to get Dad out of town. Have him fly to LA, rush from one hospital to another. He would have been gone for days. Probably even miss Midnight Madness.

No Santa at Midnight Madness?

Unthinkable!

If Mom had gone with him, then there would have been no carolers, either. Rudolph's much-vaunted Midnight Madness celebration would have been nothing more than another small-town shopping night.

We'd all assumed the killer knew the Charles Dickens cookie was made for Nigel Pearce. But what if he (or she) hadn't known that? What if the killer didn't understand the Charles Dickens and *A Christmas Carol* reference? What if they thought the beautiful, obviously very special, cookie was for Santa?

And, having failed to kill Santa, or at the least make him

ill, had they lost their nerve and tried softer or more easily available targets?

Was Santa Claus still their focus?

I glanced at my watch. It was eight thirty. Mom and Dad would still be home. Santa was off duty today, and they were going to Rochester later, meeting friends at the theater for a matinee production of *The Nutcracker* and then going out to dinner.

They'd be safely out of town all day. I'd give this all a lot more thought and call Dad tomorrow morning.

My dad would know what to do.

At midday I took advantage of a lull in customer traffic to oh-so-casually ask Jackie what she'd done the previous evening. She'd left work at seven, and I wanted to know if she'd been with Kyle at the time the fire started in my garbage.

She peered at me through narrowed eyes. "Why do you want to know?"

"Just being friendly."

She still looked suspicious, and I decided I needed to work on my friendly, concerned–employer role. Jackie glanced at Crystal. Crystal shrugged. "I had dinner at my mom's. Exciting, eh?"

"Did Kyle go with you?"

"No. It was our regular one-Saturday-a-month dinner with Uncle Jerry and Aunt Beatrice and their horrid kids. Let's just say that Uncle Jerry and Kyle don't get on too well." She sniffed. "Uncle Jerry was a recruiting sergeant in the Marines. He thinks Kyle should have a regular job, preferably a bout of *semper fi* to sort him out. Uncle Jerry doesn't understand that Kyle is *artistic*. A job would destroy all that artistic talent."

It was news to me that Kyle was an artist.

"What does he do?" Crystal asked. "I've never seen any of Kyle's art around town."

Jackie gave her a look. "He's experimenting with different modes of expression, trying to find an exact fit."

Crystal snorted. I refrained from doing the same.

Jackie ignored her and spoke to me. "You'd think Uncle Jerry would concentrate on worrying about his own layabout of a son. My cousin Gerald will be in the papers someday, mark my words, having gone on a crime spree. They're hoping no one will notice Cousin Amanda has put on a lot of weight in the last couple of months. All of it around her middle and right where she didn't need it: her boobs. But, oh no, good old Uncle Jerry's too busy pointing out everyone else's faults to look under his nose. He could start by noticing that no one in the family really believes that story about how he . . ."

"We all have difficult families to deal with," Crystal interrupted.

Jackie glared at her. "Says Miss Perfect."

"I didn't want to take violin lessons, you know," Crystal retorted. "I hate the violin. But my mother said I had to have a well-rounded musical education, and voice isn't enough."

"Well, my mom . . ."

I knew I had some reason for asking Jackie what she'd done last night, but by now I'd forgotten what that might have been.

"I was so annoyed at being lectured by Uncle Jerry about

what's the matter with young people these days, all while Gerald was wondering how much cash he could take from his dad's wallet without being noticed and Amanda stuffed her face with the dinner rolls, I went straight to my apartment after dinner. Poor Kyle has enough to deal with, after his accident, that he doesn't need to hear me complaining." She sniffed. "He went out with a couple of his buddies, anyway."

"Isn't Kyle supposed to be recuperating?" Crystal said.

"A night with his friends would have done him some good," Jackie said, although her tone of voice indicated that she didn't believe it.

The chimes over the door tinkled, and the girls cut off their conversation. It didn't matter: I'd learned what I wanted to know. Kyle's whereabouts last night were unaccounted for. I hadn't entirely forgotten that of everyone in Rudolph, Kyle had the strongest reason to want to get rid of Nigel Pearce. Simmonds had told me that GHB was a street drug. I suppose anyone, even me, could buy street drugs if they wanted to, and probably in Rudolph, too. But of all the people I was beginning to think of as suspects, Kyle was the most likely to know his way around that world.

It was possible that he'd caused the fire in the hot dog cart himself and then came around in the night to do the same to my garbage. It would be worth asking Simmonds, on the sly, if Kyle had ever been suspected of arson. I'd never thought Kyle was particularly bright: maybe he liked watching the cops run about trying to solve the problem he'd given them, and decided to do it again. Although there was absolutely no reason I could think of for Kyle to want to get my dad out of town. That had not been a police matter. All these incidents were so disparate; I was beginning to wonder if they were related at all.

Rudolph was a quiet, peaceful place. Aside from our Christmas obsession, we were a perfectly normal little town in Upstate New York. It seemed unlikely that all the crazies (murderous and otherwise) would come out of the woodwork at the same time.

It was time, I decided, that someone asked Kyle directly if he was up to something.

I told Jackie and Crystal I was off to get some lunch. Did they want me to bring anything back from Vicky's? My treat.

Jackie gave me another one of her suspicious looks.

"You've both been working so hard," I said. "I'd like to show my appreciation."

Jackie might have muttered something along the lines of "then give us a raise," before asking for soup and a salad.

"Thanks, Merry. That's so nice of you," Crystal said. "I'd like a sandwich. Anything without meat will be fine."

"As long as I'm at the bakery anyway," I said, "why don't I pick up something for Kyle? I can drop it off at his place."

"Why would you do that?" Jackie said.

"Because he's been injured. My good deed of the week." I smiled at her. "Where does he live, anyway?"

She gave me an address on Elm Street. "Basement apartment. Ring the bell for 2B."

The bakery was busy and I didn't have a chance to say hi to Vicky. Which was just as well, as I didn't want her knowing what I was up to. She would insist on coming, and then the whole thing would turn into high drama. Of course,

I didn't have to tell her, but somehow I always blurted things out to Vicky whether I wanted to or not.

I chose a roast beef on rye for Kyle, thinking he'd like something manly. Then I threw in an order of gingerbread cookies. Maybe that would jog his memory about the fatal post-parade reception.

Elm Street is not the best part of town. Most of the houses are old, many are falling into disrepair. But even here the Christmas spirit is strong, and I noticed trees and eaves trimmed with lights, and wreaths hanging on many doors. Kyle's building was broken into apartments, judging by the row of buzzers by the front entrance. I pressed 2B and waited.

"What?" said a tinny voice.

"Hi, Kyle. It's Merry Wilkinson. I've brought you some lunch."

"Why?"

"I thought you'd like something fresh."

"Leave it on the step."

I hadn't considered that. "I wouldn't want it to get stolen." Suppose he wasn't dressed? Suppose he was entertaining a woman other than Jackie? Suddenly this didn't seem like such a good idea.

The buzzer sounded, and I pushed my doubts aside and opened the door.

The hall was full of the scent of old grease, stale tobacco smoke, and Lysol. The single bulb above the entrance was dim and little light came in through the only window. I found the stairwell and carefully picked my way down into the gloom. There were two doors. 1B and 2B. I knocked, and Kyle grunted, "It's open."

I'd been expecting a filthy dump, but the apartment was moderately tidy. The furniture had been fashionable in the '70s but it looked clean. Kyle was relaxing in a La-Z-Boy, feet up, bottle of beer and full ashtray on a side table. Fortunately, he was dressed. A hockey game was playing on the giant flat-screen TV mounted on the wall. I glanced quickly around. Maybe he was an artist after all. A stack of canvases were piled against one wall, paint and brushes were laid out on a table, and an easel was set up by the high window. I sniffed, trying to be unobtrusive, but couldn't detect the odors of paint or cleaning supplies.

Did artists get artist's block?

Kyle dragged his attention away from the TV, dropped his legs, and straightened the chair. "Thanks, Merry."

I carried the bakery bag into the kitchen and put it on the table. Dishes were piled in the sink, but they didn't look as though they'd been there more than a few days. Except for a case of beer bottles, the countertops were clear.

I walked back to the living room. "How are you feeling?"

"Okay," he said.

His goatee had been shaved off and his eyebrows were singed. Otherwise his face was clear.

"You had a lucky escape," I said.

He shuddered. "Yeah."

"Do you know what happened?"

He shook his head. "Dan told me the cops have taken the grill away. Just as well. I don't want to go near the freakin' thing ever again." He reached for a pack of cigarettes, pulled one out. He lifted a disposable lighter in front of him. His hand shook so badly he had to flick it several times to get a flame. He cringed as he held fire to the cigarette. He took a deep drag. "Let me tell you, Merry, it'll be a long time before I ever have another barbeque." He rubbed his free hand over his chin and closed his eyes.

"I hope you'll be feeling better soon," I said.

"I'm fine. I just keep thinking about it, that's all," he said.

"Enjoy your lunch." I let myself out.

If Kyle Lambert had come around to my place last night and set my garbage on fire, I'd grow a goatee myself.

I was back to square one.

Crystal left at five, and at six I closed the shop. Jackie headed out to administer to Kyle. I hurried home to shower and change for my dinner date at Alan's.

Was it a date? I still didn't know.

I studied my wardrobe. Definitely not something sexy, in case he thought he was inviting a client around for a business dinner. Then again, not too businesslike as it was a Sunday night in Upstate New York. On the other hand, I didn't want to look like a country hick, either.

I settled on jeans with an unadorned blue T-shirt and a cropped black leather jacket. I wrapped a blue scarf around my neck, and added dangling silver earrings. At the door, I pulled on calf-high boots with a one-inch heel. And then I ruined the carefully crafted effect by tossing on my new winter coat. Alan's place was in the country and more snow was expected tonight. I knew better than to go even a short distance out of town unprepared for some sort of car emergency.

"You look very nice, too," I said to Mattie. I'd given him a good brushing after I'd showered, washed my hair, and dressed. Perhaps I should have brushed him before doing all that, as I'd then had to pick strands of long tan fur off my clothes and reapply the lipstick and blush he'd licked off in his appreciation of my attentions.

I hadn't had many chances to take Mattie out in the car, but the couple of times I had he'd seemed to enjoy it. Tonight, he leapt into the backseat when I held the door open for him. I owned a Honda Civic. I might need to get a bigger car when this dog finally stopped growing. If he ever did.

I'd been to Alan's house before, sourcing products for the store. He lived about fifteen minutes outside of Rudolph, heading inland from Lake Ontario. His property was deep in the woods, beautifully quiet and private. He lived in a nineteenth-century stone farmhouse, which I'd never been inside. He did all his work in a detached workshop at the end of the long curving dirt road that served as his driveway.

Snow began to fall as Mattie and I headed out of town. The bright lights of Rudolph faded behind us, and the early winter dark swallowed us up. My headlights picked out falling, swirling flakes. Trees, skeletal branches heavy with snow, closed around us. We only passed a handful of cars, but Mattie got very excited when he saw the headlights approaching. I kept an eye on my mileage indicator, counting off the distance until the turn toward Alan's house. It wasn't well marked, and I could easily miss it in the dark.

I slowed, and turned in. The road had been recently plowed, but fresh, undisturbed snow was beginning to cover it again. The path was lined by giant old oaks, maples, and tall pines heavy with snow. The trees fell back as I drove into the clearing of Alan's well-maintained property. Warm yellow lights were on throughout the house, and strands of welcoming Christmas lights, red and green, trimmed the porch railing and the eaves. I felt myself smiling. What a perfect place for Santa's number one toymaker to live and work.

All the lights were off in the workshop building. I pulled in beside it. We were going to be loading boxes into my car, so I wanted to be close. I switched off the engine, climbed out of the car, and let Mattie out. I didn't want him running off into the night woods in pursuit of little animals to play with, so I attached the leash to his collar. The front door of the house opened, and Alan stood there, a long, thin silhouette outlined in a blaze of light. He lifted one hand in greeting and began to come down the steps.

Off to my left, something caught my eye. Light where there shouldn't be any. I looked closer. A red glow flickered behind the window of the workshop. It disappeared and I thought my eyes had been playing tricks.

Then I saw it again, larger and brighter. As I watched, the light steadied, and then it began to grow. Shades of yellow joined the red.

Alan's workshop was on fire.

Chapter 20

"Fire!" I screamed. "Alan, the workshop!"

Mattie barked.

Alan was beside me in a moment. I pointed. Flames were clearly visible now, licking at the window frame.

With a shout, Alan ran for the building.

"Don't go in," I yelled. The door was on the opposite side of the workshop from the now-visible flames, but there was no way of knowing what else might be happening inside.

"Fire extinguisher," he yelled over his shoulder. "Kitchen."

I ran. On the outside Alan's house was all weathered stone and freshly painted gingerbread trim, but the inside was open spaces and sleek modern lines. The front door opened directly onto a big, open-plan kitchen. I had no trouble locating the small fire extinguisher attached to the wall next to the gas stove. I wrenched the extinguisher out of its brackets and dashed outside. Mattie was running around the yard, barking. I'd dropped the leash without realizing it. Right now, I could only hope he wouldn't run off into the woods and get snagged on something.

I ran into the workshop; waves of white smoke washed over me as they fought their way toward fresh night air. I coughed and my eyes stung. It was impossible to see much in the dark and the smoke, but I could see that the entire building wasn't on fire. Not yet. The room was warm, but not frighteningly hot.

Alan was beating at the flames with a blanket. With a shout, I handed him the extinguisher. He tossed aside the blanket, aimed the extinguisher at the heart of the fire, and sprayed. The blaze died without putting up a fight. We'd gotten it in time.

The planks of planed, golden wood stacked neatly beneath the window were a couple of inches thick, and not inclined to burn easily. Some smaller pieces on top had caught fire and acted like kindling, giving the blaze time to grow and to build. A few more minutes and Alan might well have lost his workshop, all his raw wood, and the toys and woodwork both unfinished and ready to be shipped. He tossed the empty extinguisher to one side and approached the smoldering debris. His eyes were red and a streak of black ash ran across one cheek. He coughed.

"Careful," I said, trying not to breathe in smoke. I sniffed the air, but I detected nothing but the familiar scent of woodsmoke, although thicker and much heavier than from a cheerfully burning fireplace. Mattie had followed me into the workshop. He let out a mighty sneeze and whined. He pressed against my leg and I gave him a comforting pat. The comfort, as much for me as for him.

Alan picked up a long, thin piece of wood, and with it he stirred ashes and burned scraps of wood, checking for the remains of live embers.

"What the heck?" he said as he uncovered the scorched remains of a scrap of red fabric. Using the pole, he lifted the cloth, brought it close to his nose, and sniffed. He turned and gave me a look.

"Gas."

I sucked in a breath without thinking, and choked. Through my cough, I managed to say, "You think this was deliberate?" I glanced around the workshop. A woodstove stood against the back wall, but it was dark and cold. An electric heater was not even plugged in.

"Yes," he said. "I do." He pointed to the broken window and the floor beneath. A rock, a small, ordinary gray rock, about the size of my fist, lay there, surrounded by shards of glass. "Someone deliberately broke that window. I heard a sound ten minutes or so ago, didn't pay it any mind. I hear lots of sounds in the woods at night. And then, it would seem, they tossed in a burning cloth."

"Someone tried to burn down your workshop?"

"They didn't try very hard, though. Just one cloth—might have gone out if those loose wood chips hadn't caught. If they really wanted to burn it down, why not spread gas over the exterior walls? The building's old and all wood, it would have gone up fast enough."

"Is there much damage?" I studied a row of toy soldiers and trains on the table closest to the window. The paint was blistered and the wood blackening, but they seemed to be intact.

"That's the drying table," Alan said. "I'll give them a good look, but I suspect I'll have to throw most of them out. I'm sorry, Merry, but those are the ones I had ready for you. I figured you could help me box them up after dinner. Some might be saved, if I add a fresh coat of paint. I'm so sorry," he said again.

"Don't apologize," I said. "You have to call Detective Simmonds. This is part of a pattern, Alan. Strange things have been happening around here. You could have been killed if the fire got out of control and you tried to put it out yourself."

He gave me a grin that didn't reach his eyes. The tip of his nose was gray with smudged ash. "Looks like you saved my life, Merry."

"I had good timing, that's all."

Alan grabbed a flashlight hanging on a hook next to the door beside an assortment of raincoats and umbrellas and a battered snow shovel, and went outside. I bent to grab Mattie's leash, and the dog and I followed Alan around the workshop to the side of the building where the fire had apparently begun.

Under the window, snow was churned up, but some boot prints were clearly visible. Mattie strained at the leash to get closer to give it all a good sniff. "I'd better put the dog in the car," I said. "Looks like we have a crime scene here."

Mattie didn't want to come, but I dragged him away. I opened the back door of the car and indicated he should jump up. He didn't want to but he did. Despite what was happening around us, I had a moment of pleasure at the thought that some of his training was starting to pay off.

"You wait here," I said, unfastening the leash. "I'll be right back."

I stuffed the leash into my coat pocket and returned to where Alan was balanced on his haunches, examining the prints in the snow under the window. "See anything?" I said.

He got to his feet and pointed to the double row of prints. In places they crisscrossed each other, but it was clear that some were coming, and some were heading away.

"I'm no Sherlock Holmes," he said, "but that looks to me like a clear trail. Did you see a car or anything when you came up the drive, Merry?"

"No. And no tire tracks, either. The snow was undisturbed."

"Which means our arsonist walked in."

"From where?" I asked

"That's the question, isn't it? He might have parked on an access road and hiked in. Or . . ."

His voice trailed away as he took off at a brisk pace across his yard, keeping himself about two feet to the left of the boot prints.

"Don't, Alan," I said. "Let the police handle it."

He turned and faced me. The blue eyes that I had once thought as clear and light as a summer sky were heavy with storm clouds. "I can't chance them getting away, Merry. You wait here, and tell the cops where I've gone." He reached out and touched my shoulder. The touch so light I scarcely felt it. "Get in the house, lock the doors. Take the dog with you."

"Mattie isn't exactly an attack dog," I said.

"No. But he is a dog. And a smart one." Then Alan turned and walked away. In a few steps he was swallowed up by the night woods. I glanced back at my car. Mattie's ears were up and his curious face stared out at me from the back window. I looked at Alan's house. The front door stood open, the way he'd left it when he came out to greet me. While we were inside the workshop, fighting the fire, the arsonist might have gone into the house. Was he or she in there now? Waiting for me?

I shoved my hand into the deep pocket of my coat, searching for my phone to call the police. My fingers closed on a square of paper, and I pulled out the card Diane Simmonds had given me this morning. I could call 911, ask them to contact her, but I figured I'd be better off doing it directly. Who knows when a message might get to her if she was off duty? I flipped the card over and punched the handwritten numbers into the phone.

"Diane Simmonds," said the cool voice.

I told her where I was and what had happened. I surprised myself at how calm my voice sounded.

"I'm on my way," she said. "I'll call the state police to meet me there. Do not attempt to locate the suspect yourself, Merry."

"Okay," I said. I wasn't attempting to locate anyone. But Alan was. I didn't say so before I hung up.

I glanced once again at the house and the open front door, spilling welcoming light into the yard. I wasn't conscious of making a decision, but I broke into a trot after Alan. Safety in numbers, and all that. I did spare a thought for Mattie, but decided he'd be better waiting in the car. He'd be no help to me and I'd only have something else to worry about while we stumbled around in the night woods. I found the flashlight app on my phone and flicked it on. Then I melted into the thick, dark, snowy woods. The beam of light from my phone was small but powerful as it illuminated the ground in front of me. I'd entered a path. At least three feet wide, it cut neatly through the woods. I could clearly see the boot prints we were following, Alan's larger ones running along beside. Were they from a man or a woman? Hard to tell. They were average-sized snow boots, strong and heavy, with a thick tread. They might be those of a woman with larger feet than normal, or a man with smaller ones.

"I told you to stay behind," a voice said out of the darkness.

I smothered a yelp. "I thought you might need help."

"Come on" was all Alan said.

The path got narrower as we walked, and we had to go in single file, staying close to the prints laid down earlier.

"What's at the other end of this trail?" I whispered. All was dark and quiet. No traffic from the road and no sound from wild animals, either.

"My closest neighbor. Fergus Cartwright."

"You mean our mayor?"

"The very one. The people who lived here before him had kids and the kids loved to come to visit me in the work-shop, so their parents kept this trail clear."

Fergus's house wasn't far away, and before long, thin streams of yellow light slipped through the trees. Alan signaled to me to stop at the edge of the wide, snow-covered lawn. It, and the parking area in front of the double garage, were brightly lit.

Snow was falling heavily now, not fat Christmassy flakes, but hard pellets mixed with ice. I pulled my collar up and buried my hand in my pockets. Somewhere along the way, I'd lost my gloves. Alan, who'd stepped out of his house expecting only to welcome a guest, was protected by nothing but a thick wool sweater.

Fergus's house was modern, a large building of wood and glass with a wide wraparound porch and a double garage. A stone chimney broke through the roof at the front of the house. Lights were on inside, both upstairs and down, and smoke trailed from the chimney.

The double garage doors were closed and a single vehicle was parked in the circle of light thrown off the porch. A black Suburban. I sucked in a breath.

"What is it?" Alan said.

"I recognize that car. Give me a sec." I slipped through the trees until I could clearly see the back of the vehicle and read the license plate: SUEANNE1.

I whispered to Alan, "Sue-Anne Morrow's here. I recognize her car."

Illuminated only by my iPhone app, his eyes shone in the dark. "Did you call the cops?"

"Simmonds is coming, and she's sending the state police."

"Call her back," he said. "Then give me the phone."

I placed the call and handed the phone to Alan. He spoke quickly, gave the address. And then he hung up.

All was quiet. We couldn't even hear traffic from the road.

"We can't wait," Alan said. "I have to go in. See what's going on. Fergus might be in danger."

"I'm coming with you."

"I'd rather you weren't, Merry, but I don't suppose I can stop you?"

"No," I said.

So, it was Sue-Anne after all. Sue-Anne trying to ruin Christmas in Rudolph. Sue-Anne who'd poisoned the Charles Dickens cookie, who'd tried to burn down Alan's workshop, set fire to my garbage can, disabled my float, tried to get my dad out of town.

I almost slapped myself across the head as I remembered who'd been raised on a farm. Sue-Anne's husband had told me she had. Hardscrabble, he'd called it. In that case, it was entirely possible Sue-Anne would know how to disable George's tractor.

"Let's go," Alan said. "Stay behind me."

He marched boldly across the snowy lawn and up the front steps, making no attempt to be discreet or stay hidden. I ran along behind him, my heart beating rapidly.

We hesitated on the porch. From inside the house came the sound of voices. Low, angry voices.

Alan didn't bother to knock. He simply turned the door-knob and walked into Fergus Cartwright's house, calling, "Anyone home?" as if this were a regular Sunday visit. I scurried after him.

Perhaps the first thing I noticed was that the house was not decorated for Christmas. No lovingly adorned fresh tree, no carefully preserved family heirlooms, handed down from generation to generation, no red and white flowers, no handcrafted arrangements. Not even a poinsettia or a Christmas cactus.

No wreath had hung on the front door. No greeting cards were arranged on the mantle. That was almost tantamount to sacrilege in Rudolph. I knew that Fergus's wife had left him once their kids were grown and out of the house. Still, he could make *some* effort!

Fergus's living room might have come directly from the props room at *Jennifer's Lifestyle* magazine for a featured spread on the modern western home. Burnt sienna walls, leather furniture, paintings of horses galloping across the open prairie, a fire burning in a stone fireplace so large you could probably roast an ox, if you were so inclined. And, like in an old-fashioned western, Sue-Anne Morrow and Fergus Cartwright stood in the center of the room staring each other down, legs apart, feet planted.

Fergus faced us. Surprise crossed his face when we came in. He saw Alan first, and then me. "What do you think you're doing here, walking into my home like this?" he said. "Get out."

Sue-Anne whirled around. She smiled at us and seemed almost pleased to see us. I thought that a bit of nerve. "Come on in," she said. "I'm glad you're here. I was telling Fergus that his time as mayor is finished. Let's not drag this out into a long, expensive campaign that will only divide the town. It's past time for Fergus to quit."

"Never," His Honor growled. "Rudolph is my town."

"You don't even live in Rudolph," she said. "Look at this place. You'd obviously rather be on a ranch in Montana."

I strained my ears for the sound of sirens, but outside all was quiet. Where were those blasted cops?

"Sue-Anne," Alan said, "come with me. We can talk about this another time."

"I don't want to talk about it another time," she said. "I'm here now. Trying to talk some reason into this old coot."

Alan walked slowly across the room, across the huge, exquisite Navajo rug that, if it was authentic, must have cost in the tens of thousands. He kept his eyes on Fergus, but he reached out and placed his hand on the woman's arm. "Come with me, Sue-Anne, please," he said in a low, firm voice.

Wasn't it Fergus who needed to be taken out of danger? I was about to yell at him, tell him to run, find cover. Who knew what Sue-Anne might have hidden under her coat? I opened my mouth, but no warning shout came out, because I had noticed two things.

Sue-Anne's fashionable size-six boots had pointed toes and stiletto heels.

Fergus's head and shoulders were damp with melting snow.

"No," Fergus said. "It's time to settle this. Here and now. This is my town. Mine. People like you need to understand that. I'm the only one who can keep Rudolph strong and prosperous. Folks need to be reminded sometimes."

"Absolutely," Alan said. "You have my vote, Fergus. Yours, too. Right, Merry?" He threw me a glance, jerking his head toward the door behind us.

Sue-Anne looked as though she were going to argue. But then I saw comprehension slowly cross her face. "Uh, yeah. Okay," she said.

"Folks around here think I'm Noel Wilkinson's puppet," Fergus continued. I doubt he'd even heard Alan say whom he'd be voting for. "Santa Claus indeed. If only that blasted Noel would get out of my way, everyone would see that I'm the power in this town. No one else. I can break it. And only I can fix it."

Alan and Sue-Anne had been backing up slowly, leaving me closest to Fergus. The mayor's eyes widened, and then they focused and he saw us.

He lunged for the fireplace and grabbed an iron poker. Alan shouted a warning. Sue-Anne screamed. Fergus held the poker, blackened and dusted with cold gray ash, aloft.

"You!" He turned on me. "You're as bad as your father. Couldn't mind your own business, could you? Had to keep nosing around, asking questions." His eyes were wild and mad. He charged.

"Merry!" Alan screamed.

Sue-Anne just screamed.

I ducked. I tried to run, but my foot caught the edge of the Navajo rug, and I went down, landing hard on my butt. Fergus closed on me, the poker raised high. My hand found something in my pocket. I didn't think about what I was doing as I pulled it out and whipped it upward. It sliced through the air with a hiss. The metal clip on Mattie's leash got His Honor hard in his left cheek. He howled and staggered backward. He dropped the poker and lifted a hand to the wound, shocked at the sudden pain.

Then Alan was on him and Fergus went down.

Outside, an engine rumbled, and bright lights poured through the living room windows.

"Go see who that is, Merry," Alan said, his voice calm, in control. "I'll stay here."

"Welcome. You're just in time," I said as I opened the front door.

"What's happening?" Diane Simmonds asked.

"We're all in the living room," I said. "Come on in."

She gave me a long look, and then pushed past me.

Fergus was on the floor, Alan standing over him, armed with the poker. Sue-Anne was curled up on the couch, weeping noisily.

"It was him?" Simmonds said to me. "Fergus?"

"We think so. We followed boot prints from the site of the fire directly here. When we confronted Fergus, he suggested he was responsible for all the other awful stuff that's been happening."

"Including the murder of Nigel Pearce?" she asked.

I shook my head. "That didn't come up."

Simmonds pulled handcuffs off her belt. Alan stepped away, and she quickly and efficiently cuffed the groaning mayor.

Chapter 21

Russ Durham arrived seconds behind Simmonds. He burst into Fergus's house the moment the detective snapped on the cuffs and hauled Fergus to his feet, giving him the expected warning.

"It's my town. Mine!" His Honor bellowed as state police burst through the doors. Long after the excitement was over they'd finally showed up. Accident on the highway, they said with somber shakes of their bald heads—terrible stuff.

"Whatever," Diane Simmonds had said.

"Want to tell me what happened?" Russ Durham asked me.

"Why are you here?" I said. The minute Diane had the cuffs on Fergus, my legs had given way. I would have fallen to the floor had not Alan grabbed my arm and led me to a chair.

"A good reporter knows everything that's going on in his patch." Russ lowered his voice and gave me a grin, slow and private. "I was listening to the state police radio. Your name was mentioned, Merry. How could I not respond?"

"Respond?" I said. "In pursuit of a story? Or to help me?"

"I can't say I forgot about being a newspaper man. But I was worried about you."

"Thanks," I said. "I think."

We watched as Fergus was hustled out the door. He was handcuffed, escorted by cops, followed by a stern-faced Detective Simmonds. "It wasn't my fault!" His Honor protested. "He had a heart attack or something. How was I to know he had a bad heart?"

"To whom are you referring, Mr. Cartwright?" Simmonds asked.

"That ridiculous Englishman, of course. Now, you seem like a sensible young lady, I'm sure you'll understand. This is my town. People were forgetting that. I had to remind them, didn't I?"

"Why?" I shouted. I couldn't help myself. "Why? Nigel Pearce was going to do a feature on Rudolph. It's what we've been wanting for so long. To be officially recognized as America's Christmas Town. But you killed him. You almost killed Christmas!"

Fergus blinked. "Merry, dear. You'll understand. You must know what it's like living under Noel Wilkinson's shadow." Simmonds stopped walking. She let the man talk to me. I'd noticed Russ slip a digital recorder out of his pocket and press buttons.

"Any problems in Rudolph and everyone rushes to ask Noel what to do," Fergus said. "They forget that I'm the mayor, not Noel. I showed them, didn't I? I gave them problems, and I solved them, too."

"You killed a man," I said.

Fergus shrugged. "That was an accident. He was only supposed to get sick. It was Noel who'd written to that fancy foreign magazine suggesting they write something about Rudolph."

"I didn't know that," I said.

Fergus snorted. "Noel said it would be good publicity for Rudolph but our so-called Santa Claus would have ended up getting all the credit. I had to show them, didn't I, that Rudolph doesn't need Noel Wilkinson anymore. I'm in charge here. I am!" As he spoke, Fergus's voice began to rise and then he was screaming. The cops tightened their grip on his arm and at a nod from Simmonds they led him away, yelling at the top of his lungs that he was in charge.

Sue-Anne Morrow was still rolled up into a ball on the leather couch. "Is he gone?" she asked as Fergus's voice faded away.

"Yes," Russ said.

She uncurled herself. Her hair was a tumbled mess, and instinctively she began to rearrange it. Russ held out a hand, and she accepted it. He guided her to her feet. She plastered on a smile.

"Goodness me. Wasn't that odd?"

"Looks like the field's wide open for you, Sue-Anne," I said.

"I can't so much as bear to think of my election prospects at a time like this," she said. "Such a tragedy. Ambition taken to extremes." She shook her head. "I'm far too upset to drive myself home. Russ, be a dear."

"You can come with me, Mrs. Morrow," Simmonds said. "We can talk in the car." The detective turned to me. Alan was standing on one side of me, Russ on the other. It was a lovely, safe place to be. "I want to hear what brought you two here tonight, but that can wait until tomorrow. They're taking Fergus into the Rudolph police station now and I want to interview him while he's still in the mood for true confessions. Can you come down to my office first thing in the morning?"

"Yes," Alan and I chorused.

"Do you want a ride back to town, Merry?" she asked.

"I'll take her," Russ said quickly.

We all went outside. Lights from the cruisers threw swirling beams of red and blue into the steadily falling snow.

I shivered and buried my hands in my pockets. I'd lost Mattie's leash. Taken away as evidence.

"You okay, Merry?" Russ and Alan said in unison.

"I'm fine. I guess it's all starting to hit me now. Imagine, Fergus Cartwright, of all people."

"Come on, Merry," Russ said, "My car's over there. Catch you later, Anderson."

"Mattie," I said. "I left the dog in my car. I'm okay to drive."

I set off at a trot. Poor Mattie would be frantic, locked in the car while police cars screamed up the road and people shouted and wept. The dark woods closed around me. Behind me, a light came on, illuminating the trail, and I didn't bother to turn my flashlight app on. Two sets of footsteps followed me.

I burst into the clearing at Alan's house. Everything seemed so calm and peaceful. The fresh snow, a circle of welcoming yellow light spilling out of the house, the scent of woodsmoke. Overhead the clouds were drifting away, and a bright white moon was coming out.

I ran to my car, expecting to see my dog frantically trying to scratch his way out, trying to speed to my side. Instead, the car was as peaceful as the rest of the scene. I peered in the back window. The Saint Bernard puppy was nothing but a ball of tan and brown fur, curled up, nose to tail, breathing heavily, fast asleep.

"Oh," I said.

Russ and Alan each peeked over one of my shoulders.

"He looks okay to me," Russ said.

"Me, too," Alan said.

"If you're sure you're okay to drive," Russ said. "I'll follow you back to town."

I glanced at Alan. Weren't we supposed to be having dinner?

"Looks like," the toymaker said, "I'll be working through the night. I need to check over the stock for your store, Merry. I should be able to salvage some of it. I can rearrange my other deliveries so you're covered."

"But . . ." I said.

"Let's go, then," Russ said. He walked around my car. Put his hand on the passenger side door. "Merry can drop me back at my car. I'll follow her to town, make sure she gets settled in okay. Shock can be delayed, you know."

"Good night, Merry," Alan said. He turned and walked across his yard, heading for the workshop. I wanted to call out. To tell him I didn't care about the blasted toys. To tell him that he was as much in danger of delayed shock as I was. That he needed someone to watch him tonight, too.

He opened the workshop door and disappeared inside. A light came on.

"Ready?" Russ said.

"Ready," I replied.

Mattie woke up when the doors opened. He greeted Russ with a slobbery kiss.

Chapter 22

Monday was a quiet day at the shop in terms of customers, but nothing close to quiet when it came to locals wanting to hear all about the dramatic arrest of Fergus Cartwright.

As the day progressed, the tale grew in the telling. The forest on fire, a terrifying standoff between His Honor and a SWAT team, Sue-Anne Morrow held hostage with an explosives belt strapped to her chest.

Jackie was supposed to have the day off, but she came in shortly after opening, to tell me she'd help out if I needed time to recover.

My mom and dad were next through the doors, the visit so important Mom had risen before noon. "You might have been killed!" she screeched, wrapping me in a hug.

"But I wasn't," I said, very sensibly.

Dad shook his head so hard his beard quivered. "Fergus. Of all people" was all he said.

I'd phoned my parents when I got up this morning and let them know what had happened. Dad had been so shocked he'd been without words.

I'd dropped Russ off at Fergus's house, where he picked up his car. He followed me back to town and parked on the road while I put the Civic in the garage. He'd met me at the door at the bottom of the stairs. "I'll see you up," he said.

I hadn't protested. Shock was beginning to settle in. All the way back to town, I'd had the image of Fergus with that iron poker held high, coming toward me. Russ had settled me at the kitchen table, grabbed a throw off the big chair in the living room where I usually curled up to read, placed it around my shoulders, filled the kettle, and plugged it in. He then filled Mattie's food and water bowls and made hot sweet tea when the kettle was ready.

He placed the steaming mug in my hand and said, "Drink."

I drank, and immediately felt a bit better.

He sat on the couch and watched me drink the tea. Neither of us said anything until I'd finished.

When I had, he got to his feet. "I'll get you settled into bed."

I gave him a smile. "Don't you have a story to write or something?"

"Story can wait."

"I don't think so. Thanks for taking care of me, but I'm okay now."

He looked at me for a long time. He reached out and touched my cheek. "If you're sure?"

"I'm sure, Russ."

I walked him downstairs to see him out. When I got back to the kitchen, Mattie had knocked over his water bowl. I'd wiped it up, refilled the bowl, and fell into bed to sleep a long, dreamless sleep.

Now I assured my parents I was fine, told Jackie that as long as she was here she could work today, as I had to be at the police station later to make my statement.

Sue-Anne made the rounds, ensuring everyone knew we would be in good hands during the temporary absence of a mayor. With much girlish giggling and waving of hands, she halfheartedly tried to quell the rumor that she'd fought Fergus in a life-and-death battle of unarmed combat. Such was her humility that the story only grew and spread.

She popped into my shop to superficially thank me for saving her.

I left Jackie to mind the store and went to the police station.

I was shown into a small but comfortable room with sub-dued lighting, nice furniture, a colorful painting of a field of sunflowers hanging on the wall, and several boxes of tissues scattered throughout. Not what I'd imagined a police interview room to look like.

Simmonds noticed me admiring my surroundings. "We talk to the perps elsewhere."

She took a seat and switched on a tape recorder. A tall man in the uniform of the state police crossed his arms and leaned up against the wall.

It didn't take long for me to give my statement. I simply recited what had happened last night. Arriving at Alan's, spotting the fire, putting it out, following the trail to Fergus's house. Simmonds thanked me for my time. I left and walked back to my shop. The sun had come out and the sky was a brilliant blue. Everyone seemed in a good mood, smiling and waving and exchanging season's greetings. I glanced into Vicky's bakery to see that almost every table was full and there was a line at the counter. People were popping in and out of shops, carrying laden shopping bags.

The convenience store had copies of today's *Gazette* prominently displayed. "Caught!" declared the bold headline, above a picture of Fergus with his head down, his hands behind his back, being loaded into a cruiser by two stern-faced cops.

I walked past Mrs. Claus's Treasures and went home.

Mattie and I were heading for the park when I became aware of a car pulling up beside me. Diane Simmonds parked and got out. "Mind if I join you?" she said.

"Not at all."

She exchanged effusive greetings with Mattie and then she fell into step beside me, the dog trotting happily between us. The park was an expanse of sparkling snow. Near the bandstand a man was helping three kids build a snowman, and a couple holding hands were gazing out over the ice-tossed bay.

"Christmas in Christmas Town," I said. "And all is right with the world."

"You truly love it here, don't you?" Simmonds said.

"I guess I do at that. I followed my dream to Manhattan. I found the dream and I lived it. But like all dreams it didn't last, and I know I'm very lucky to have been able to come home again."

"You deserve to know what Cartwright had to say, before

a hastily summoned lawyer arrived and managed to convince him to shut up."

"Did he confess to killing Nigel?"

"He confessed to putting the drugs onto the cookie, but says he didn't intend to kill anyone. He'd been told that GHB was a common street drug. He only wanted to make the man sick and thus not say nice things about Rudolph in his magazine. I suspect that's the truth. What Fergus didn't know is that Pearce was on an anti-insomnia drug that reacts very badly with GHB, and that he would go for a walk in the park alone. Fergus also told us he sabotaged your tractor, as you suspected, and added a couple of splashes of lighter fluid to the edges of the hot dog cart when Dan's attention was momentarily diverted."

I remembered the bright yellow stain I'd seen on Fergus's shirt that day. Mustard.

"He placed those anonymous calls to the newspaper. He's rather proud of that. Thinks he was very clever disguising his voice. He also set fire to your garbage can," she said. "He wants me to tell you that he didn't plan on anyone getting hurt."

"Why? Why on earth would he do that?" I said. Mattie whined at the tone of my voice.

"He was afraid of losing the next election. Apparently some people want Noel Wilkinson to run again. Fergus decided to be proactive and try to discredit your dad. First, by making you appear to spoil the parade, then spoiling the visit of the magazine reporter who'd come at Noel's invitation. He had some crazy idea of ruining everything so he could rush in and save the day. Unfortunately, he seems to have better ideas for doing damage than fixing things, and found himself, once again, being helped out by your dad. So he hoped that by threatening you with the garbage fire, he'd distract your father. He said he tried to get your parents out of town, but that hadn't worked."

Fergus's daughter lived in Los Angeles. It wouldn't be a stretch to think that she knew Eve there, and she told Fergus my sister was going into the mountains for a few days, giving Fergus the idea of sending Dad on a wild-goose chase to California.

"And Alan's workshop?"

"He'd overheard people talking about Rudolph's toy-maker and how popular he was with visitors." Simmonds pulled her collar higher around her neck.

"What happens now?" I asked.

"Whether or not Fergus intended to kill Nigel Pearce doesn't matter one whit to me. The man died as a direct result of Fergus's actions. He's been charged with murder."

We'd reached the park. We stood in silence, watching the happy family building their snowman.

"I'd better get back," Detective Simmonds said. "We've a ton of paperwork to do."

"I appreciate you telling me," I said.

She bent over and gave Mattie a hearty rub behind the ears. "You just take care of this big guy."

Mattie voiced his agreement.

Jackie left a few minutes before closing, but not until she told me she was thinking of breaking things off with Kyle. He was getting too needy, she said. Expecting her to rush around to his apartment to bring him something for lunch, and then come when she got off work and cook his dinner.

She was beginning to think, she told me, he was malingering. The doctor had sent him home after all of one hour in the ER, and it had now been three days since the exploding barbeque incident. His eyebrows were even growing back.

I refrained from rolling my eyes.

On her way out, she held the door for Alan. He carried a large cardboard box.

"Where do you want this?" he said. "I've more in the truck."

"Put that one on the counter, and I'll unpack it right here. The others can go in the back room."

In all he brought in three large boxes full of wooden train sets and toy soldiers. We unpacked them together and arranged the toys on shelves. "You've done a wonderful job," I said. "You must have worked all night."

"I did," he said. "Because you needed them."

I turned and faced him. "Thank you," I said.

I might have said something more, but a knock on the door had us both jumping.

Russ Durham was peering in at us, grinning.

I hurried to unlock the door.

"Hope I'm not interrupting anything," he said in that slow, sexy Southern accent.

"No!" Alan and I chorused.

"I'd like a statement for the paper from you, Merry. What it felt like to confront a vicious killer. That sort of thing."

"It felt terrifying," I said. "But you can't quote me. I have no comment." I've always wanted to say that.

"Come on, give me a tidbit, anything I can use. You're finished for the day, why don't we talk about it over dinner."

"I'm . . ." I said.

"That's a great idea," Alan said. "And as I was there to also confront the vicious killer, I'll come along. I'd be happy to give you some good quotes. You don't mind, do you, Russ?" He smiled.

"Mind? Why would I mind?" Russ smiled back.

I glanced between the two men, each of them more handsome than the other.

Why did I feel like I was playing tug-of-war with Mattie? And this time, I was the ball.

It was Christmas in Rudolph, and all was right with the world once again. I might even have time to figure out what on earth I was going to do with not one, but two, delightful admirers.

M2G0610

M7G0610

WELL-CRAFTED MYSTERIES
FROM BERKLEY PRIME CRIME

- **Earlene Fowler** Don't miss these Agatha Award–winning quilting mysteries featuring Benni Harper.

- **Monica Ferris** These *USA Today* bestselling Needle-craft Mysteries include free knitting patterns.

- **Laura Childs** Her Scrapbooking Mysteries offer tips to satisfy the most die-hard crafters.

- **Maggie Sefton** These popular Knitting Mysteries come with knitting patterns and recipes.

- **Lucy Lawrence** These brilliant Decoupage Mysteries involve cutouts, glue, and varnish.

- **Elizabeth Lynn Casey** The Southern Sewing Circle Mysteries are filled with friends, southern charm—and murder.

M5G0610